Reason in Revolt

Book Two of the
Revolution Trilogy

by
Alan Gibbons

Circaidy Gregory Press

Copyright Information

Reason in Revolt text © 2018 Alan Gibbons, cover photo Rhiannon Barton © 2017, cover design and content under this cover © 2018 Kay Green. All rights reserved. No part of this publication may be reproduced, stored in a retrieval system, rebound or transmitted in any form or for any purpose without the prior written permission of author and publisher. This book is sold subject to the condition that it shall not be lent, resold, hired out or otherwise circulated without the publisher's prior consent in any form or binding other than that in which it is published.

ISBN 978-1-910841-48-8

Printed in the UK
by Catford Print

Published by
Circaidy Gregory Press
45 Robertson Street,
Hastings
Sussex TN34 1HL

www.circaidygregory.co.uk

Contents

About the Author
page ii

Glossary of historical characters
Page iii

Part One
Enemies of the People
page 1

Part Two
The Revolution Besieged
page 73

Part Three
Children of the Revolution
Page 153

About the Author

Alan Gibbons has been a published writer for 27 years, mainly in the children's and Young Adult field. He is the winner of The Blue Peter Book Award 2000 'The book I couldn't put down' for his best-selling book Shadow of the Minotaur and he has won seventeen other awards.

Before becoming an author Alan was a teacher for 16 years. Alan is a full time writer and independent educational consultant. He is the organiser of the Campaign for the Book, which promotes libraries and the culture of reading for pleasure. He is a member of the Speak up for Libraries coalition and initiated National Libraries Day. He is the recipient of the Fred Jarvis Award for services to education. Alan visits 150-180 schools and libraries a year in the UK and abroad, working with young people to encourage their interest in reading and writing.

If you would like Alan to visit your school, library or youth group
email: mygibbo@gmail.com

Reason in Revolt is the second volume of the Revolution trilogy, Alan's first work for adults. It follows on from Book One, **Winds of October** and Book Three, **Spurn the Dust**, will follow.

Glossary of real life figures in Reason in Revolt

Some real-life participants in the Russian Revolution appear in this novel. I have made every effort to portray them accurately. Where I include their words in the novel, they are re-imagined using their real-life speeches as a basis.

Gleb Ivanovich Boky, Communist, succeeded Uritsky as head of the Petrograd Cheka.

Lev Davidovich Bronstein, member of the Communist Party and organiser of the October insurrection.

Felix Edmundovich Dzerzhinsky, Polish-born Communist. Head of the security police, the Cheka, when it was founded.

Moisei Markovich Goldstein, known as Volodarksy, was a leading Communist and editor of the *Red Gazette*.

Fania Yefimovna Kaplan, Socialist Revolutionary activist who attempted to assassinate Lenin.

Alexandra Mikhailovna Kollontai, leading Communist Party member and writer.

Yakov Khristoforovich Peters, Latvian Communist and a founder of the Cheka state police.

Anatoly Vasilieyvich Lunacharsky, Communist, People's Commissar for Education.

Grigory Ivanovich, Semyonov, Socialist Revolutionary activist.

Vyacheslav Mikhailovich Molotov, member of the Military Revolutionary Committee and Bolshevik militant.

Larissa Mikhailovna Reissner, Bolshevik activist and writer.

Fyodor Fyodorovich Raskolnikov, leader of the sailors at the Kronstadt base and Bolshevik. Married to Larissa Reissner.

Ludmilla Stahl, Communist activist.

Vladimir Ilyich Ulyanov, known as Lenin, main theorist and leader of the Bolsheviks (later Communist Party), Chairman of the Council of People's Commissars (Sovnarkom), the government of the new workers' and peasants' state.

Moisei Solomonovich Uritsky, Communist. Led the Petrograd Cheka when Dzerzhinsky moved the headquarters of the organisation to Moscow.

Jukums Vatsetis, Latvian officer who became the first commander-in-chief of the Red Army.

Grigory Yevseevich Zinoviev, member of the Communist Party Central Committee. He was in charge of the Petrograd regional government and, in 1919, Chairman of the Executive Committee of the Communist International.

Part One

Enemies of the People

Svetlana

Ludmilla Stahl was making her way to the rostrum. Stahl was a friend of Lenin and his wife Krupskaya and she was just the woman to shake things up. Sveltlana wasn't disappointed by her speech. From the very first moment, Stahl delivered a fiery address, defending the seizure of power.

'You've heard the stories, I suppose,' she said. 'Comrade Kollontai arrives at her office, People's Commissar of Welfare, no less, a government minister and the concierge locks her out.'

There was laughter from a couple of delegates, but when nobody took it up, the hall fell silent.

'The civil servants are on strike. They think they still run the show. They refuse to accept the rule of the Soviets. They object to the dictatorship of the proletariat. Some of you might ask, what dictatorship? We've got office workers taking the nibs out of the pens to stop us carrying out our work. Imagine that, a revolution fails for want of a quill!'

She cast a stern glance in the direction of a row of delegates to her right.

'There are some in this hall who want us to take a step back, to come to terms with those who opposed taking power. They talk about meeting the enemies of the revolution half way.'

There were one or two shouts of: 'Shame!'

'You are right,' Stahl said, nodding in agreement with the voices from the floor. 'Comrade Trotsky introduced himself as the new Minister and his officials laughed in his face. Can you imagine it? The workers, peasants and soldiers carry out a revolution and an army of pen-pushers stands in their way.'

Stahl spoke for the mass of party members before her. Everyone was working long hours, trying to bring some order to the social neurosis that had seized red Petrograd since the revolution. Everyone was tired, surviving on a few hours of restless sleep. She left the platform to loud applause. As she passed, she darted a critical glance at Svetlana.

'Well, don't just stand there listening, Comrade,' she snapped, in no mood to say please. 'I expected more from you. Get yourself to the platform to support my position.' She noticed Kolya and delivered the next line acidly. 'This eager, young lover of yours will be waiting for you when you get home.'

Svetlana blushed and took the comment on the chin. She knew her relationship with a man twenty years her junior had set the tongues wagging in Party circles, but if Comrade Kollontai could ignore the comments about her and sailor Dybenko, she could do the same.

'I have to go,' Kolya said, very aware of Stahl's withering stare. He whispered in Svetlana's ear. 'I will see you later.'

Svetlana nodded and did as Stahl had instructed. She succeeded in attracting the attention of the chair and made her way forward. After Stahl's speech, she would surely be kicking at an open door.

'Comrades,' she said, 'women workers, heroes of the February days, fighters for the revolution....'

OK, she decided, that's buttered them up. Now to business.

'I am here to support Comrade Stahl,' she growled, swinging her gaze to the row of Lady Kamenevs gathered to her right. 'We have delegates who want to conciliate. Let's be fair, they say. Let's have a socialist coalition, they say. Let's get into bed with the SRs. Weren't these Socialist Revolutionaries the same comrades who turned down a chance to join the new Soviet government in the first place?'

Svetlana was well aware of the discomfort she was causing to those Bolsheviks who had opposed the insurrection.

'What do we have here, revolutionaries who set their faces against revolution? Next thing you know, there will be swimmers who don't fancy the water.'

She adopted the pose of a reluctant swimmer dipping her toe in icy water. It earned her appreciative laughter.

'Who gave our government ministers, our Sovnarkom, their mandate? Who said 'All Power to the Soviets'? – the workers!

Now there was loud applause. Svetlana saw Stahl nodding.

'We have decrees on peace, bread and land as we promised. That's right, this is a republic of equals and we keep our promises. '

By now, she had the delegates eating out of the palm of her hand.

'Would these historic decrees exist without our October revolution? Would they? Oh, you can't have the Bolsheviks holding the power, our opponents say. Well, why not? Did we not win a majority in the Soviet? Do other parties not have the right to participate freely in it? Did we not take the power as the vanguard of the working people?'

She delivered each rhetorical question in a harsh, almost metallic voice then stalked across the stage.

'We will talk to these fine Menshevik and SR comrades on one condition.' She paused, picking out faces in the crowd and making eye contact. One or two squirmed uncomfortably. 'It is this. We do not relinquish state power. We do not offer the Kornilovites and the counter-revolutionaries a way to drown red Petrograd in blood. We defeated them at Pulkovo Heights – yes, I was there, a woman worker with a rifle in her hand – and we will do it again.' She pounded her fist on the lectern. 'Again...again...again.'

Some of the delegates joined in the peroration, but Svetlana wasn't quite finished.

'Until we consolidate the revolution our Party will hold the reins of power, with support from others if possible, alone if need be.'

Comrade Stahl had turned the tide with her speech. Svetlana had only to reinforce her arguments. She felt relaxed as she delivered her final argument.

'To those who would walk away from the Central Committee, to those who would surrender the forward positions of the revolution, I say this. Until all Russia is safe and free from counter-revolutionaries, we demand unity behind the leadership. We will not hand power back to the land owners and the capitalists.'

There were shouts of: 'Absolutely!' and 'Well said.'

Svetlana was encouraged by the response. 'People say there must be a socialist coalition government. We say, on what basis? If it is on the programme of the October revolution, then there is room for discussion. If it is to be the programme of the defeated bourgeoisie, then there is nothing to talk about. Let these so-called moderates create their Committee of Public Safety and appeal to the troops to overthrow Soviet power. We will meet fire with fire. We demand comrades with steel conviction. Anything less is treachery.'

There were a few isolated protests and some gasps of 'outrageous!' but the hall was with the supporters of Lenin. Svetlana ended with a shout of defiance.

'Long live the world socialist revolution!'

Stahl was complimentary about Svetlana's speech. There was no mention of the departed Kolya. 'You have earned great respect among the women workers, Svetlana. You have toiled alongside them for many years, sharing their troubles. They trust you.'

Svetlana was aware of her daughter Anna making her way over. Anna saw who Svetlana was talking to and waited at an appropriate distance. Stahl had a fearsome reputation.

'I sense a *but*,' Svetlana observed.

'You are an intelligent woman,' Stahl answered. 'You know I have something to ask you. We hold power by the thinnest of threads. We had to beat back Kerensky. The Right SRs say we will be overthrown in a matter of days. Gorky says two weeks. Don't forget, it took a bitter struggle to gain control of Moscow. The old state machine is hostile to us. We will need talented people to fill the gaps.'

Svetlana took a moment for this to sink in. Was Comrade Stahl offering her a job?

'I don't understand.'

This produced a chuckle. 'Oh, I think you do, Svetlana. You are a good organiser. You can read. Our revolution could perish for lack of culture. There are libraries to organise, literacy programmes. I think you could make a great contribution.'

'I am a worker,' Svetlana protested. 'My place is in the mill.'

Stern eyes met her own.

'Your place is where the Party needs you, Comrade Svetlana.'

'Without the Vyborg, there is no revolution. It is the beating heart of our power. It is where I belong.'

Stahl was having none of it. She gave another of her withering looks.

'Without reliable people running the workers' and peasants' state, we shall not survive the winter, Svetlana. The German Army remains on our soil, armed to the teeth. We are surrounded by hostile nations. The very apparatus of government is against us. None of us can abstain from our responsibilities.'

Svetlana was about to protest that she took her responsibilities as a party militant very seriously, but Stahl brushed away her objections.

'There are six thousand Party members in the Vyborg district alone, Svetlana. We have plenty of good people to take your place. When revolutionaries carry out their revolution, they become rulers.'

'This is not about individuals,' Svetlana argued. 'The working class is the ruling class.'

This earned a sympathetic smile. 'The working class and the revolutionary movement is made up of individuals, Comrade.' Svetlana could see Anna looking on, perplexed. They worked on the same section. The thought of leaving her daughter and her workmates behind to become a Party bureaucrat left Svetlana's heart heavy.

'I know, but....'

'The individual plays a driving role in the making of history, Svetlana. Would there have been a successful revolution without Comrade Lenin, an almost bloodless insurrection without Comrade Trotsky?'

'You can't compare me to them!'

'We all play our part, Svetlana. The dying Tsarist bureaucracy would crush the hopes of the workers' state at its birth. We will need an army of worker-leaders to replace the functionaries of the old order. You and I must do our duty.' She winked. 'Don't expect any privileges. Do you know what the People's Commissars earn for running the country, five hundred roubles a month, the average wage of a skilled worker.'

'That is how it should be,' Svetlana observed.

Comrade Stahl rested her hand on Svetlana's arm. 'It is how it is and how it is going to be. We will talk again.'

Svetlana watched Stahl walk away down the aisle to listen to the continuing business of the conference. Anna finally joined her mother.

'What was that about?'

Svetlana felt as if she was sleepwalking. 'I am to leave the factory.'

Anna's eyes, brown as nuts, opened wide with surprise.

'They want me to teach people to read. I will organise literacy classes, libraries, cultural events.'

Anna embraced her mother and kissed her on both cheeks.

'Why, that is wonderful. It is such an honour.' She saw the sadness in Svetlana's eyes. 'You should be happy.'

'I will miss the comradeship of the mill. I will miss you.'

Anna was bright, full of the optimism of her nineteen years.

'Oh, get it into perspective, Mama. You are teaching people to read. It's not like you are going to exile in Siberia.'

Svetlana folded her daughter in her arms and pressed her lips to the top of her head, the way she had when Anna was a little girl.

'How can somebody so young be so wise?' she asked. 'Do you know I love you so much it makes my heart break?'

'Your heart should break when you lose somebody,' Anna reminded her, 'not when you see her every day. You're so sentimental, Mama.'

The delegates were breaking up to get something to eat, buffeting mother and daughter as they filed out.

'What do you think we'll be eating today?' Anna asked.

Svetlana played along with the game. 'I think it could be, let's see, oh...thin cabbage soup with black bread?'

They joined the line and burst out laughing as the thin, green gruel slopped into bowls.

'Yesterday, today and tomorrow,' Svetlana announced to her fellow delegates. 'All hail Comrade Cabbage, saviour of the revolution.'

Amid sympathetic smiles, they sat down to eat. Gradually, the humour drained from Svetlana.

'We have ten days' food supplies in the city,' she murmured. 'There is no central government. Everything depends on the initiative of the working people.' She glanced at Anna. 'Is it very wrong of me to wonder if we are up to it?'

'Mama,' Anna said, stroking Svetlana's face, 'my beautiful Mama, with people like you we will storm the heavens and conquer the whole world.' Tears started in her eyes. 'You must not be afraid. You are the strongest person I know.'

'And you, my beautiful daughter, are the gentlest and warmest.' Finishing her chunk of bread, she said, through the bulge in her cheek, 'What is your brother up to?'

Anna shrugged. 'You know Volodya. If he isn't at work or at home, you can be sure a woman is involved.'

Svetlana found this amusing. 'Do you disapprove of his behaviour?'

'I wish he treated women as comrades rather than his personal playthings.'

'It takes two, you know,' Svetlana reminded her. 'I don't see any of his women putting up much resistance. They're falling over themselves to get at him.'

Anna was not convinced. 'That's true, but men don't get pregnant.'

Svetlana stretched. 'Well, I can hardly disapprove, can I?'

'Meaning?'

'I have my own plaything, Anna. Or have you forgotten about Kolya?'

Anna refused to accept the comparison.

'You are comrades. Kolya treats you as an equal. Oh Mama, don't be obtuse. You know what I am talking about. The Russian man thinks he can do what he wants with a woman. He thinks nothing of beating her. Do you remember the old saying: a chicken is not a bird and a peasant woman is not a human being?'

'There is no need to remind me,' Svetlana told her daughter. 'Volodya would never say anything like that. He is a gentle soul.'

Anna gave a little nod. 'You're right. I could never accuse Volodya of being a brute. He wouldn't raise his hand to a woman, but he gets what he wants and moves on to the next. Aren't relationships meant to be equal now?'

'Sovnarkom will make a start when it decrees that marriage is a free, voluntary union, Anna. We will not change human psychology overnight.'

Anna pursed her lips. 'You indulge him too much.'

Svetlana planted her splayed fingers on Anna's head and wagged it back and forth. 'I indulge you both. Come on, let's get some air.'

They stood on the steps outside, breath misting in the November chill. There were red flags everywhere, and banners that snapped in the wind from the Neva. There were slogans on walls. Here and there, Red Guard units drilled or simply lolled against railings, smoking and chewing sunflower seeds. A small child emerged from the mist and damp and held out a scrawny hand.

'Do you have any bread, Comrades?'

Anna stared at the outstretched palm. 'Is there nobody with you?'

Azure eyes blinked at her as if she had just spoken in a foreign language.

'Where is your father?'

'Dead in the war.'

'Your mother?'

'She went away.'

Svetlana felt a kick in her chest. 'She went without you?'

A nod, as casual as it was wretched. 'She was sad all the time. She stopped talking to me. Then one day she was gone. I don't know where. I think I did something wrong.'

Anna gestured to the child. 'Stay there.' With that, she scampered up the steps. 'Wait here. I will find you something.'

'Where do you live?' Svetlana asked.

The child continued to stare dumbly.

'Do you have a home?'

Finally, there was an answer. 'You're not stupid, Comrade. There's no roof over my head.'

Svetlana lowered her eyes, as if admonished by a schoolmistress. 'So you're living on the street?'

'It's my only home now.'

Anna arrived with a bowl of soup and two chunks of black bread.

'One to eat right away,' she said, brandishing the bread. 'One for later.'

'I will eat both immediately,' the child answered emotionlessly. A chunk disappeared into a greedy mouth. 'There are people who would take it off me.'

While the child was mopping up the last of the soup with the hard, crusty bread, Svetlana asked, 'What's your name?'

'I am Dina.'

Svetlana and Anna exchanged glances. It didn't escape Dina's attention.

'You thought I was a boy, didn't you?'

'I'm sorry,' Anna replied. 'It's because your head is shaven.'

'That's the nits,' Dina explained, 'and the lice. They like long hair.'

Svetlana came to a decision. 'Where will you be later?'

That produced a frown from Dina. 'Why are you asking?'

'We have a friend,' Svetlana explained. 'She works for the Commissariat of People's Welfare. She will help you.'

'Nobody helps the *besprizornye*.'

'We gave you food.'

Dina looked down at the bowl. 'I will tell you my whereabouts, but nobody will come.'

'Somebody will,' Svetlana insisted. 'I promise.'

Without another word, Dina went on her way. Her shoulders sagged and she moved with little purpose or energy. This was a child who was used to disappointment.

'Do you remember what I asked?' Svetlana said.

'You wondered if we were up to the task of making the socialist revolution. That's what you mean, isn't it?'

'That's right,' Svetlana answered. 'We must not fail. We have to succeed, for the likes of Dina. She is the future.'

Kolya

Flanked by Pavel and Mikhail, he strode into the editorial office, bringing the members of staff to their feet. One man fled instantly, leaving just two of them: a balding, middle aged man with a drooping moustache and round, steel-rimmed glasses and – next to him – a painfully thin, young woman wearing her hair in a tight bun.

'Collect your things,' he told them. 'The newspaper is closed down until further notice.'

'This is outrageous!' the editor cried, his diminutive frame trembling with indignation. 'On whose authority are you ordered to do this?'

Kolya waved a sheet of paper under his nose.

'I am acting on behalf of the Military Revolutionary Committee. If you wish to register your objections, I will give you an address.'

The editor stood to attention, thin chest thrust forward in a show of defiance.

'I demand that you leave these premises forthwith,' he declared, in a voice just this side of hysteria.

'Forthwith,' Kolya repeated, picking up the latest edition of the paper. '*Forthwith*. Not the kind of word we hear in the Red Guards, eh, Comrades?'

Mikhail honoured the question with a half-hearted laugh. Pavel simply looked on with a bored expression.

'Get out of this office!'

To the editor's surprise, Kolya tapped his chest with an outstretched finger, causing him to stumble against the desk.

'Violence,' his assistant cried. 'You struck him!'

Kolya examined the offending index finger then cast a glance in the direction of his companions. 'I must be stronger than I thought. Imagine if I had used my pinky.' He waggled his little finger then fixed the editor with a contemptuous stare. 'What's your name, little man?'

Scrambling together what was left of his dignity, the editor mustered a reply. 'I am Anatoly Petrovich Tar...'

'Name and patronymic will do, Citizen,' Kolya said. 'These premises are closed until further notice.'

'On what grounds?'

'The Military Revolutionary Committee has passed a resolution temporarily forbidding the publication of bourgeois papers and counter-revolutionary publications.'

'Counter-revolutionary!' came the indignant cry.

Kolya made a great show of reading the sheet of paper. 'Let's see. Yes, there it is in black and white. Counter-rrrrr-evolutionary. Now, will you clear your desk like a good boy and piss off.'

'How dare you talk to Mr Tarkovsky like that!' his assistant cried.

'I appreciate your loyalty and courage, Alexandra,' Tarkovsky said, 'but I think I had better deal with this.'

'You might be better letting her talk,' Pavel said, speaking for the first time. 'She's got more balls than you will ever have.'

Alexandra's eyes narrowed with fury. By way of response, Pavel winked at Mikhail. 'She fancies me.'

'You are a crude brute,' Alexandra snarled 'My brother is with General Krasnov. If he were here now, he would split you in half with his sabre.'

Tarkovsky winced visibly at her show of anger. Kolya seized on her words.

'What was that word again? Oh yes, counter-revolutionary.' He leaned closer to Tarkovsky. 'Any complaints about us closing you now, Citizen?'

'Alexandra's views are her own. This is a democratic socialist newspaper.'

'Is that right?' Kolya answered. 'Democratic and socialist, eh? So let's have a look through a few back issues, Citizen Tarkovsky. What did you say about the Red Guards when we were marching on the Kornilovites?'

Tarkovsky looked uncomfortable.

'Oh yes, you called for us to be disarmed. Maybe you wanted the Red Guards to fight the enemy with flowers. How did that work out?'

'Really, I....'

'Proceed,' Kolya said. 'I am interested to hear what you have to say.'

'I was on the street alongside the women of the Vyborg in the February revolution.' He tilted his head to display a scar on his bare scalp. 'The Pharaohs gave me this for my pains.'

Kolya was unimpressed.

'What about this article from just a couple of days ago? *The only solution now is a democratic government from which the Bolsheviks, especially Lenin and Trotsky, are excluded.*' He examined the ceiling. 'Now remind me again, who were the main figures in the victorious revolution?'

'You may not like what we say,' Tarkovsky objected, 'but we have every right to say it.'

'There is no absolute right to press freedom,' Kolya told him, his voice a register lower. 'Your words assist the counter-revolution. You make the propaganda while the generals prime their guns. When the revolution is safe, your doors can reopen.'

'When will that be?'

Kolya noted that Tarkovsky had just made a major concession, accepting that the office and printing press were going to close.

'That, Citizen Tarkovsky, will be the subject of a fierce class struggle between the Soviets and their enemies.'

'You don't represent the Soviets,' Alexandra yelled. 'The Soviets include all the socialist parties, not just one. You are usurpers. You carried out a coup.'

'We hold a majority in the Soviets,' Kolya retorted. 'Across Russia, the great cities declare for the revolution. The regiments rally to our demand for peace. The peasants welcome the land decree.'

'It is evident that there is no point arguing with you,' Tarkovsky said, his voice heavy with resignation. 'As with all zealots, you are immune to reason. Get your things, Alexandra. We are leaving.'

There were tears in her eyes. 'But it is wrong.'

Tarkovsky pointed at the weapons in the hands of his three tormentors. 'They have the backing of the Soviet and the Military Revolutionary Committee. Most importantly, they have that most persuasive of arguments, the barrel of a gun.'

While Tarkovsky buttoned his waistcoat and shrugged on his jacket, Alexandra placed personal items in her bag. Kolya noted the painstaking, precise why she arranged the objects. She saw him watching her.

'Do you have nothing better to do?'

'Not really, no.'

She stopped packing and planted her hands on her hips. 'Men like you are cowards. Do you know that?'

'I didn't,' Kolya answered. 'Please enlighten me.'

'You seize power in a coup. You butcher boy soldiers. You....'

Kolya crashed a leather-gloved fist on the desk.

'Enough! The Bolshevik party gained the majority in the Workers' Section on September 25th. That day, Trotsky was elected chairman of the Soviet.' He indicated his companions. 'The soldiers rally to the party banner. Those cadets you talk about so fondly rose in insurrection. They fired first. They caused the fighting, not us. I saw our dead littering the street where your fucking cadets gunned them down.'

'So you say!'

Kolya sneered.

'Do you know why there was no fighting when we took power?'

Alexandra backed away, intimidated by Kolya's show of fury.

'Well!'

'You had the guns. You have them now. You use them against a woman and a man of peace. You are wicked.'

Kolya paced up and down, like a bear harried by a wolf.

'Kerensky had guns. The *Stavka* had guns.' Kolya swung his arm. 'Why didn't they use them? Here's why. We had the backing of the people. When the Red Guards marched on the Winter Palace there was nobody left to defend the Provisional Government. It fell without a fight.'

Alexandra finally summoned all her reserves of defiance.

'Next time you come up against opposition, it won't be the Women's Battalion,' she promised. 'Our brave lads will defend Mother Russia to the death.'

'Is that right?' Kolya said, nodding away in his anger. 'Well, know this Citizen. We will crush our opponents with an iron fist.' He pointed to the door. 'Now get out!'

When the door finally slammed and Kolya was alone with Pavel and Mikhail, he let out a raw cry of frustration.

'Did you hear how she spoke to me?'

Mikhail perched on the edge of Tarkovsky's desk. 'You shouldn't let her get to you. You've heard it before. These people are impotent.'

Pavel fanned out the newspapers on the desk and examined the headlines.

'I wouldn't be so sure.'

'Meaning?'

Pavel laid his rifle on the table in front of him.

'She wasn't just speaking for herself, you know. Did you hear what she said about her brother? The Red Guards defeat the Cossacks at Pulkovo Heights and what do we do? We get General Krasnov to promise not to rise against us. Now, I don't know much about revolutions, but I've read Comrade Lenin. It's revolution against counter-revolution. There's a word for that and it's civil war. You watch that bastard Krasnov turn up somewhere with an army at his disposal.'

'So what were we supposed to do?' Mikhail asked. 'Shoot him?'

'Throw his sorry arse into prison at the very least,' Pavel said.

Kolya was more definite.

'No, Mikhail was right first time. You can't have a revolution without firing squads.' He ran his hands through his hair and straightened up. 'Anyway, board the place up. It's time to stop up the mouth of the counter-revolution.'

Pavel watched Kolya prowl to the door.

'Where are you going?'

'Our job's done here,' Kolya told him.

Mikhail slapped Pavel on the shoulder. 'He's going to show his Svetlana a good time.'

Kolya paused at the door. 'Something like that.'

But it wasn't Svetlana's solace Kolya sought. He waited impatiently at the apartment lent to him by the party, gazing out at the gleaming river. Alexandra's show of resistance still angered him. Somewhere deep inside him he felt the urge to strike down her resistance, to throw her to the floor and stamp on every peppery word of protest. He waited for Klara and he yearned for Svetlana.

'Svetlana, my love.'

She represented everything that was good in him. She was true. There was no sturdier Bolshevik in the whole of Petrograd. If she had doubts, she buried them deep. While he remained an outsider, an intellectual, the seabird that rode with the storm, people like Svetlana were the very storm itself.

'So why can't I love you as you deserve. Why do I crave another?'

There was a day, not so long ago, on a hillside looking north towards great Petrograd. Svetlana had been there, face smudged with the dirt of conflict. The counter-revolution rose at Gatchina and Svetlana marched to meet it without a moment's hesitation.

'Because that is who you are.'

He became aware of a squealing door hinge, a light tread on the floorboards.

'Talking to yourself again, Kolya?'

He relaxed. Klara had finally arrived. She was as dainty and as beautiful as ever. There was the same haughtiness, the same air of danger.

'Here she is,' he said, 'the prettiest, little whore in all Petrograd.'

She frowned. 'I thought you Bolsheviks weren't supposed to talk to women that way. The comrade-whores went on strike for dignity, you know.'

'What's this, Klara? Have you been doing some homework? We'll make a Communist of you yet.'

Klara snorted, unlaced her boots, seized his arm and guided him to the bed.

'Fat chance of that,' she said. 'The day before the revolution, people went hungry. The day after the revolution, people queue for bread. Nothing changes.'

'Not in a day it doesn't,' Kolya said, 'but look what we are doing. Women have the vote, divorce rights, equal pay...'

'Save your propaganda for somebody who wants to listen,' Klara told him. 'We are both here for the same thing.'

She started to lazily unbutton his shirt. He sat up so she could strip it from his body. When she flung it across the room, she saw his black leather jacket, hanging on the peg.

'Why do you all have to wear those ugly things?' she complained. 'If you are so keen to create a new world, you should be wearing bright colours.'

Kolya roared with laughter. 'What would you have me wear when I go arresting counter-revolutionaries?'

She pressed her lips to his stomach.

'Anything would be better than that thing. It makes you look like a crow.'

On impulse, she wriggled out of her dress and stripped naked. She grabbed the jacket and wrapped herself up in it.

'You are such a tiny thing,' Kolya commented. 'My jacket reaches halfway down your thighs.'

'Maybe you would like to take it from me,' Klara teased, insolence written all over her face.

Kolya was out of bed in a flash. There was laughter and play-fighting then the brush of the jacket's lining against soft skin and a hungry, needful mouth on small breasts and hard nipples. They grunted. Bodies bucked and sweated until they were both spent.

'Do you ever think about me once we've fucked?' Klara asked.

Kolya watched the daylight dying along the ceiling. 'Not for a moment.'

She punched him in the stomach and he doubled up, laughing and coughing simultaneously.

'You're too rough!' he complained.

'You deserve it, you monster. You don't care for me at all. You don't care for anybody.' She pinched his skin just below the breast bone. 'I have a good mind to tell Svetlana what you get up to with me.'

At that, the humour drained from Kolya's face. He grabbed her wrists and threw her on her back.

'The day you go telling tales to Svetlana is the day they fish your scrawny carcass out of the Neva.'

Klara's eyes searched his face.

'You mean it, don't you?' she said.

Tears started in her eyes.

'Well, if you care for the old bitch so much, what brings you running to me like a randy mongrel?'

Kolya released her. 'I only wish I knew. You're bad for me, Klara.'

'And Svetlana? Is she good for you?'

Kolya took his time answering.

'Don't you know?' Klara asked.

His head shook slowly.

'In a way, she is everything to me, my lover, my comrade, the beat of my heart....'

Klara was pouting, infuriated by the words of endearment.

'You are wrong to call her old, Klara. At forty-five, she is as beautiful as any woman I have ever met.'

In that moment, he cursed his own inconstancy. Svetlana was his life. Klara was his weakness.

'Yet you come to me.'

Kolya ran his finger along her plump, sulky lips.

'That's right, I come to you.'

'Why?'

'Why do people tear off their clothes and plunge into an icy river? It's the shock, Klara. When I make love to Svetlana, it is warm. It is fond and secure.'

Klara was beginning to beam, anticipating the praise to come.

'What is it like with me?'

He gave a shake of his head.

'That is the question I keep asking myself. You are unsettling. You sell your body to other men. You are unreliable and as mischievous as any spoilt adolescent...'

'I am the same age as you,' Klara reminded him. 'I am a grown woman. I make my own choices.'

'That's right. We are the same age. We have no ties, no children, no baggage at all. Klara, we are free in a way Svetlana never will be. That's what makes you so exciting. You are as dangerous and unpredictable as a forest fire.'

Klara laughed. 'And I make you tingle with desire. You couldn't cast me aside if you wanted to'

Kolya nodded. 'You're my drug.'

Klara settled herself in his embrace and sighed happily.

'Do you have influence?' she asked. Kolya found the question disturbing. He didn't want her wandering out of her world into his.

'In what way?'

'Your bloody revolution is ruining trade,' Klara told him. 'We've got your comrades telling us we should find proper work rather than demean ourselves, but that's not the main problem.' Kolya imagined the Red Guards confronting the prostitutes, harrying them off the streets. He didn't need them causing him problems

'So what is the problem?'

Klara turned her face to look at him.

'It's what you're doing to these poor bourgeois. It's them I fuck, not your dirt-poor proletarians. How are the rich supposed to pay for a good, cultured screw, if you take everything from them?'

Kolya rubbed his chin against the top of her head.

'See,' he said, 'things do change, for all your scepticism. Sovnarkom is going to decriminalise adultery. Good job for us, eh?'

'Neither of us is married, Kolya.'

'True, but I am still cheating on my Svetlana.' He considered Klara, so slim and wide-eyed in the half-light, like a cat woman. 'So you're complaining about the revolution because we are calling the bourgeoisie to heel?'

'That's right. They came to me to get away from their boring wives and their suffocating lives and now they don't have the money. You're even taking their houses off them.'

'Why should a family have all those rooms while people live in lousy barracks or on the streets? Tell me that.'

Klara wasn't interested in Kolya and his politics. She was the most selfish creature he had ever met, the opposite of his brave, generous Svetlana. He felt like kicking Klara out that minute and going to find his dear, sweet love, but Klara interrupted his thoughts.

'You and your bloody Bolsheviks are going to make me starve.'

'So you're looking for a job, are you?'

There was a pout of distaste at the word *job*.

'I am looking for an income if whoring goes tits up.'

'Right now,' Kolya told her, 'I am just another Red Guard trying to defend the revolution. I don't see how I can help.' He remembered the unwelcome message he got from Comrade Anishin earlier. 'Oh, the owner of this flat is returning to Petrograd in a few days. We'll need somewhere else to meet.'

Klara smiled. 'Why don't you go back to Mrs Turisheva's place?'

Kolya remembered his landlady with distaste. 'What, and put up with her infernal whining every day? Anyway, she's talking about going back to her village. If she does, the party will move people into her rooms *en masse*.'

Klara's smile was saccharine. Behind it lay untold mischief. Klara's words didn't sit easy with him. He imagined her in the same room as Svetlana. The thought of Klara being able to keep tight-lipped about what they did here in this flat was absurd.

'But there are jobs, aren't there? Your beloved party has got to pull people out of the factories to run the country.'

'You're a clever, little scorpion, aren't you?' Kolya murmured.

Klara snuggled up against him. 'Oh yes. Just watch out for my sting.'

He remembered what she had said about talking to Svetlana. She was clever, all right. Maybe too clever by half.

Raisa

'There is no need to talk to Raisa about the *besprizornye*.' Elena told Svetlana as her fingers stole along Raisa's forearm. 'She knows all about life on the streets.'

Raisa wondered how much Elena had told her aunt.

'This child you met,' Raisa asked. 'How old is she?'

'She looks seven or eight,' Svetlana replied, before adding a rider. 'She is probably older. The emaciation has that effect.'

Raisa listened to Svetlana and remembered the hollowed eyes and starvation-hollowed cheeks of the street children among whom she had once lived.

'Svetlana,' she ventured, 'tell me the truth. Did you come to me because I am attached to the Commissariat for Social Welfare or because I have this place available?'

The guesthouse was modest in size, but there were four rooms standing empty. Raisa knew Svetlana was curious about how she came to be in possession of it in the first place. After all, at barely seventeen, Raisa somehow owned an entire house, at least occupied it, yet her parents had worked in the factories of the Vyborg. No wonder Svetlana was suspicious. Imagine how it looked. When she met Svetlana, she had been able to pass herself off as an office worker or civil servant, even a bourgeois, so demurely was she dressed. Nevertheless, she had rushed to join the February revolution without a moment's hesitation. She had lived many lives in one and that obviously intrigued Svetlana. One day, Raisa would tell her the whole tale, of an act of self-defence that had changed her entire life.

Svetlana's reply didn't answer Raisa's question. 'I came to you because I made a promise to a desperate child.'

Raisa was struggling with her emotions. 'There are thousands, tens of thousands of these children in Petrograd, Svetlana, millions in Russia. The Commissariat is trying to address this issue. We are beginning to draw up plans for homes for them, but....'

The way she turned up her palms indicated the scale of the problem.

'Are you telling me nothing can be done?' Svetlana asked, steel in her voice. 'Did we not make a revolution to change the world? Is October not about making Russia a beacon of hope?'

Raisa smiled at the passion in Svetlana's voice.

'I didn't say there was nothing we could do.' Raisa straightened her back and looked across the room at the older woman. 'After the February revolution, there were people who made rooms available to the *besprizornye*. In a way, these works of charity are a bandage bound round a great wound, but some of the children have had food and a roof over their heads, thanks to these individual acts of generosity. I will come and meet Dina.'

She left the room and took her winter coat from the peg. She was tucking her hair into her fur hat when Elena appeared. 'Are you all right?'

Raisa was trembling a little. 'How much does Svetlana know about me?'

'She knows you were once poor. She has suspicions about the money.'

'Does she know I killed to get it?'

Elena buttoned her own coat. 'I have never told her and she will never ask.'

Raisa stroked Elena's cheek and kissed her on the lips. Simultaneously, Svetlana appeared at the door and dropped her gaze.

'There is no need to be embarrassed, Comrade aunty,' Raisa said, teasing.

'I am not embarrassed,' Svetlana answered. 'I know that there can be love between two women, just as there can between two men. I just find it…unfamiliar.'

'Yet you have known me all my life,' Elena said. 'Did you not suspect?'

Svetlana smiled. 'It made sense when I saw you and Raisa together. You are my sister's daughter, Elena. You are my blood. I am proud that you have found someone with whom you can share your life.'

This earned another kiss from Raisa, but consciously on the cheeks, which produced laughter.

'So what is Comrade Kollontai like?' Svetlana asked.

'She is tall and striking,' Raisa replied then, in a whisper. 'A little scary too. She is intense, but she has the most gentle, blue eyes. I like her. That said, it is like being in the company of a legend. She has been a revolutionary for eighteen years. Can you imagine? She witnessed Bloody Sunday, all those years ago. She has been in exile. She knows Martov, Luxemburg, Liebknecht. She knows *Lenin*.'

'You sound quite infatuated with her,' Svetlana observed.

'Don't tease,' Raisa countered. 'I love only Elena.'

'Good to hear it,' Elena said, wrapping an arm round her lover's shoulders and squeezing.

They passed a drowsing *droshky* driver, arms crossed on his lap. The horse in the shafts looked weary and emaciated. Red Guards lounged against a motor truck. One of them recognised Svetlana and waved. They had gone a few yards when Svetlana stopped and retraced her steps.

Raisa turned. 'What's she doing?'

Elena rolled her eyes. 'I think she is getting us a lift.' She pointed towards the Troitsky Bridge. 'There…and back.'

'So we are taking these kids in?' Raisa asked. 'You don't mind?'

Elena's eyes sparkled with amusement. 'You are an open book, Raisa. Don't tell me you haven't already made your mind up.'

There was a gruff shout and the driver started the truck. Svetlana joined him up front. Raisa and Elena scrambled into the back and sat with their backs against the wooden sides. One of the Red Guards was watching them. He ran an appreciative look over Raisa.

'Are you with anybody, Comrade?'

Raisa's instinct was to point at Elena and say *her*, but she didn't live in a world that understood or accepted who she was, not even after the revolution. There was talk about legalising homosexuality, but the moment you said the word homosexual, people automatically imagined a man. There was always this question in people's eyes: what do two women *do*? She erred on the side of caution.

'I am with somebody,' Raisa answers, 'and my lover would eat you for breakfast, *Comrade*.'

Without any hesitation, the Guard switched his attention to Elena.

'What about her? Is she with anyone?'

'Aren't you the charmer?' Elena snorted. 'Raisa turns you down and I'm seconds.'

The Guard grinned. 'No offence, Comrade.'

Elena turned away. 'Fuck you, Comrade.'

Laughter filled the truck and they travelled through the darkening city. Presently, the truck came to a halt. There was a child standing on a street corner, the November wind riffling through her thin clothes. Svetlana appeared round the back of the truck and took down the tail gate.

'Come and meet Dina.'

They were walking towards the shaven-headed, little girl when she whistled and half a dozen other children scampered from the shadows. Dina wagged her head to the right and the left.

'They come with me.'

'Dina…'

'They come with me now,' Dina continued, 'or you will have thirty kids here in the next five minutes, swarming all over that vehicle.'

One of the Red Guards found this funny. 'She's not kidding, Comrades. This area is plagued by the little buggers.' He seemed wary of Dina. 'They don't just beg, you know. Some of them are expert thieves.'

Dina glared at him. 'Screw you, Comrade Fuck-Face.'

'Will you listen to that little scamp. She's insolent and Red.' He rubbed Dina's scalp. 'I like this kid.'

Dina gave him a humourless stare. 'Watch where you put your hand. I've got lice.'

The Guard reacted as if he had been electrocuted, earning the derision of the rest of the unit.

'The way things are, Comrade, we are all going to get lice. The lads coming back from the Front are crawling with them.'

Half an hour later, Raisa was opening the guesthouse door. One of Dina's friends was looking around, wide-eyed.

'You live *here*? Are you a bourgeois?'

'I am a Bolshevik.'

'Are you a rich Bolshevik?'

Raisa saw Elena looking at her, wondering how she was going to answer.

'I am a Bolshevik who knows how to survive.'

Dina was exploring the ground floor, peering into every room. 'Who lives here?'

'Sometimes it is just me,' Raisa told her. 'Sometimes Elena stays.'

'What about the other rooms?'

Svetlana rested a hand Raisa's shoulder. 'If you are wondering whether Dina is always so direct, the answer is yes.'

Raisa saw things in Dina's face Svetlana couldn't imagine. She knew the numbing cold that wouldn't go away, the intense pain of her bones against the cold, hard cobbles, the men who come in the dark. This little girl knew things no child should.

'There are two beds in the room next to mine,' Raisa explained. 'Three of you in one, three in the other.'

Dina led the other children upstairs. They inspected their room and, satisfied that they had found somewhere warm and safe to shelter, they made their way back down.

'When do we eat? You had cabbage soup and black bread at your meeting.'

This produced a tremor of expectation from the other children.

'There is no soup,' Raisa told them, 'but I do have sausage....and black bread.'

The smallest of the children, a little girl with hair like straw, tugged Dina's sleeve. 'I like it here.'

Everyone ate together. Svetlana, Raisa and Elena talked. The children didn't. The smallest of Dina's group pointed at Svetlana.

'Her jaw clicks when she eats.'

Raisa leaned forward. 'You shouldn't say things like that.'

'Why not? It does.'

'But you don't say it.'

'Why not?'

Raisa had just run out of things to argue when Svetlana intervened.

'Do you know why my jaw clicks when I eat?'

There was no answer.

'Well, I will tell you.' She peeled back her lip with her little finger. 'Do you see these teeth? They're my canines, my dog teeth, my *wolf* teeth. I use them to eat bourgeois for breakfast.'

'You do not!'

Elena joined in. 'It's true. She does. Show her, aunty.'

Svetlana played along, stuffing imaginary people into her mouth and making a loud, gobbling noise. 'Prince Lvov. Yum yum. Kerensky. Yum yum. General Kornilov. Mm-umm.'

Finally, there was laughter. It rang around the room. Only Dina kept a straight face. Raisa inspected the flat, pale mask of a face and wondered what thoughts lay behind it. She had had a face like this once.

After Bagrov came into her life, to sell her like a piece of meat?

The smallest girl tugged Dina's sleeve. 'She does not eat bourgeois for breakfast, does she, Dina?'

'Of course not,' Dina said.

The face was still white, still flat and featureless. Then there was a twitch, a smile.

'Breakfast is too early to munch bourgeois, little Iskra. Svetlana waits until dinner.'

The laughter now was hearty and prolonged. The children rolled on the floor, kicking their legs. Even Dina was joining in, tousling Iskra's hair. Svetlana knelt in front of the smallest child.

'Your name is Iskra?'

There was a nod of acknowledgement. 'Mama said I was her little spark.'

Dina was no longer smiling as she remembered her abandonment.

'What happened to your Mama?'

Iskra answered without hesitation, without a flicker of sadness.

'The Pharaohs killed her.' The little girl swung a stick-thin arm. 'They went like this, and this, and this then she fell to the floor.'

A tear spilled down Svetlana's cheek, but Iskra's eyes were dry.

'You witnessed it?'

Iskra finished her story. 'I tried to make her get up, but she didn't. Then the Pharaohs charged and I ran.'

'Oh, my poor baby,' Svetlana sobbed, taking Iskra in her arms. 'Don't you have anyone?'

A light filled Iskra's face. 'There's my *babushka*.'

'You've got a grandma. Where is she?'

Iskra looked at Dina for help. Dina simply shook her head.

'She doesn't know. Iskra thinks her grandmother works in a factory.'

'Which one? Where, darling?'

Iskra shook her head. 'I don't know. It's a big one.'

Dina met Svetlana's eye then Raisa's. 'You cry because she's little. We all have stories like that.'

Raisa came to a decision. 'It's time you went to bed, children. I will take you up.'

She watched them scrambling between crisp, clean, white sheets. There was play-fighting and giggling.

'Goodnight,' Raisa said before leaving the room.

She was halfway downstairs when she heard the chorus of goodnights coming from the room.

'Goodnight, darlings,' she murmured. 'I promise to keep you safe.'

In the hall, Svetlana and Elena were buttoning their coats.

'Must you go?' Raisa said.

'You may have a job at the Commissariat,' Elena answered, 'but Svetlana and I still have to turn up for work at the mill.'

'But you are going to work for the Commissariat of Education soon,' Raisa said, directing her words at Svetlana.

'I haven't left yet,' Svetlana reminded her. 'Until I do, I must turn up on time for work.'

Elena raced up the stairs and wrapped her arms around Raisa's neck. Her mouth was by her lover's ear so that Svetlana couldn't hear.

'Two days, my love, then we will be together all night.'

Soft lips brushed Raisa's ear lobe.

'You are doing a beautiful thing for those children.'

'It is not enough,' Raisa answered. 'There are so many like them. Our worker's state will be judged by what we do for the weakest among us.'

Elena raised her voice.

'We will prevail. Isn't that right, aunty? We will crush the counter-revolution. The workers of Germany, France and Britain will come to our aid.'

Svetlana was nodding.

'We will make the world anew or perish in the attempt.'

Pavel

'Have you got a problem with Kolya, Pavel Sergeyevic?'

They were leaning against an armoured car, watching Kolya talking to Comrade Anishin of the Petersburg Committee.

'Why do you ask?'

'I see the way you look at him. There is suspicion in your stare.'

Pavel flicked his cigarette to the ground and screwed it out with his boot. 'He reaches for brute force a bit too readily for my liking.'

'Odd thing for a soldier to say.' Mikhail had an inkling what this is about. 'Are you thinking about yesterday?'

'Did you see how he talked to that editor? As for his assistant, Christ, she was the same age as my Nina.'

'When are you two getting married?'

Pavel took note of the abrupt change of subject. Mikhail was a survivor, a pragmatist. He didn't like it when people rocked the boat.

'As soon as these bloody pen-pushers arrange the civil ceremony. The speed things work, Nina will be dropping my sprog before I can make an honest woman of her.'

Mikhail patted Pavel on the arm. 'Do we even say things like that anymore? Marriage is a free and voluntary union. Divorce is the right of either partner. We're creating a new world, my friend.'

'We're creating a new world with the same, shit people,' Pavel reminded him. 'It's going to take time.'

Mikhail was intrigued by the conversation taking place across the road. There had never been much love lost between the old Bolshevik Ashinin, a metalworker, and the former student Kolya.

'What do you think they're talking about?'

'I don't know, but it usually means some crap job for us grunts to do. I came out of that newspaper office with a bad taste in my mouth. See, I've got a Party leaflet from before the revolution demanding freedom of the press. So how come we're shutting down newspapers the moment we take over?'

The same guarded expression as before stole across Mikhail's features.

'You heard Kolya. It's a temporary measure against the counter-revolution.'

'How temporary is that, Mikhail? You've been a member longer than me, remember. Maybe you've got used to swallowing every titbit they throw your way. Me, I'm just a moody, suspicious *muzhik* at heart. No matter who's talking to me, I get to thinking, why's this bastard lying through his fucking teeth?'

The snow was fine and wind-tossed, but there was already a sheen of white on the streets of the city.

'Don't you trust the Party yet?'

'The way I see it, you've got a right to your say. We didn't make a revolution by acting like nodding, fucking donkeys. We made a revolution by Bolsheviks arguing with Bolsheviks. Remember when Lenin wanted Kamenev and Zinoviev chucked out of the Party?' He saw Kolya coming over and took a step away from the vehicle. 'The day I hear people swallowing everything the Party bosses tell them is the day I tear up my card and walk away.'

Kolya arrived just in time to catch the last snippet of conversation.

'What's this about tearing up your Party card?' he asked, half-seriously.

Pavel was a combustible kind of man, prone to fiery outbursts and impulsive actions. Kolya was willing to put up with his prickly personality so he could employ his undoubted military talents.

'It was a joke,' Mikhail interjected.

'Don't go talking for me as if I'm some imbecile,' Pavel retorted. 'I said the day people start taking orders instead of arguing the toss is the day I walk away from the party. Fierce argument is the lifeblood of the workers' movement.'

'Then there is no reason for concern,' Kolya replied. 'The debates in our Party are fierce and long. Svetlana gives me a right tongue-lashing from time to time.' Kolya saw the two soldiers looking at him with smirks on their faces and grasped the sexual innuendo. 'Oh, do fuck off. I'm just

24

telling you our Party is based on free and open debate. Nobody tells another comrade what to think.'

Pavel gave Kolya's words a guarded welcome. 'So what's the word from Comrade Anishin?'

'Everybody is worried about the developing situation. Bolsheviks are being withdrawn from the factories to keep the city running. Anishin says the level of political work is declining. Our cadres are in charge of revolutionary tribunals, food supply, doing paperwork, every fucking thing except educating the workers that made the revolution.'

Pavel knew there was more to it than another complaint about Bolsheviks having to take over the state machine.

'And?'

'And there is talk about a permanent body to guard against counter-revolution. Anishin is asking if we're interested.'

Pavel wasn't happy with the word *we*.

'Is that right, Comrade? Well, I didn't see him coming over to talk to me. Or Mikhail here. It seems to me you're the only one getting any information round here.'

Kolya's answer was blunt and firm. 'He talked to me as the elected officer of this unit.'

'Well, I was standing twenty yards away,' Pavel growled back, 'and I would have appreciated being treated with some respect.'

The silent confrontation continued for some moments, tension between the two men taut as elastic. Finally, Kolya held up his hands.

'Fine, you may be right. I should have consulted you and the other men. I apologise.' He tilted his head. 'Are we good?'

Pavel's face was unreadable. He shoved a thumb under his rifle strap and let the cold wind pinch his face. He closed his eyes for a moment, his way of telling Kolya he was thinking about it.

'You remember to tell the men what's happening and I will say no more about it.' He picked at the rifle strap. 'So what's this new unit? How is it different from the Military Revolutionary Committee?'

'They are talking about a commission with the sole purpose of suppressing counter-revolution. The MRC is trying to do every fucking thing, maintain food supplies, control the bourgeois press, keep order, arrest counter-revolutionaries. It can't go on like this. The whole thing goes to the Soviet Executive in a few weeks.' He knew he was walking on egg shells when it came to talking to Pavel. 'So what do you think?'

Pavel nudged Mikhail in the ribs. '*Now* he wants our opinion.'

Mikhail ignored his friend. 'The way I see it, the revolution remains in peril. It took a thousand dead to secure Moscow. The generals are regrouping in the Don. I'm in.'

Kolya nodded with satisfaction. With Mikhail's support, the agreement of the unit was virtually guaranteed. Only Pavel stood in the way.

'Do we still elect our officers?' he asked.

'I am elected,' Kolya said. 'There has been no discussion of this issue, but I don't see why that should change. Why, would you like to challenge me, Pavel?'

'You know what I'd like,' Pavel answered. 'I'd like the things we promised when we made the revolution – peace, bread and land. As soon as I know there will be no more fighting, I am taking Nina back to my village where we can bring our kid up happy and free. How does that sound?'

'That sounds like an admirable ambition,' Kolya replied, 'but a revolution is a civil war between the classes. There will be no compromise. The proletariat has to impose its democratic dictatorship over the defeated bourgeoisie and landlords.'

'Funny thing,' Pavel noted, 'I am hearing a lot about dictatorship and bugger all about democracy.'

'Comrade,' Kolya said sternly, 'what are the Soviets and factory committees but democracy? Tell me when there was such a hornet's nest of debate and argument under the Tsar? When was there ever democracy in Russia before the 1905 Soviet?'

Mikhail decided it was time to interpose himself between them.

'So what about this new commission?' he asked. 'It's all down to you now, Pavel Sergeyevich. The lads will go along with what you say.'

Pavel beat his hands together against the winter cold.

'Down to me is it? Very well, it's like this, there's no future for my kid if the generals bring back the autocracy. My sons and daughters will still grow up on the verge of starvation. Us peasants have risen against the landlords all over Russia. The sons of the peasants, the soldiers in uniform, are saying they're pissed off with dying in their millions on account of the bloodlust of the rich. Damned right, I want to stamp out counter-revolution.'

Kolya held out a hand to shake Pavel's, but Pavel wasn't finished.

'The moment I think somebody is pulling the wool over my eyes, betraying the revolution, I'll put a bullet between his fucking eyes. We don't take orders without having our say. Got that, Comrade?'

Kolya nodded. 'Got it. Now will you shake my hand?'
Pavel took his time, but he took Kolya's hand.

Nina was waiting for Pavel when he returned to their cramped tenement room, with its damp walls, crumbling plasterwork and air of dank melancholy.

'Why must you be out so late all the time?' she asked. 'I miss you terribly. Now that Nadezhda has found the other girls somewhere to live, I get lonely.'

Pavel took her in his arms and ran his palm over her baby bump.

'Doesn't this little one keep you company, kicking and squirming all the time?'

Nina nuzzled her cheek against his, instantly placated. 'Do you think it will be a boy or a girl?'

'Which would you like?'

'Which would you?'

'I asked first.'

Pavel hated these games. Nina was gentle and loving, but her every question gnawed away at him, making him want to scream as if she were caging him with words.

'Very well,' he said, suppressing his irritation. 'Girl.'

'Why a girl?'

'Then she can be my little princess.' He grimaced. 'Listen to that. There's me, a bloody, republican communist and I still talk about the autocrats as if they are our betters. I wonder how many years it will take before we stop using the language of our exploiters.'

Nina frowned. 'I like the word princess. It's just an endearment for a little girl.'

Pavel was unimpressed. 'If you say so. Comrade Kolya would probably shoot me for saying it.'

'You don't mean that!'

Her shocked expression entertained him. Nina was always so literal, taking his outbursts at face value.

'Of course not. There's been fighting and some arrests, but this isn't the French revolution or the Paris Commune, you know. Maybe, for once, the working people can put their case without bloodshed.'

Nina turned to look at him, her face upturned because of the difference in height.

'Are you still arguing with Kolya?'

'All the time. He's a cocky little prick.' He perched on the bed that had to serve as a chair in the tiny room, pulling her onto his knee. 'To hear him talk, you'd think he was some Old Bolshevik, steeled through years of struggle. I remember him when he was hanging round the back of meetings in his blue student cap.'

Nina was leaning against him. She was as thin as ever. He could feel her ribs under his fingers, the flat little breasts. He had tried to get her what food he could, but how could a Bolshevik demand special treatment when so many were going hungry?

'I wish you wouldn't rub him up the wrong way. Nadezhda says he is Anishin's lieutenant. Important men like Shlyapnikov think he is one to watch.'

'I should think he is,' Pavel admitted. 'He is strong-willed and single-minded. That goes a long way in this world. I just wish he had more of a conscience. He's messing Svetlana around.'

Nina's eyes lit up. Pretending to be shocked, she was quite the gossip.

'You mean he is seeing somebody else?'

Pavel uttered a long sigh.

'Either that or he's a counter-revolutionary spy. He leaves us early and turns towards the Nevsky Prospect, but there's Svetlana saying how he is always working into the dead of night. Where is he the rest of the time, that's what I want to know?'

Nina was concerned. 'Are you going to say anything?'

'To Svetlana?' Pavel shook his head. 'I don't know anything. Why plant doubts in the poor woman's mind when I don't have any proof? It would break her heart. She doesn't like to admit it, but she needs Kolya.'

He lay back on the bed, staring up at the shadows on the ceiling, and Nina was grateful to lie with him.

'Revolutions would be a lot more successful if we could make them with the people of the future, not the flawed, self-centred specimens we have now.' He was stroking her neck and her breasts. She was becoming aroused at his touch. 'Do you remember Bakholsky?'

Nina shook her head. 'No, who is he?'

'One of the lads at the barracks. He's got leave to go back to the village for his father's funeral. It is eight *versts* from home. He is going to take my family a letter.'

'Do you miss your village?'

His hand was moving over her stomach. They would make love when he was done speaking.

'I miss it more every day. I always said I would return and grow rye and have children, milk some cows and watch the river flow. I was not made for city life.'

'So why do you stay?'

'The peasants have lived in ignorance for all of time, always fearful of the onset of famine. The revolution offers us a chance to change. There is machinery now that lessens our toil. I can teach the children to read. Nina, there will be a golden future.'

Doubt was written all over her face.

'So we are to leave Petrograd?'

He had his hand under her skirt. Her eyes were shut, her lips parted. Her breathing was coming faster now.

'I can't say when for definite,' Pavel replied. 'We have only just fought a bloody battle to stop the counter-revolution's advance on the city. The German Army remains on Russian soil. There is so much to do.'

Nina pressed him for a straight answer.

'But we will leave?'

Oh, we will leave, Pavel thought. He longed for the blush of the sun on the wheat fields, the scent of the threshing floor and the rhythm of the seasons. To the likes of Kolya and Svetlana, the city was everything, but for him the land was eternal. In spite of everything, war, famine, revolution, drought, the peasants endured.

'We will go home just as soon as the revolution is safe. Will you come with me?'

Nina was moving her hips in time with the rhythm of his hand.

'You know I would follow you to the end of the Earth, my love.'

He studied her face as he touched her. No matter how he tried, no matter how determined he was to repel the image, whenever they were in the throes of passion, Nina's face always dissolved into that of Raisa. How could life be so cruel?

'And you, Pavel, would you follow me?'

Every time she spoke this way, every time there was talk of the future, he wanted to answer with the truth and dispel the doubts that haunted her. She was no fool. She saw the faraway look in his eyes,

'Pavel, my love, would you follow me?'

He kissed her on the forehead.

And lied.

'Of course.'

Raisa

Rising early, she rinsed her face with cold water from the washstand in the corner of the room. She always rose early these days, in the wake of the revolution. There was so much to do. Most of the Bolsheviks she knew were assigned three or four tasks and drove themselves to the limits. It was as if they thought they could change everything by a pure act of will. Working for the embryonic state consumed their every waking moment. Her heart tugged as she thought of Elena. There was precious little time for love when they were straining every sinew to hold on to power.

She listened for some sign of life from the room across the landing, but there was none. There were no giggles, no yawns, no bare feet pattering on the floor. The children were still sleeping.

It was strange having these six kids under the same roof. For months, Raisa had done everything possible to suppress memories of her own time on the streets, but the thoughts kept seeping back, like putrid swamp water under her boot. Did little Dina have her own Bagrov? Was she storing up her own bank of nightmares? In her mind, Raisa was staring up at his fleshy, sweaty face the way she had done when he had found her shivering in a shop doorway. She remembered his first words.

'How long is it since you last ate?'

Yesterday, she had told him.

'What if I told you there was a nice, hot *borscht* waiting for you?'

What's the catch, she had asked.

'No catch. I'm fond of kids. I don't like to see you suffering like this.'

I'm fond of kids. She should have known then. She was not yet sixteen when he raped her for the first time. That was the start of her journey into night, all those men, all that humiliation. She survived it because even survival in Hell is easier than death. Life can be no life at all, but few are ready to snuff out its precious candle. They dream, often against all odds, that a bright, new dawn is possible.

'And I made that dream come true.'

It was a dream born in blood, but the man who died had been a piece of shit. He would have beaten her, crushed her skull, thrown her body into the Neva to join the rest of the pollution. To this day, she felt no regret for what she did to Andrey. If that killer, that sick, sadistic monarchist pig came at her again, she would reach for the razor once more. Yes, and if she met Bagrov again, she wouldn't hesitate to use it on him. In a world where millions were being maimed and killed, even the sweetest spirit can be a monster.

Within minutes, there was *kvass* and hot, sweet porridge waiting for her dirty-faced guests. Raisa was surprised that the children hadn't come running at the first whiff of piping hot food. Yesterday, it was all they could talk about. She climbed the stairs and that was when she noticed, for the first time, that there was a picture missing from the wall at the bottom of the stairs, one bought for Mrs Kuznetsova by her husband. That was the first signal that anything was wrong. Raisa rushed into the children's room. She saw the tumbled beds and no sign of their occupants.

'Dina, Iskra?'

Heart leaping, she pounded down the stairs and searched the downstairs rooms. The children had gone and, with them, some of Mrs Kuznetsova's trinkets and ornaments. This came as no surprise. Innocence doesn't last long on the streets. Starving human beings will do just about anything to satisfy the craving in their bellies. Dina was no different. She had probably had it all planned the moment she saw the boarding house. Raisa had been a fool not to expect it, but she felt the loss keenly.

She forced herself to be practical. There was no blame attached to the children. Maybe there was a gang master to whom they brought the things they stole. Maybe they saw more of a future in some lousy criminal than they did in her promises of a socialist future. She ate her porridge, staring at the snow on the rooftops outside. Finally, she buttoned her coat and put her hat on. She gave the house one more backward glance, wishing she could have said goodbye before the children left. With sadness in her heart, she walked to the Smolny, glancing up at the familiar Palladian façade. She was making her way to the Commissariat when Svetlana intercepted her.

'I thought you were at the mill,' Raisa said.

'Not today,' Svetlana answered. 'Comrade Stahl was waiting for me.'

'So your literacy project has started?'

'Not quite yet,' Svetlana told her. 'The party is turning its attentions to the elections for the Constituent Assembly.'

'More elections?' Raisa said. 'Didn't the Soviets vote in favour of revolution?'

She read the other woman's expression. Svetlana had just been reminded how recently Raisa had joined the party.

'Before the revolution, we Bolsheviks campaigned long and hard for a bourgeois parliament, a Constituent Assembly. We accused our opponents when they delayed the elections. That was all before there was

Soviet power, of course.' She adjusted her kerchief. 'What is it they say, Raisa, Rome wasn't built in a day. Our trials did not end with the seizure of power. They have only just begun. There is no time to relax, dearest. We must renew our efforts. Nothing has really changed until the conditions of the people change.'

Raisa listened intently, trying to make sense of a bourgeois parliament and a workers' government.

'We campaigned for this Constituent Assembly. Now it could be a rallying point for the counter-revolution.'

'So are the Red Guards going to close it down?'

Svetlana shook her head.

'It is not that easy. We campaigned for the Assembly. We can hardly set our faces against it now. We would look like complete hypocrites. No, we will campaign for Bolshevik candidates. Elena is already at work in Anishin's office. You are going to join us.'

'What about the Commissariat?'

'Comrade Kollontai has other staff. She will understand.'

When Svetlana and Raisa entered the office, faces turned their way. One of them belonged to Elena.

'Ah, there you are Comrade Svetlana. You have brought Raisa, I see. The leaflets are ready to pick up at the printers. We are drawing up a list of factories to visit. It is not just handing out flyers. We expect you all to speak on behalf of the party.'

'Speak?' Raisa said, her voice a petrified croak. 'I can't.'

'You spoke once before,' Svetlana reminded her, 'and you did very well. You will not let anyone down.'

Raisa caught Elena's eye and blushed. Before long, the leaflets arrived and they sat side by side, putting them in piles ready for the election campaign.

'How are the children this morning?' Elena asked.

Raisa hesitated, wondering how to break the news.

'They're gone.'

'What?'

'They must have sneaked out of the house while I was still asleep.'

Raisa took a deep breath and explained about the empty beds and the stolen things.

'We should have expected it, I suppose,' Elena said, 'but it is still disappointing. I thought they liked us.'

Raisa devoted herself to the task in hand. 'I would rather not talk about it. What are we supposed to say at these meetings?'

Elena was ready with the party line. 'The elections are a test of the class struggle. A victory for the Bolsheviks in the elections will be a recognition of the successful revolution and backing for the Soviet government.'

'But there must be thousands of villages that have never even seen a Bolshevik. What if we lose?'

'Then it will be another aspect of the emerging civil war.'

The prospect of renewed conflict terrified Raisa.

'Comrade Trotsky is publishing secret correspondence about the War. He will demonstrate that it was an imperialist war. Peace talks are about to begin. At last, the revolution will have a breathing space, Raisa. We can fulfil our dreams.'

Raisa felt a catch in her chest. 'Do you think so? I am weary of conflict.'

Everyone was, well, almost everyone. She wondered about the people who seemed to thrive on it. Did they have no fear? Did they never lie awake in the early hours, hollow inside at the great dark abyss before them?

'First things first. Anishin is going to assign us an election meeting each. We will go in twos.'

'I hope I am with you,' Raisa said.

In the event, as the least experienced of the comrades in the room, she was assigned to Comrade Anishin. On the way over to the engineering factory where the meeting was to take place, he went over the main points. Raisa reacted with dismay.

'Do you mean I am speaking, not you?'

'That's right, Raisa. Don't fear, I will be standing right beside you.'

'Can't you do it, Comrade?' she asked. 'Please. The last time, I spoke on impulse. The words came straight from my heart.'

'You impressed us all. The party needs comrades like you, young fighters who can speak directly to the women workers.'

So it was that she came to be standing on the platform, with Anishin at her side. She began slowly, haltingly, daunted by the mass of factory women before her.

'I am speaking in favour of List 4, for the Bolsheviks,' she said.

A voice boomed from the crowd. 'Speak up. I can't hear you from back here.'

'I am here on behalf of the Bolsheviks,' Raisa said, thrown completely off her stride. 'I am speaking in favour of List 4. This election is an expression of solidarity with the October revolution and Soviet power.'

'That's straight out of *Pravda*,' somebody shouted. 'We know the Bolsheviks are for the revolution and power to the Soviets. Tell us something we don't know.'

Raisa glanced at Anishin, a flash of terror in her eyes. He kept a straight face. Out of the corner of his mouth he hissed a garbled comment about the role of women. Raisa clawed after something, anything to offer to the expectant audience in front of her. She had nothing but the story of her life and started talking about the woman who raised her.

'My mother was a factory worker like all of you, toiling long hours in terrible conditions. She gave birth to me behind a curtain in a bed next to the machines.'

The women recognised the picture she was painting.

'Two years ago, cancer took her. My father died at the Front. I have no other family. My mother made profits for the capitalists. My father shed his blood in their pointless, imperialist war. How was their sacrifice rewarded? Comrade sisters, I will tell you. I was reduced to living on the street.'

Should she make it so personal, she wondered. Raisa sensed Anishin watching her, but averted her eyes. There was no more whispered advice to be had from that quarter. Maybe he was angry with her.

'I had no hope until the women, women like you, took to the streets on International Women's Day, demanding bread. You gave me courage when you presented your bodies to the sabres, whips and bullets of the autocracy. You gave me something to live for.'

Applause followed, steadying her nerves.

'Some of you may know Comrade Svetlana.'

Murmurs of recognition followed the mention of Svetlana's name.

'She took me under her wing that day. She explained that there could be another better world for all of us. Comrades, there are nineteen electoral lists you could vote for. Of these, only the Bolsheviks stand unconditionally for the defence of October. Only the Bolsheviks stand for Soviet power. The party promised you peace, bread and land. Peace negotiations are about to begin with the German imperialists. We will fulfil our promise. The Military Revolutionary Committee is fighting to stop counter-revolutionaries interrupting bread supplies. The peasants will have the land, not the landlords.'

She was encouraged by the warm reception the meeting awards her. Though her stomach was churning and her legs were barely holding her up, she struggled on, words heaving themselves out of a chest so tight she could barely breathe, never mind speak.

'There is more, so much more. The Bolsheviks' opponents would take a step back, disband our Red Guards, let the bourgeoisie crawl back into government through the back door. Is that what you want?'

There were shouts of *no*.

'The Bolsheviks offer hope. There will be laws giving us maternity leave, health benefits and old-age pensions. Together with our brother workers, we women will make common socialist cause. All our children will learn to read, not just the children of the rich. There will be a factory inspectorate paying attention to the rights of women.'

She fought to be heard over the applause and shouts of approval.

'Lists like those of the Kadets represent your enemies. Even now, the Kadets want to continue the war so your husbands, brothers, sons perish on the battlefield. Even the Left SRs want a government without Comrade Lenin or Comrade Trotsky. Don't be fooled. Vote List 4. Women will only be fully emancipated through the victory of socialism. Defend the proletarian revolution!'

After that, Raisa stumbled from the stage. Her heart was slamming and she was so overwhelmed with emotion there were tears in her eyes. When she finally emerged from the crowd, she sought out Anishin.

'Did I do all right?'

'Was all that stuff true?' Anishin asked. 'Did you really live on the streets?'

She was shocked that he could even ask such a question.

'I would not tell a lie.'

Anishin found that amusing. 'There are plenty that do. You remind me of a young Svetlana.'

Raisa was flattered.

'You mean that as a good thing, don't you?'

Anishin nodded. 'A very good thing. There is no better comrade in all Petrograd.'

Raisa had never heard the normally colourless Comrade Anishin talk so warmly before. She ventured a daring comment.

'You sound as if you are a tiny bit in love with her.'

The way his neck reddened told her she had struck a chord. Until this moment, she had always thought of Anishin as much older than her, but he was barely in his mid-thirties himself.

There was a certain sadness in his eyes.

'Is something wrong?'

'Promise you will never breathe a word of this to anyone,' he said. Comrade Anishin had feelings, after all.

'I would never betray a confidence,' Raisa told him.

'I think Svetlana is wonderful,' he confessed. 'She deserves better than that scoundrel Kolya.'

The way he talked about Kolya set off alarm bells. Svetlana was Elena's blood and one of the most caring people Raisa had ever known. She would kill anyone who tried to hurt her.

'Why scoundrel?'

She asked the question while fearing the answer. Anishin took Raisa by the sleeve and led her to one side where nobody was listening.

'Normally, I would not say a word against a fellow comrade, especially one as dedicated as Kolya, but he is not true.'

'Comrade....' Raisa's voice trailed off. 'I don't know your first name.'

'It is Vassily.'

'Vassily, what do you mean. In what way is he untrue?'

'I assume you know that he has been staying at the apartment of a party sympathiser.'

'Yes, Svetlana told me.'

'I have seen him there, with a young woman. I called unexpectedly on a party matter and I saw them enter together. There were the sounds of intimacy. Some days ago, I saw her again. Comrade Raisa, this woman is a prostitute.'

At the word *prostitute*, so many feelings boiled up inside Raisa. Bagrov did not rape her out of lust, but in order to put her to work in his whorehouse. Every day, she dreaded being recognised by one of the men who used her.

'You should not judge a woman who has no other means of earning a living, Vassily.'

'I don't,' he answered. 'I judge the man who uses her services.'

'Do you know this woman's name?'

'No. Why?'

'Because I must talk to her. I will not allow anyone to betray Svetlana.'

Anishin nodded grimly. 'I wish I had never said anything.'

Raisa could still feel her skin crawling as she relived her time in Bagrov's brothel and what she endured there.

'We are Communists, Comrade Anishin. We should never hide the truth.'

There were two more factory meetings on Raisa's itinerary. By the third, she was quite exhausted and Anishin spoke in her place. Raisa had heard the likes of Anishin before, confident, competent, but devoid of passion. She reached the Smolny just as a watery, yellow sun melted into the evening murk. Elena greeted her with a welcoming smile.

'Good news,' she said. 'I am coming home with you.'

'How's that?'

'Aren't you pleased?' Elena asked, sensing something.

Raisa planted a kiss on her lover's cheek. 'Of course I'm pleased.'

Elena still seemed alert to the thoughts haunting Raisa.

'I know you, Raisa my angel. There is something on your mind.'

'We will talk on the way home.'

In the event, Elena was impatient to hear the news and they stopped halfway down the Nevsky Prospect. They found a quiet spot.

'It is Kolya. I think he is seeing somebody else.'

Elena's eyes flashed. 'How could he? What kind of man would hurt our beautiful Svetlana?'

Bit by bit, Raisa explained what Anishin told her.

'I'll rip the bastard's balls off and shove them up his arse!'

Raisa pulled her close. 'I don't doubt that you could do it. You will wait until we know for sure. Not a word to Svetlana.'

Elena had her arms folded. Rage smouldered in her eyes. Raisa insisted.

'You must promise.'

'Very well. Not a word until we know for sure.'

They completed the ten-minute walk to the guesthouse without exchanging another word. Raisa unlocked the door and led the way inside. No sooner had she set foot on the stairs than a high-pitched voice announced the return of the children.

'Dina! Iskra!'

They emerged one by one from the sitting room, guilt etched on every face.

'How did you get in?' Raisa demanded.

Dina was ready with an explanation. 'You left a window open upstairs. We sent Iskra up the drainpipe. She's as agile as a monkey.'

That's when Raisa realised that Mrs Kuznetsova's picture was back on the wall.

'I'm sorry about your stuff,' Dina said. 'It's habit. We were going to fence it then Iskra said she wanted to come back here. Is that all right?'

'Dina, I longed for your return with all my heart, though how I will feed us all, I have no idea.'

Dina dropped her eyes.

'Dina?'

'There was a Red Guard unit. They had cabbage rolls.'

Raisa knew what was coming next. 'And?'

'We stole them.'

'Dina, that is wrong.'

There was the ghost of a smile on Dina's thin, almost bloodless lips. 'So I shouldn't have taken them?'

Raisa could feel her stomach grumbling. 'That isn't what I said.'

'So stealing is all right sometimes?'

'Well, you can loot the looters, take from the bourgeoisie, but Dina, this was Red Guards, the protectors of the revolution.'

Dina had an answer. 'While I am eating, I will make sure I feel very guilty.'

Raisa found it impossible to suppress a smile. 'Well, see you do.'

Kolya

'Shit!'

The campaign was over. The results of the Constituent Assembly elections, with the exception of some of the most remote areas of Russia, were in and they were posted on the wall in one of the Smolny's many rooms. Kolya was reading them in the company of Anishin and Svetlana. There were other party members milling about, trying to digest the significance of all these numbers. Kolya had already come to a firm conclusion.

'Do you know what this means?'

Svetlana ran her finger down the Petrograd results. 'Kolya, calm yourself.'

'Calm myself? Think about it, Svetlana. In the whole of our history, there has never been a single genuinely democratic election. Now, under cover of these results, the same monarchists who blocked any thought of free elections dare to wave the banner of democracy. It makes my blood boil.'

Privately, Svetlana thought too many things made Kolya's blood boil.

'You must get it into perspective. Red Petrograd is our fortress. Just look at the vote, almost a million citizens, 80% of eligible voters and they have rallied to the Bolshevik cause in their hundreds of thousands. We are the clear winners with almost half the vote. We dominate the Vyborg, Peterhof and the other working class districts. The soldiers are with us too. Our hold on power is firm.'

Anishin rushed to agree with her, nettling Kolya. He had been aware for some time of Anishin's feelings for his Svetlana.

'It is the same with Kronstadt,' Anishin said. 'Two-thirds of the Baltic Fleet support the Bolshevik list. It is true in Moscow too, where there is an even higher mandate than Petrograd. We are the clear winners in the urban centres.'

Kolya gave him a pitying look. 'What about the rest of the country? Where does the counter-revolution sit waiting, Comrade Anishin?' There was scorn in his voice. 'Not in the Vyborg. Not on Vasilievsky Island. In Siberia, we have barely ten per cent, five per cent in Transcaucasia. The SRs have almost double our vote across the country. You must face facts. This is serious.'

'Kolya…'

There was a wave of the hand, expressing impatience.

'Our opponents have the Constituent. We have the Soviets. We will never cede power. They will never accept our right to rule. What if they reject the programme of the October revolution? Then it is civil war.'

'These figures don't tell the whole story,' Svetlana said, putting a positive gloss on the results.

'Really?' Kolya answered. 'So what am I missing?'

'The SRs are two parties now,' Svetlana reminded him. 'The programme of the Left is similar to ours in many respects. There is some talk of a coalition.'

Kolya was not to be placated. 'It is still printed as one party on the ballot paper. The Right will claim the victory and there will be no coalition with Chernov.' His fists were clenched, his knuckles white. 'Comrade Lenin was right. The vote should have been delayed to take the new circumstances into account. Our agitators could have gone to the villages where we have no organisation. Did we not promise them land?'

Svetlana refused to accept that the results of the election amounted to a crisis. 'Look at the workers' vote, Kolya. The working men and women stand with us. These are the heroes who made the revolution.'

Anishin listened while his comrades chewed over the result. Kolya sensed a change of heart.

'Say what you think, Comrade Anishin.'

Anishin spoke in a subdued voice. 'I fear Kolya is right. There is no way to distinguish between the Right SRs and the Left SRs and town and country are divided. The counter-revolution will rally around the Constituent Assembly.'

Theirs was one of many arguments raging in the Smolny. The rank and file members knew that somewhere in the former school, Lenin, Trotsky and the rest of the Central Committee would also be digesting the news. Kolya was aware of Anishin scrutinising his every move. As the first rush of blood caused by the election results ebbed, he began to wonder what was going on in Anishin's head. There had been a time when Anishin had dismissed Kolya as just another bookish idealist, but Kolya had won the factory militant's grudging respect during the July Days, proving himself as a man of action. Now there was a change. What was the significance of those brooding looks? Kolya had seen Anishin creeping round Svetlana like a lovelorn hound, but it was more than that. When Svetlana crossed the room to talk to another of the comrades recruited by Stahl to work under Lunacharsky at the Commissariat of Education, he turned to Anishin.

'Do you have something to say to me, Comrade Anishin?'

In Svetlana's absence, Anishin dispensed with any show of civility. 'I have nothing to say to you, Kolya, nothing at all.'

For a few moments, Kolya stood there, blinking with surprise. He followed the engineer to the door with a puzzled stare, then caught him up in the corridor.

'Would you like to tell me what this is all about, Comrade?'

Anishin checked that nobody was eavesdropping. 'I know, you son of a bitch. I *know*.'

A prickle of unease travelled down Kolya's spine, but he controlled his face.

'Know what?'

'I know about you and your whore.' Anishin waited a beat. 'Do you want me to tell you her name? Klara. I dare say there are others. There usually are with men like you.' Kolya's senses were spinning. He should have been more careful.

'Is this some kind of blackmail? What do you want?'

'Oh, I don't want anything, Comrade,' grinned Anishin. 'You see, I am not like you. I don't betray people. I don't treat them like shit.'

Kolya was still struggling to maintain a show of *sang froid*.

'Are you going to say anything…to Svetlana?'

Anishin folded his arms, leaning back against the wall.

'No, I won't say anything. I won't be the one who breaks her heart, you bastard. I can't for the life of me tell why, but she loves you.'

Kolya digested the engineer's answer. 'You don't understand.'

Anishin wasn't interested in explanations. 'I think I understand perfectly, Kolya. There is a coldness inside you. You use people. You are driven by your appetites. Well, maybe that's all right if it only affects your personal life. It might not be a problem if you are just one more party comrade getting up to a bit of naughty.'

'Comrade…'

Anishin wagged a finger.

'No, Kolya, you're going to hear me out. I recommended you for a position of responsibility. That's right, I put in a word for you. Suddenly, I see something in you I don't trust, a flaw in your character.' Anishin was poking a finger in Kolya's face. 'No, I don't trust you one fucking bit. So you be honest with Svetlana or maybe I'll change my mind. I could make life very uncomfortable for you.'

With that, Anishin walked away. Kolya was finding it hard to breathe. Klara was a game, an obsession. Svetlana was the embodiment of the party. She was life. Kolya stood there, clawing at the collar of his shirt, trying to steady his nerves. At that moment, he heard a familiar voice.

'Are you unwell?'

He hadn't heard Svetlana approaching. She laid a cool, welcome hand on his forehead. Her touch reassured him, as though everything was going to be all right, but it wasn't. Nothing would ever be right again.

'You look upset.'

'It's nothing.'

Svetlana's face was clouded by concern. 'Kolya…?'

'I told you. It's nothing!' His voice faltered. 'I'm sorry. I shouldn't have raised my voice.' Finally, he was able to throw her a bone. 'Maybe I've been working too hard. The things we have to do.' He remembered the editorial office and decided to use it to distract her attention. 'We closed down a newspaper, one with Menshevik sympathies. I have doubts about closing socialist publications.'

Svetlana seemed surprised. 'You do? I always thought you were quite without conscience, my Red monster.'

He put an arm around her waist. 'Don't mock me, Svetlana.'

'It's true,' she told him. 'Everyone I know has their doubts, even Comrade Anishin, but not you. I always thought it was because you got your socialism out of books and not from life at the factory bench.'

'You think me too cerebral?'

She laughed heartily at his choice of words. 'If you mean, do I think your mind is always up in the clouds, yes, I do.' She touched his nose fondly with her finger. 'Do you know what people call you?' She let the question hang. 'Robespierre. I suspect you will find it flattering.' She ran her hands down his upper arms. 'Listen, we are done here for today. Do you really need to go out again?'

'No,' Kolya answered. 'I am done for today.'

Svetlana clapped her hands and did a dance as if she was a little girl again. Lights danced in her eyes.

'When do you have to hand back the keys to the apartment?'

'Tomorrow.'

Svetlana took his hand in hers. 'Then we should make the most of our last evening there.'

She showed him what was in her bag.

'I have food enough for the both of us and even a little Vodka. We shall have ourselves a party, my darling Kolya.'

Still, he was unable to play the game of the faithful partner.

'I don't deserve you, Svetlana.'

'Yes, you do, my love. My days would be bleak without you. You make me whole.'

They were on the way out of the building when they saw Anishin waiting alone at a tram stop. Svetlana waved gaily. Seeing them together, Anishin waved back, if a little hesitantly.

'I feel sorry for Vassily,' Svetlana said. 'He agitates among all these factory women, but you never see him with any of the girls. He seems so alone. Maybe I should try to make him a match.'

'No,' Kolya said hurriedly, 'leave well alone.'

Svetlana seemed a little confused. 'Whatever is wrong?' She examined his features. 'There's something going on between you and our Comrade Anishin. What is it?'

'There are disagreements about what will replace the MRC when it is disbanded.'

'And that's it?' She scoffed. 'I don't believe it. There are times when the two of you are like a pair of rutting stags.'

Once more, Kolya was unable to disguise his feelings. Svetlana understood. At least, she understood something.

'Does Vassily hold a torch for me?' she asked. 'Is that it? I'm the point of conflict?'

Kolya seized on the idea. 'I don't like the way he looks at you.'

'Are you jealous?' Svetlana danced ahead of him and did a twirl. 'Oh, isn't this wonderful? Here I am, a forty-five-year old mother of two with spreading hips and stretch marks and I have two young bucks fighting over me. It is like something in a Tolstoy novel.'

'You shouldn't make light of it, Svetlana,' Kolya told her. 'I don't want him near you.'

She took both his hands and kissed him warmly.

'Oh, you stupid young fool,' she told him. 'I love you. Surely you know that by now. Why, I have never given Vassily a second glance. He is a comrade. That is all he is.'

Kolya was keen to press home his advantage, to put distance between Svetlana and Anishin.

'I would feel more secure if you spent less time around him.'

Svetlana evidently found Kolya's supposed jealousy flattering.

'If it makes you feel any better, I will try to arrange to be elsewhere when Vassily is around. When I start my work at the Commissariat, I will see less of him anyway. Hey, here's our tram.'

They raced after the streetcar and clambered on board. Svetlana's lips brushed Kolya's ear.

'Do you want me to give you a demonstration of my fidelity when we get to the apartment? I swear, it will take your mind off Comrade Anishin.'

An hour later, Kolya was lying awake in bed, his chest against Svetlana's back. He had his arm round her, his hand cupping a familiar breast. The moonlight was milky and washed them, as if with cold water. Kolya gave a shudder. This was so natural, two bodies that knew each other well, that clung with such intimacy. *Christ, you're a fool, Kolya*, he thought. Why would he throw away what you have with Svetlana on a mere whim?

He resolved, just as he had many times before, never to see Klara again, to treat her like a pariah and somehow survive Anishin's infernal snooping. Svetlana stirred in her sleep and he considered her face. In many ways, she was still young. How she had survived the work in the mill, the death of a husband and the raising of two children without it wasting her, he couldn't imagine. He had asked her once whether she was worried about falling pregnant. She had explained that she nearly bled to death having Anna. There would be no more children.

'So many trials,' he said, stroking her.

She stirred.

'I am sorry, my love,' he murmured. 'You deserve better than me.'

It was an hour since Svetlana had fallen into a deep sleep. He envied her the peace of mind she seemed to possess. His demons were still there. All kinds of strange thoughts crowded into his mind after dark. He heard the tolling of a bell. It was midnight and the world was slipping into cold, dead silence. It made him think of the counter-revolution rousing itself in the vast lands beyond Petrograd. Terror and blood were two hounds that had been let off the leash. Their hunger would not easily be satisfied.

He was still brooding on these matters when the door handle turned at the entrance to the apartment and he saw a slim figure silhouetted by the dim hall light outside. It was Klara. He wanted to warn her that they were not alone in the flat, but how could he without waking Svetlana? Luckily, Klara did not shout a breezy obscenity the way she usually did. She took a couple of steps forward, her tread causing the floorboards to creak. Kolya came to a decision and scrambled into his trousers before padding across the room in his bare feet to intercept her. A shaft of light fell on Klara's face and he saw the amused look. He waved in the direction of the door.

'Well, well, lover boy,' Klara said once they were out on the landing. 'Just been shagging Svetlana, have you? Who's been greedy? I thought you were done with that old cow.'

'Don't talk about her like that.'

'Why? Do you *love* her?'

In that moment, Kolya detested her.

'Your face!' Klara said. 'You hate me, don't you? Do you know why? It is because we are alike, Kolya.'

'You're not fit to kiss that woman's feet,' Kolya snapped, desperately trying to keep his voice down.

'I bet her feet are not all you've been kissing tonight,' Klara answered mockingly.

She peered through the half-closed door. 'She's got a nice arse, I'll give you that. I can see the attraction for a man. I bet it quivers like jelly when you're banging her.'

'Stop it!' Kolya snarled. 'What are you doing here?'

'It was slim pickings out tonight. Your Red October has screwed up my living. I thought I might come and have some fun with you instead.' She ran her fingers down his chest. 'I bet you wouldn't dare take me here, like this.'

Her hands reached his trousers and the unbuckled belt. She had his cock in her hand. 'This little solider has done one tour of duty already tonight,' she whispered, 'Let's see if we can stroke some life into him.' She felt the way his member jerked in her grasp. 'Oh look, he seems keen.'

'Stop it.'

Klara snorted in his face. 'I don't see you going back inside, lover boy.'

'I hate you, Klara.'

Already, she was hoisting her dress up to her waist and planting her feet apart.

'No, you don't Kolya. Just think about our names, Klara and Kolya. We are like two peas in a pod. We complement one another, my Romeo.'

'I could kill you,' Kolya whispered, his voice thick with lust.

Klara pulled him close so that his erect penis was pressing into her.

'But you're not going to, are you? I know exactly what you are going to do to me.'

Their passion was quickly spent. Kolya trembled as he pulled away.

'The owner is back tomorrow. I will be sharing a place with some other guys, party cadres. I can't see you again.'

Klara adjusted her clothing.

'Oh, you'll find a way.'

Patting his cheek, she made her way down the stairs and out onto the street. Kolya buttoned his trousers and slipped inside the apartment. He was halfway across the room when Svetlana sat up, knuckling her eyes like a little girl.

'Kolya?'

He adopted a reassuring voice. 'I'm here.'

Svetlana was watching him, sitting cross-legged. 'What are you doing?'

'Oh, it's nothing. You know what I'm like.'

To his relief, she relaxed and rolled onto her back. She didn't hear anything.

'Is it your insomnia again?'

Svetlana stifled a yawn. 'You think too much. You allow yourself to be tortured by that restless mind of yours.'

Kolya climbed back into bed and gazed down at Svetlana's trusting face.

'How do you do it?' he asked. 'With so much happening, how do you maintain your peace of mind?'

Svetlana's answer was characteristically pragmatic.

'I have a cause that is just,' she told him. 'I have two children I adore and a lover who makes me feel young. What do I have to worry about?'

Kolya watched her roll over and glimpsed his reflection in the mirror opposite. It would be hours before he could sleep.

Pavel

'Six weeks of Soviet power,' he grumbled, 'and it comes to this.'

He watched the marchers moving southeast along the Nevsky Prospect. Compared to the watching soldiers in their greatcoats and the Red Guards in their motley attire, the crowd looked well-dressed. There were swaying banners announcing the Union for the Defence of the Constituent Assembly.

'The boot is on the other foot,' Mikhail observed. 'The bourgeoisie does the protesting and we do the ruling.'

'Enemies of the fucking people,' was Pavel's verdict as he watched the well-shod feet tramping on the compacted snow.

Mikhail was not always as ready to judge as his friend, but this time there was no argument from him.

'Not many workers or soldiers here,' he grunted dismissively.

The leather-clad figure of Kolya was just down the road, reviewing the march. He had his hands clasped behind his back as he kept watch.

Pavel stamped and blew into his hands. 'He says there are going to be arrests.' Then a gruff laugh. 'I bet he wants to shoot them all.'

This time, Mikhail looked at him askance.

'You're not serious, are you? They don't pose any threat.'

'No.' Then an additional comment. 'Not yet, at least. Do you know what he calls the Kadets?' He quoted from memory. '"The living embodiment of the bourgeois counter-revolution."'

'He'll have got it from Lenin or Trotsky or some such,' Mikhail replied. 'I used to think our Kolya was a deep thinker, but I reckon he filches most of what he says. We could do it too....'

'Only we don't read enough,' Pavel interjected.

A grin. 'Yes, there is that. Read a book and shoot a counter-revolutionary.'

He saw one of the marchers staring. His words had evidently been overheard.

'What's the matter, Citizen? Does the truth hurt? How many of you bastards were backing Kornilov when he mounted his coup?' He pretended to screw his knuckles into his eyes. 'Aw, did we spoil the party out at Pulkovo?'

The retort was quick and indignant. 'General Kornilov only wanted to restore order to this city. Why does that terrify you Reds so much?'

Shrugging off Mikhail's restraining hand, Pavel marched forward.

'Order, is it? And what does that mean? More Bloody Sundays? More Lenas? You like your massacres, you lot. Well, things have changed. We don't go marching behind priests any more, entreating our Little Father to understand our sad plight. That all ended with our two revolutions. These days, we don't ask, we demand.'

The march slowed. Amid the peal of church bells, another demonstrator registered a protest.

'What right do you Bolsheviks have to delay the Constituent? The people of Russia have spoken.'

Pavel ignored Mikhail's pleas to move away.

'Oh, it's democracy, is it? Well, we didn't hear much about democracy from the Romanovs when they were gunning petitioners down like rabbits. I'll tell you about democracy, Citizen. Democracy is when the working people decide they've had enough exploitation and they start to organise themselves. Ever heard of a Soviet?'

Now, there were wagging fingers, contorted faces. Two interpretations of representation confronted one another, the votes of the bourgeois republic and the assemblies of workers', soldiers' and peasants' deputies, the Constituent Assembly and the Soviets.

'You block our way because you fear the will of the people,' one woman shouted.

'Your majority is rigged,' Pavel barked back at her. 'The Right SRs don't speak for all the peasantry. The Left is with the Soviets.'

Suddenly, there were ten, twenty protestors trying to have their say.

'Mother Russia has spoken. Stand aside. Your time is done. The Constituent will meet.'

Fury swelled up from the marching ranks.

'What are you going to do, you Bolshevik swine, shoot every one of us?'

Pavel was twisting this way and that, countering the objections. His attention was drawn to the pealing clarion of bells from the nearby churches.

'Listen to that,' he shouted. 'What, you think you've got the blessing of God? You've got nothing. You want to fight the war to victory, don't you? Well, forget it. We've signed an armistice with the Central Powers. It's peace.'

The clamour rose.

'Shameful surrender!'

'The cowards' peace will not hold.'

Then there was a new note of bitterness and accusation. 'These Bolsheviks, they're in the pay of the Kaiser.'

'German gold.'

'Is that the best you can manage?' Pavel yelled. 'You want to talk about Germany. Your beloved Tsar Nicky is third cousin to the Kaiser. You don't like talking about that, do you?'

At that moment, Kolya arrived. 'Step back, Pavel Sergeyevich,' he advised. 'You're just feeding their appetite for victimhood. We'll deal with them at the appropriate moment.'

His words didn't go down well.

'Deal with us? What do you mean by that?'

'Is that a threat?'

Kolya spun round to answer his interrogator and found himself looking at a familiar face.

'Remember me?' she said. 'Alexandra.'

'You're the secretary from the newspaper offices.'

'I was the secretary,' she said pointedly. 'You put me out of work, you arrogant bastard.'

His eyes narrowed.

'Just keep moving.'

She wasn't done. 'I meant what I said about my brother. The sabres and lances of the Cossacks wait for you scum in the Don. This time you will face real fighting men.' She rejoined her friends behind one of the banners and glanced back. 'We'll see how you red ruffians handle the warriors of the steppe.'

As the march continued along the Nevsky Prospect, there were gaily coloured banners rippling in the wind. Flags hung over the street, welcoming the uprising of the revolution's opponents.

'How many do you reckon?' Mikhail wondered out loud.

'Ten, twenty thousand,' Pavel answered. 'I'm not much good with numbers.'

Kolya shook his head. 'You're wrong. It's more like forty. The votes for the Constituent have emboldened the reaction.'

'That Alexandra remembered you, didn't she?' Pavel said pointedly. 'It seems you have a way with women.'

'What's that supposed to mean?' snapped Kolya.

'Oh, nothing.' Pavel sauntered away, leaving him to chew on the remark.

Presently, Mikhail caught up with him. 'Was that about his whore?'

Pavel was still staring, cold-eyed, at the marchers. 'What do you think?'

As the throng snaked north, it continued along the Liteiny beneath an enormous banner, proclaiming: '*Make way for the electors chosen by the people.*'

'Gravediggers of the revolution more like,' Pavel said.

Mikhail stood beside him, digesting the importance of this moment. 'You're sounding like Kolya.'

Pavel was glum. 'Just because I don't like the fucker, it doesn't mean he's wrong about everything. Maybe if the young had been allowed to vote, maybe if the difference between the Left and Right SRs had been clear in the election, maybe if they'd updated the electoral roll, all this wouldn't pose such a threat. As it is....' He spat on the ground, earning looks of distaste from some of the women marchers. 'This is turning nasty. I don't like it.'

The marchers' destination was the Tauride Palace. Pavel gazed at the vast building with its columns and domes.

'The gates are padlocked. Let's see how determined they are now.'

The answer wasn't long coming. Enraged by the sight of the wrought-iron fence and padlocked gates, the soldiers and Red Guards blocking their way, some of the crowd surged forward. They were clambering into the palace gardens. Already, there was the sound or the orators, Right SR leaders Chernov and Sorokin among them. Some of the delegates elected to the Assembly were making their way inside.

'Look at them,' Pavel said. 'There's Miliukov stirring up the counter-revolution in the Don with Alexeev and Kornilov and we're just standing here, letting them set up an alternative to the Soviets.' He was grinding his teeth as he took in the growing revolt. 'They've got Kaledin on board, Ataman of the Cossack Host. Tell me this isn't serious.'

Mikhail was less concerned. 'The Left SRs are moving towards the Bolsheviks. Whatever happens in the Don, there is nothing they can do to overthrow the Soviets here.'

'You're right about Petrograd.' Pavel conceded. 'We'll shut the fuckers down. That's not what worries me.'

'So what is bothering you?'

Pavel lit a cigarette and squinted through the acrid smoke. 'I've got a wife and there's a kid on the way. If it's up to the likes of Kolya and Anishin, forget about joining the Cheka. We're going to be on the first train south to fight the counter-revolution.'

He had his friend's attention.

'Do you think it's in the offing? We're going to the Don?'

Pavel continued to observe the scenes outside the Tauride, but it was the shadows of galloping Cossack warriors that danced in the deepest corners of his imagination.

'See this?' Pavel answered. 'It is nothing but a sideshow. They're raising the banner of counter-revolution in the Tauride, but the guns are being primed in cities like Rostov and Novocherkassk. You need to see the big picture.' He recognised the look of shock in Mikhail's face. 'Funny thing, my friend, you've been a Bolshevik longer than I have, but in many ways, I think you're new to this game. The slogan on our lips was peace, bread and land, but there are things written in Lenin's pamphlets you should remember.'

Mikhail continued to listen, sullen with the realisation that his comrade was right.

'Revolution is civil war, Mikhail, my brother. I don't think I understood it until now. These generals, they were never going to make peace with the revolution. Pulkovo Heights was only a skirmish.'

'Some skirmish,' Mikhail muttered. 'It was bloody enough for me.'

'I didn't realise at the time,' Pavel told him, 'but that fight was nothing, nothing at all. Kolya understands it. The real thing is coming.' He waved his arm at the furore around the Tauride. 'This is a rumble of thunder before the storm.'

Mikhail rubbed his face with his sleeve. Were those tears in his eyes, Pavel wondered.

'Are you OK?'

Mikhail snatched his arm away.

'Am I fuck!'

Pavel shouldered his rifle and took a few steps before turning.

'Bad news doesn't go away just because you stop talking about it.'

An hour later Pavel was alone. Mikhail's temper hadn't improved and he had gone to get drunk. Pavel found that his steps had taken him towards Mrs Kuznetsova's boarding house. He stood, gazing at the lighted windows, remembering a conversation with Raisa, a time there had seemed to be an unexpected warmth between them. He was about to turn towards home when the door creaked open. There she was, standing on the step, watching him with a question in her eyes.

'Pavel Sergeyevich?'

'I was at the Tauride,' he mumbled. 'I found myself in the area.'

'The palace is quite a walk from here,' Raisa reminded him. 'It is cold. Would you like to come in? You could have some tea.'

Pavel nodded and followed her inside. He was instantly greeted by six curious faces. The children watched the soldier hanging up his coat.

'I heard you had…guests.'

Raisa did the introductions, finishing with Dina and Iskra.

'How do you feed them all?' Pavel asked when the children vanished into the next room, ushered away by Dina, the oldest.

'It is hard, but I get some help from the Commissariat. This is now officially a state children's home.'

'What makes it official?'

Raisa laughed. 'I signed a form. Somebody got Comrade Kollontai to countersign it. Until we get access to proper accommodation it doesn't mean much.'

'Don't run yourself down,' Pavel said. 'You've done well.'

Raisa seemed less sure. 'I have a feeling there will be many more children coming my way. There is an urgent need to shelter these kids.' Instinctively, she turned towards the sound of children's voices. 'Do you remember Dina?'

Pavel has no problem bringing her to mind.

'Yes, her head is shaven.'

'That's her. How old do you think she is?'

'I don't know, eight, nine maybe.'

'She is twelve. She will be thirteen soon. She is nearly a woman. That's the effect of malnutrition.'

Pavel was shaken by the information. 'Poor kid. It's not much of a childhood, is it, living on the streets?'

The wind whipped against the windows, reminding them of the conditions.

Raisa lowered her gaze. 'No, it is no life at all.' Pavel put down his cup and asked the inevitable question.

'Where is Elena?' he asked.

'She went to the Tauride with Svetlana to watch the march,' Raisa answered. 'There is real concern about this crisis. Kolya thinks it will spur the counter-revolution to action.' She plucked at a thread on her dress.

'Maybe it should have been delayed so that people understood the Left and Right SRs were different parties. The election has sowed confusion.'

'That's what I said to the marchers.' Pavel said.

'You were on duty?'

Pavel nodded. 'Yes, I just came from there. There's going to be bloodshed. They hate us and some of our lads are itching to teach them a lesson. I tell you, Raisa, there is no end to this thing. I didn't quite grasp it at the time, but the day we took power, we declared war on all the past generations of Mother Russia and all the Great Powers. You know what we did, we kicked a hornet's nest many times bigger than all of us put together.'

Raisa listened with her hands folded on her lap, wondering what had brought him here. He had declared his love for her once before and his voice sounded the same as it did then. The noise of the children playing rose suddenly in volume. Pavel spoke over the tumult.

'It is hard what happens to children out there on the street.'

Raisa held back from explaining the horrors she had experienced.

'The reason I am here, the reason I need to talk to you…'

'Don't.' It was too much. Raisa couldn't bear to discuss Pavel's infatuation.

'No, please hear me out. I feel the same as I did when I professed my love for you once before, maybe more so, but I know it can never be. We are comrades in the cause of socialism.'

Raisa held herself back from interruption, but why would he turn up like this when he understood her feelings towards Elena? Why humiliate himself again?

'You will always be in my heart, Raisa. I had to talk to you face to face, be honest with you. You see, I saw the counter-revolution today. Those crowds at the Tauride, it isn't just this Assembly they want, it is Russia cleansed of Soviets, of Bolsheviks, of people like us. War is coming and it will be more savage, bloodier than the conflict with Germany.'

'You mustn't say that. It's unimaginable.'

'It's only too real, for a peasant like me. I've seen the landlords at first hand, bastards the lot of them. The war of classes will always be more brutal than the war of nations.'

Raisa gave the briefest of nods. He was only confirming what she had feared for so long.

'The generals are raising an army in the Don. We don't know how strong they are or how much backing they have from the Great Powers, but they are arming.'

Raisa finally cut him off with a wave of her hand.

'Pavel Sergeyevich, I am a Bolshevik just like you. I hear the same talk at the Smolny. Let us be honest with one another. What brought you here?'

Pavel thought of Nina waiting for him, the new life growing inside her.

'There are times in life when you need to draw a line, to make up a balance sheet and move on. I am a soldier, Raisa Alexeyevna, I would like to think a bloody good one. I am earmarked to lead a detachment being sent to the Don.'

Without knowing why, Raisa felt a sudden sense of loss. Pavel could never be a lover, but he was a friend on whom she had come to depend.

'I see.'

'It is possible that my child will be born while I am gone. Maybe I will never return.'

Without thinking, Raisa reached out and took his hand.

'I shouldn't be here,' Pavel said. 'I have a wife, the mother of my unborn son. My feelings for you are a betrayal of her love for me. For all that....I have to be true to my feelings. I love you still, Raisa. I will love you until my dying breath.'

He withdrew his hand gently and made his way to the door. Her eyes followed him.

'That's it? That's what you had to say?'

He pulled his scarf up over his mouth. His voice came out muffled.

'That's it. I have said everything I wanted to. I may see you again before I leave. Maybe I won't. Have a good life, Comrade Raisa.'

Raisa's voice was soft and coloured by melancholy.

'You too, Pavel Sergeyevich. May good fortune go with you.'

Kolya

He walked from the direction of the Admiralty and strode through the door of Number Two, Gorokhovaya Street in a forced show of confidence, saluting the sentry, a man he remembered from the night they guarded the bridges over the Neva together, the night of the insurrection.

It still wounded Kolya that he had not been at the Winter Palace, which would forever go down as the focal point of the revolution. He made his way to the front desk of the Cheka's new headquarters and stood to attention in front of the clerk, a pale, rigid woman who took her own good time to register his presence.

'Name and patronymic?' she asked without even looking his way.

He suppressed the instinct to laugh and announced himself in clipped, neutral tones.

'I am Nikolai Nikolayevich Markov. I am here to see Comrade Peters.'

The clerk treated him to a cool stare. 'Take a seat, Comrade.'

Kolya turned and saw a row of wooden chairs. He sat and crossed his legs, watching a procession of leather-coated men coming and going. While he was clad in his short jacket, the one that was nevertheless voluminous around the slight frame of his diminutive temptress, Klara, they were wearing long coats that billowed out as they walked. Presently, a clock chimed. He had been waiting for ten minutes. A second bell followed. It was a moment before he realised that the clerk had just slapped her palm on the counter bell to get his attention. For the first time there was some expression in her face. She seemed amused that she had caught him in the middle of a daydream.

'Comrade Peters is ready to receive you now, Comrade Markov.' She made her fingers walk. 'Move along. He doesn't like being kept waiting.'

Kolya stared at the building's bewildering interior. 'Would you mind directing me to his office?'

The fingers walked again, indicating the way. 'When you reach the staircase, it is the third door on the left.'

Kolya had almost reached the staircase when he heard her voice behind him.

'Remember to knock before you enter.'

Kolya nodded, found Peters' office and rapped on the glass panel before him.

'Come in.'

He found himself in the presence of the notorious veteran of a London robbery in which three policemen were killed. Peters was a man of some notoriety.

'I am....'

'Comrade Kolya. Yes, I know. You are a friend of Vassily Anishin.'

Kolya hesitated, wondering how to answer. 'Yes, I know Comrade Anishin.'

Peters had a broad face and a shock of dark hair. 'Boring fucker, isn't he?'

Kolya stared for a moment, before laughing out loud. 'A bit, yes.'

'A lot, I'd say. Dull as fucking dishwater.' The Latvian continued. 'Comrade Anishin is the one who recommended you.'

'I am grateful to him.'

'I expected two other comrades, Pavel Sergeyevich Kirilenko and Mikhail....'

'They have been reassigned to the Transcaucasus.'

Peters frowned. 'They're going to the Front? I was not informed.'

Kolya preferred not to go into his recent disagreements with Pavel. 'They volunteered. They will be leaving in the near future.'

Peters considered Kolya's answers for a few moments, made a note and continued his remarks. 'I assume you are familiar with the remit of the All-Russian Emergency Commission for combating Counter-Revolution and Sabotage?'

'I am familiar with the remit of the All-Russian Emergency Commission for Combating Counter-Revolution and Sabotage,' Kolya echoed.

Peters raised a bushy eyebrow.

'Fancy yourself as a wit, do you, Comrade?'

Kolya scrambled to redeem himself. 'I apologise, Comrade Peters. It just popped out. I'm...rather nervous.'

To Kolya's surprise, Peters grinned. 'I know. I'm taking the piss.'

Kolya relaxed.

'Comrade Dzerzhinsky put it better than I can,' Peters said. 'The Cheka requires hard, dedicated comrades who are prepared to do anything in defence of the revolution. Have you met Comrade Dzerzhinsky?'

Kolya shook his head. He knew Dzerzhinsky's reputation, of course. The head of the Commission was legendary as a selfless Polish revolutionary. Kolya had glimpsed the tall, lean Dzerzhinsky at meetings, but had never been in his presence. He remembered Iron Felix's angular features and dark, intense eyes, a beard, a receding hairline and a high domed forehead.

'You will meet the Comrade-Director presently,' Peters informed him casually.

'It will be an honour.'

Peters nodded. 'Of course. So are you?'

Kolya hesitated, wondering what he is being asked. 'Am I...?'

He had an idea that Peters was playing a game of verbal cat and mouse with him.

'Are you ready to do anything in defence of the revolution? It's in the job description.'

Kolya felt like an idiot. He rushed out his answer.

'Of course, Comrade Peters. I feel that we have been handling these counter-revolutionaries with kid gloves. We released the cadets during the insurrection and they promptly shed Red Guard blood at the military schools. We released General Krasnov on parole after he promised not to foment counter-revolution and he immediately rushed off to the Don to join Alekseev and Kornilov. We…'

Peters cut him off in full flow. 'I know the record, Comrade. You are right. Soft hearts don't win revolutions. The opponents of the proletariat are a many-headed hydra. The time for leniency is over. We intend to meet force with force. Those who rise against the revolution will be struck down with an iron fist. Are you prepared to deliver the blow, Kolya?' Before Kolya could answer, Peters added a second question. 'Are you happy with me calling you Kolya?'

'Kolya is fine. Yes, I am ready to crush our enemies.'

Peters nodded with satisfaction. 'Good. Then we will get to work. How would you characterise the political situation?'

Kolya tried not to hesitate. 'The immediate challenge is that the counter-revolution is grouping around the convening of the Constituent Assembly. If the majority votes against the decrees of the Soviets on the issues land, peace and workers' control they are effectively demanding the dismantling of the gains of October.'

'Succinctly put,' Peters observed. 'Anything else?'

'The Kornilovites are raising an army in the Don. The nationalists are challenging our power in the Ukraine.'

Peters continued to nod.

'I…' Kolya searched his thoughts. 'Things may not be as bad as initially thought.'

'How's that?'

'The counter-revolution claims authority because of the SR vote in the Constituent elections, but the Left SRs have now completed their formation as a distinct political party.' He paused, expecting a further nod of encouragement, but Peters was busy scribbling a note, which put Kolya slightly on edge. 'The Left SRs are now in a coalition with the Bolsheviks in government.'

'So we can trust them to support us?'

Kolya sensed that a trap was being laid. 'The Bolshevik-Left SR coalition is enough to justify our defence of Soviet power in the face of the challenge from the Constituent, Comrade Peters.' He was about to ask whether that was right, but decided that asking such a question would be a bad idea. Instead, he ploughed on. 'Nonetheless, the Left SRs have in the past criticised the Military Revolutionary Committee. By implication, they may try to limit the freedom of action of the Cheka.'

Peters slapped his palm on the desk in front of him. 'Precisely! Well put, Kolya. Our Left SR friends may soon be joining us as members of the Cheka, but the initiative has to come from us Bolsheviks.'

The news that the Left SRs might join the Cheka came as a surprise to Kolya. Peters continued without a break.

'We will not allow the Left SR handler to slap a collar and lead on the Bolshevik dog. These bloody civil servants are still trying to paralyse Soviet rule. The last thing we need is endless negotiations about how to deal with opposition. When we call a spade a spade and label the Kadets enemies of the people, they squeal like pigs.'

He thumped his forefinger down.

'We know some of the Kadets, including as prominent a leader as Struve, are in contact with the counter-revolutionary conspiracy in the Don, but the moment we exercise the right to arrest suspects, the SRs, the likes of Commissar Steinberg, demand a review of where and how we hold them. This is intolerable, Kolya. We will not fight our enemies with one hand tied behind our back.'

Kolya wondered whether he should say something, but it was as if Peters had become oblivious to his presence.

'We have reports of junior army officers planning an uprising against Sovnarkom, but still Steinberg seems more interested in controlling the defenders of the revolution than arresting its opponents.' Finally, he turned his gaze in Kolya's direction. 'What do you think we should do, Kolya, faced with such obstruction?'

Kolya thought carefully before answering. 'We must retain our freedom of manoeuvre, Comrade Peters. That is essential.'

'Good. That is the view of the Cheka's leadership. Our personnel must not be diluted by idiots who are blinded by bourgeois liberalism.'

Encouraged, Kolya added to his opinion. 'We must be prepared to take pre-emptive action to behead conspiracies before they come to a head.'

Peters thumped the table.

'Absolutely! Give me a concrete example.'

Kolya was delighted to be asked. Hadn't Peters already outlined the obvious scenario?

'These army officers,' he replied. 'Simply waiting for them to take arms against the Soviets would be suicidal. It is just two months since we took power. We can't afford the luxury of gathering evidence. There could be countless dead before we have the proof to put before a tribunal.'

Kolya was sure that he had answered the questions to Peters' satisfaction. He had been reading everything written by Lenin, Trotsky and Dzerzhinsky on the matter, taking painstaking notes and practising his answers to a potential interview in front of the mirror. He had even roped in his beloved Svetlana to help him rehearse.

'Which brings me back to my question, Kolya,' Peters said. 'This is the land of the knout and the pogrom. We do not have the luxury of decades of parliamentarism and open bourgeois democracy. The fight to retain power will be bloody and harsh. If we lose, we can expect no quarter from our enemies. I asked you if you were willing to undertake any action necessary to defend the revolution. It is the same question Comrade Dzerzhinsky and I, indeed all the members of the presidium of the Cheka ask. Are you ready to fight the enemies of the revolution to the finish?'

Kolya leaned forward. This was his kind of language. At last, the gloves were coming off.

'I am more than ready, Comrade Peters. I am eager to get started.'

Kolya left Number Two, Gorokhovaya Street after dark, head buzzing with Comrade Peters' words. He stood in the street outside, looking up at the subdued lighting that came bleeding from the building's windows. He tramped across the snow newly-fallen snow, the bloom of enthusiasm from his first day with the Commission draining away as he anticipated an evening in the company of his new roommates. A cramped, dingy flat had replaced the spacious apartment where he had entertained both Svetlana and Klara. It was a considerable step down. He had a choice – to go looking for Svetlana in the hope that she would invite him home or to retire to his new lodgings and listen to the dismal snoring of the other occupants.

Snow was spiralling against the clear, starlit sky. He watched the scene for a while, captivated by the elegance of it all, yet crushed by its vast emptiness. There was a third option, one he had tried to force from his mind. He recalled the urgent, furtive fucking on the landing that last night at the apartment and he craved Klara's touch. Maybe that was what he needed at this moment. She had her own place after all, tiny, damp and unwelcoming, but at least it was a room with a bed. With any luck, she would not be entertaining. She would be ready to relieve the sudden depression that had descended upon him on leaving the Cheka headquarters.

A brief walk took him to the Nevsky Prospect and the bitter-sweet promise of Klara. He wandered her usual haunts, expecting to see her at any moment, but there was no sign. So he waited. Presently, he heard footsteps crunching on the show and turned, face lit with expectation, only for his momentary ecstasy to be dispersed in an instant. Brown eyes blazed with accusation and betrayal.

'Waiting for somebody, Kolya?'

His flesh crawled. This moment was always going to come, but there was no reassurance in inevitability.

'Svetlana!' His heart was like lead in his chest. 'It is wonderful to see you, but what brings you here at this time of night?'

Though he already knew the answer, he willed it not to be so.

'I should cut that lying tongue out of your head, Kolya.'

Kolya painted a look of shock and wounded innocence on his face.

Svetlana held her arms wide. 'What could bring me to this corner at such an hour, I wonder. Maybe I decided to prostitute myself on the street like your little friend.'

Horror welled up inside him. She knew!

'Svetlana, I don't...'

'Please don't think about constructing another mountain of lies, Kolya. I have had doubts before, you see, but you always had plausible explanations. Do you know what love is? It is the willingness to suspend disbelief long after you know in your heart of hearts that you are betrayed.'

'It was Anishin, wasn't it?' said Kolya, weighed down by despair and consumed with rage. 'He told you. Don't listen to the lying bastard. He wants you for himself, Svetlana. He is jealous.'

For several moments, Svetlana didn't speak, confining herself instead to tracing lines in the snow with the toe of her boot.

'I don't doubt it, Kolya. I am quite aware of Vassily's feelings for me.'

'That's it then,' Kolya cried eagerly. 'It isn't what you think. I happened to meet Klara and we got into a conversation. I told her that whoring is no life, no life at all.' He searched Svetlana's face, hoping to see doubts forming. 'Yes, I felt sorry for her and said I might be able to get her some clerical work at the Commission, anything to pluck her off the street. I know it must seem far-fetched, but it is true. Svetlana, I love you and only you.'

Svetlana continued to make patterns in the snow. She gazed intently at the marks she was making as if they contained some magic formula by which she could judge the veracity of his words.

'Svetlana,' Kolya said when she failed to respond, 'you must believe me. Don't trust Anishin. He would do anything to prise you away from me.'

Finally, she met his eye. 'It wasn't Anishin who told me, was it Elena?'

Kolya heard movement and turned to see Svetlana's niece shoving a frightened-looking Klara forward.

'Svetlana....'

Before he could say another word, Svetlana strode forward. She swung her felt boot and he felt a searing pain between his legs. With a groan, he crumpled to the ground, knees punching twin holes in the newly-fallen snow. He felt strong fingers wrapping themselves in his hair and jerking his face upwards. Svetlana crashed her fist into his face and his whole head was numbed. For a moment, the only sensation was the sweet taste of blood in his mouth. Svetlana wasn't done. Klara broke free of Elena's grasp and tried to run, but Svetlana outflanked her and sent her to the floor with a backhanded slap. Klara cried out and knelt sobbing at her attacker's feet.

'I should apologise to you,' Svetlana panted, nursing her throbbing fist. 'You owe me nothing, you pathetic, little bitch. What possessed you to get involved with a selfish prick like Kolya anyway? I would have thought this trade would have sickened you of men. Are you in love with him?' Svetlana liftted Klara's tearstained face with her thumb. 'Oh, you poor, wretched fool. You are. He has played us both.'

Kolya was rising unsteadily to his feet. Svetlana turned, eyes blazing.

'My advice to you, Nikolai Nikolayevich, is to get the fuck back on your knees before I knock you down again.'

Kolya did as he was told. 'Svetlana, please don't hate me.'

'Hate you?' Svetlana said. 'You really are full of yourself, aren't you? I despise you, you prancing buffoon, with your leather jacket and military boots. What's more, I am disappointed in myself for not seeing through you earlier. Do you know what I did when Elena told me about you and your piece on the side? I told her to get out of my sight. That's right, I lost my temper with my own niece.' She took a long, deep breath. 'But I knew. The moment she said it, I knew she was telling the truth.'

Elena reached for her aunt. 'Come away. Don't waste your breath on the lousy shit.'

Svetlana nodded and the two women walked away, arm in arm. Kolya stayed where he was, spitting blood onto the snow. Before long, Klara approached on her knees.

'You look ridiculous,' Kolya told her.

'Don't be cruel,' Klara pleaded. 'Not after this.' She worked her jaw. 'That bitch hits hard.'

He inspected her face. 'You'll mend. I suppose this was always going to happen, wasn't it? We were hardly discreet.' There was blood at the corner of her mouth, which he wiped with his sleeve. 'Don't worry, she hasn't spoiled your looks. She could have, you know. Svetlana is the kind of woman who could snap a man in half. A matchstick like you, hah, she would have no problem doing lasting damage.'

Klara began to sob and Kolya wrapped an arm round her shoulders. 'That's right, get it out of your system.'

Klara reacted angrily, shrugging his arm away. 'Stop being so fucking patronising, you monster. She hit me. All on account of you.'

To her horror, Kolya started to laugh. 'Yes, she did, didn't she? It was nothing compared to the treatment she gave me. My balls still haven't recovered. They'll be swollen like beetroots. He shoved his little finger between his split lips. 'That's not all. I think she loosened a tooth.'

Klara was staring at him. 'What's wrong with you? She hurt us both, the rotten cow.'

Kolya sat on the snow, with fresh flakes falling on his face.

'Oh, we hurt her a lot worse than she did us, my little scorpion. She's putting a brave face on it, but we just broke her heart. Shit, I am a complete bastard, a real pig.'

Klara was staring at him as if he had just torn off his clothes and started dancing naked on the snow.

'You're mad!'

'No, not mad, just a little bit...what am I trying to say here? Yes, I am a little bit fucking human, that's what I am.' He shook his head. 'That's the trouble with this revolution. It needs noble, incorruptible heroes and what's it got, stupid fuckers like me.'

He leaned across and planted a kiss on Klara's swollen cheek.

'That hurts,' she protested.

Kolya grunted. 'Yes, and so does life. It hurts like a bastard. I'm sorry, Klara, sorry for dragging you into my poisonous sea of crap.'

Klara struggled to her feet and held out a hand.

'You can come back to mine,' she said. 'Don't worry, there won't be any men coming knocking. I'm done with whoring.'

'When did this happen?'

'I've been wanting to get off the streets since I met you.'

'Found love, have you?'

Klara's eyes glistened with tears. 'Don't mock me, Kolya. Please don't make fun of me.'

Kolya took her hand, skidding as he got to his feet. He wrapped a hand round her thin shoulders.

'I'm not going to add to your troubles.' He pressed his lips to hers. 'Well, at least tonight has done away with one complication. It's just the two of us from now on, Scorpion. I might even be faithful.'

Klara pinched him. 'You better had be.'

They hadn't gone far when she put another question to him. 'Do you love me, Kolya?'

He skidded to a halt and took her pinched, pale face in both hands.

'Now that's one hell of a question to put to a man with aching balls. What's love, Scorpion? I thought I loved Svetlana, but I treated her miserably. The war has done many things to those in its path. It has abolished decency and humanity. It has broken the family. Maybe it has destroyed love. All that's left is survival, revolution and screwing.'

'You don't believe that.'

He kissed her. 'I believe in revolution. It is the only way out of the mess we keep making of our wretched lives. Beyond that, I am struggling to know what I believe, Klara. I have been left with few certainties. Let's say I am reconciled to two. The first and most solid is that I will defend the revolution to my dying breath. It is the hope of the world.'

'And the second?'

'Ah, the second,' Kolya said. 'It's you.' He let it sink in. 'I can't tell you I love you, but right now I need you. Is that enough for you?'

Klara returned his kiss.

'It will have to do,' she said, 'for now.'

Pavel

Hitherto, Pavel had considered Comrade Anishin a time-server. Didn't he side with Kamenev and Stalin in accepting the Provisional Government before Lenin arrived to shake things up?

'Men change,' he murmured, the wind catching at his words

'What's that?'

Pavel's words weren't really meant for Mikhail, but he continued anyway.

'None of us stay the same, do we? I always knew Kolya saw Vassily Ashinin as a rival, but there's something else just lately. Do you think it's about Svetlana?'

Mikhail shrugged. 'You mean Kolya's got a rival?'

'That's exactly what I mean.'

Mikhail wasn't interested. He was more concerned about what was happening outside the Tauride Palace. 'What do you think he's got planned for us this time?' he asked, watching Anishin wandering around the barracks yard. Armoured cars and trucks were shuddering to life, ready to move out. Exhaust fumes hung in the damp, cold air.

'We're going to clean out the Constituent,' Pavel told him, 'sweep away the rubbish. This is our last job before they ship us south to fight the generals. We're going to slap two arse-cheeks of the counter-revolution, one here and one in the Don.'

Mikhail had reconciled himself to the idea of leaving Petrograd. He had no ties binding him to Peter. Like Pavel, he had roots in a village many miles out in the vast, frozen heart of Russia. Presently, Anishin mounted a flat back truck and the soldiers shuffled forward to hear what he had to say.

'Comrades,' he began, breath misting before his face, 'your fortitude and loyalty is needed again. Two powers face each other here in red Petrograd. The Constituent Assembly is a bourgeois parliament. It represents a step back from the republic of Soviets we created less than three months ago on these streets. When you elect a delegate to the Soviet, you can remove him if he fails you. There is no such power of recall in a bourgeois parliament. This Constituent has no future. This is not just the position of the Bolshevik party, but of our new coalition partners, the Left SRs. All of those who rallied to the Soviets are against the Constituent.'

Mikhail listened to his speech and shifted his feet uneasily.

'He's no orator, this Anishin. Most of the guys here don't give a damn for the ins and outs of party allegiances. They just want what was promised, peace, land and a full stomach.'

'Maybe,' Pavel replied, 'but Comrade Anishin means what he says. I trust him.'

'Like you trusted Kolya?'

'We all make mistakes,' Pavel answered. 'I'll be glad to be out of the city so I don't have to see the fucker's face.'

Anishin was ploughing through his speech, trying to stir some enthusiasm in the soldiers' ranks.

'These bankrupt men at the Tauride, what do they have to offer? The Soviets are the guarantors of the decrees on peace and land, workers' control and national self-determination, an eight-hour working day and a minimum wage. We will not let them dismantle our hard-won gains.'

He was finally having an effect on the men before him. Pavel took the opportunity to give Anishin some much-needed support.

'Enough talk,' he shouted suddenly. 'Comrade Anishin is right. The Constituent Assembly is made up of the enemies of the people. Some of them are using this crisis to prepare an insurrection. You know what happened on New Year's Day, don't you? Only this week, the bastards tried to assassinate Comrade Lenin, fired on his car. Some of us were at the meeting where he'd been speaking, preparing us for the journey south to deal with Kornilov and Kaledin. It's a miracle he wasn't badly injured. Well, if that's how they want to do things, we're ready for them. Do you know what the counter-revolutionaries' slogan is?'

He waited a beat. 'All Power to the Constituent Assembly, that's what they're saying. Thieving buggers. They're taking our words and twisting them. Well, we know the real slogan, don't we lads? All Power to the Soviets. We can sack our delegates. Try getting rid of anybody elected to the Constituent. Their fat arses will be glued to their seats.'

The other men were nodding. Pavel had rallied them to the cause of defending the workers' state.

'Tell us what to do, Comrade. We are ready.'

Anishin located him in the crowd and gave him a grateful nod.

'Move out.'

Clambering into the transport, Pavel glanced back at Mikhail. 'This isn't going to end peacefully.'

Mikhail shrugged. 'So long as it ends. If they stick to marching and no funny business, I'm happy. Let's get it over with. You know these bourgeois. A well-aimed kick up the backside and they will limp away home. They've no stomach for a fight. They didn't even defend the Winter Palace.'

Pavel spotted Anishin sliding into the front seat of the truck, seated next to the driver.

'So what's the plan?'

'Supporters of the Constituent Assembly are meeting at nine assembly points. From there, they are going to converge on the Field of Mars and join together for the approach to the Tauride Palace then it is back out to the Nevsky Prospect to disperse. The Red Guards and the Baltic sailors are out in force. We're there to support them.' He twisted round to look at Pavel. 'When do you leave for the Don?'

'It can only be a few days now. Other units have already gone.'

Anishin nodded. 'It won't be a walk in the park. They're tough bastards, these Cossacks.'

Pavel inspected his rifle. 'Tell me something I don't know. They're expert horsemen and we'll be descending on their home territory. They will have something to defend.'

He took hold of Mikhail's shoulder and gave him a shake.

'My good friend Mikhail thinks we'll wind up buried in some corner of the Don or the Kuban. Isn't that right?'

That earned a soldier's scowl.

'If I am, there will be ten counter-revolutionaries rotting next to me.'

Anishin laughed out loud then he saw a column of demonstrators forming up behind two large banners. As the regiment formed up on the snow, he gave his final instructions.

'This is it, Comrades. Anybody who refuses to obey your orders will be arrested. If shooting breaks out, return fire without mercy.'

The men exchanged glances. Pavel was the first to speak.

'Say that again.'

'Are the marchers armed?' Mikhail asked. 'Why are we talking about returning fire?'

'My information,' Anishin said, 'is that it is possible.'

Pavel didn't like the evasive tone. He had always thought Anishin was a straight-talker.

'But do we *know* they are?' he demanded.

Anishin seemed evasive. 'I do not have that information.'

'What's going on here? Either they're armed or they're not. You must have an idea.'

Anishin failed to meet his look. 'Counter-revolutionaries just tried to assassinate Lenin. If they give us any trouble, we let them have it.'

'You mean if they shoot first?'

Suddenly, the entire atmosphere had become oppressive. The Tauride gardens looked like an armed camp, full of bivouacs, field kitchens, machine gun posts and artillery emplacements.

'This is how the city looked when Kornilov was coming,' Pavel observed. 'So it isn't just a demonstration?'

'The Cheka has uncovered plans for a rising. The word is the counter-revolutionaries lack the strength and will restrict themselves to a demonstration, but we are prepared for any eventuality.'

Like Mikhail, Pavel craved a straight answer, but none was forthcoming. Soon the marchers started to arrive. Mikhail found a vantage point to view the throng.

'There aren't as many as last time,' he called. 'No, the ranks are thinner. They can't even raise the numbers to protect their own bloody parliament.'

'How many do you reckon?'

'Hard to say. Half the size of the last one.'

'The Petersburg Committee of the party has been putting out appeals not to join the demonstrations,' Anishin reminded him. 'A lot of people have stayed at home. As you say, they don't seem that keen to rally round the Constituent.'

Pavel indicated the approaching throng. 'There are still enough of them to cause trouble.'

The Marseillaise was being sung, reminding him of the February days. Blood red banners flaunted slogans such as 'Away with Political Terror!' and 'Long Live the Brotherhood of Peoples.'

'Nothing there about the Soviets,' Anishin murmured.

'Is it any wonder,' Pavel said. 'There aren't many workers here, just one banner from the Obukhov plant as far as I can see. It's the same crowd as last time, only fewer of them.'

Suddenly, there was a surge forward. Anishin gave the order to bar the way.

'Block their advance!' he roared.

The marchers nearest the front were yelling at the Red Guards and sailors, demanding to be let through. Some tried to disarm isolated soldiers.

'You are ordered to turn back,' one sailor shouted.

His eyes were wild. He was surrounded by at least twenty marchers, some of them making a grab for his rifle.

'Lower your weapon, Citizen.'

The sailor snatched his gun away and rasped a command.

'Move back!'

As the marchers pressed towards the Tauride, the confrontation became heated. Eyes bulged with indignation. Faces became taut with frustration.

'Put away your weapons. We wish to pass.'

Then there was a shot, fired into the air, followed by a scream.

'Hold your fire!' Pavel ordered. He shouldered his rifle and pushed back the men nearest him. 'Control yourselves, Citizens or we will arrest you.'

The soldier to his right was less patient. 'If they don't back off, I will show them how a soldier deals with counter-revolutionaries.'

There was a young woman, smartly dressed, right in front of Pavel. He would always remember her eyes, the way they sparkled with determination. 'The people voted for the Constituent,' she said. 'You Bolsheviks came second. Move aside.'

The sailors and soldiers guarding the palace were stern-faced. They started tearing banners from poles and trampling them underfoot. A Red Guard unit moved forward, clubbing a man to the ground by a rifle butt. In retaliation, a banner pole was swung. This time Red Guards didn't fire over the heads of the crowd, but into it. Panic rose like a winter squall.

'Stop!' Mikhail yelled. 'Cease fire.' He looked at Anishin. 'Tell them.'

There was no answer. The crowd was beginning to scatter, some into the palace gardens, others in the direction of the Liteiny Prospect.

'Clear the street,' Pavel barked. One of the bluejackets from Kronstadt came running towards them, eyes wild. He was breathless. 'Some of them are building barricades on the other side of the square.'

'Are they armed?' Pavel demanded of the sailor.

The sailor shook his head.

'What did you see?'

'There's hundreds of them, dragging stuff into the street.'

Anishin's mind was made up. 'Treat it as an armed insurrection against the power of the Soviets.'

Mikhail was beside himself. 'What the fuck? How do you know anyone is armed? You can't give that order.'

Anishin grabbed Mikhail. 'These bastards tried to shoot Comrade Lenin. Do you think this is a fucking game?'

Mikhail was wide-eyed. 'Have you seen a single weapon?'

Anishin was stubborn. 'We had information about a rising.'

67

'Do you see any bloody guns?' Mikhail repeated. 'Pavel, you know they're unarmed. Say something.'

Pavel wiped the sweat from his brow.

'Vassily, this getting out of hand..'

In the middle of the confrontation, a vehicle screamed to a halt and Kolya got out.

'I order you to disperse the counter-revolutionaries.'

'They're unarmed,' Mikhail protested.

Kolya wasn't listening. 'What are you waiting for? Clear the street. As for you, Comrade Anishin, where's your leadership?'

When the crowd failed to disperse, shots rang out. The first to fall was the woman who confronted Pavel. A band of scarlet was spreading across her chest. He remembered the blue eyes that blazed before him. They recalled Raisa's. Already, she was being bundled into an ambulance, arms flopping.

'Is she alive?'

The ambulance pulled away from the scene. He would never know.

'Cease fire!' Mikhail roared until his throat was sore. 'Cease fucking fire!'

The Red Guards were now moving forward, pushing the demonstrators back. There was more firing. Blood stained the snow over to their right. By the time they reached the Liteiny there were people escaping onto the frozen river, trampling abandoned banners in their desperation to escape the gunfire.

'Like the February revolution,' Pavel murmured, 'only we are the Gendarmes now.'

'What just happened?' he demanded. He confronted Anishin. 'Did you know we were going to fire on the march?'

Anishin had his eyes averted.

'Answer me!'

'I knew there was a chance.'

Mikhail walked past Pavel, barging his shoulder.

'He knew there was a chance.' He had only gone a few steps when he turned. 'Maybe I will give Anishin the benefit of the doubt, but Kolya knew we were going to shoot for sure. What have we become?' When nobody spoke, he continued. 'Do you remember what happened here in Petrograd sixteen years ago? Do you?'

Anishin's response was indignant.

'Of course we do. You do not have a monopoly on conscience, Mikhail Vasilievich. Everybody is haunted by the folk memory of Bloody Sunday. My parents were there that day.'

'Then you should know better. The Tsar's troops gunned down hundreds, thousands of innocents.'

'Are you trying to compare this to Bloody Sunday?'

'So what's the difference?'

'The people here today weren't innocents,' Anishin retorted. 'They were out to overthrow the Soviets. There was a plan for a rising, but they were too weak so they decided on a demonstration instead. Are you fucking naïve?'

'I don't care,' Mikhail snapped. 'You don't shoot people for a plan. You *arrest* them.'

Anishin shook his head stubbornly. 'Do you see *hundreds* dead? That's how it was under the Tsar. Don't let your imagination run away with you, Mikhail Vasilievich. There is a handful of casualties.'

'So it's a Maths lesson now, is it? Even if there's only one, it's unnecessary. You saw that woman, same as me. She couldn't have been more than twenty.'

'We don't know anything about her.'

Mikhail stared in disbelief.

'The point is we fired on an unarmed demonstration. How does that make us any better than the fucking Tsar?' He turned to Pavel. 'You're quiet. Don't you have an opinion?'

Pavel finally gave his answer. 'It shouldn't have happened, not like this.'

'Well, it did happen,' Mikhail told him. 'We could have cleared them without reaching for our weapons. People got hurt and I feel ashamed.'

Pavel blew out his cheeks. 'He's right Vassily. We could have done this without any gunfire. The march was pathetic.'

'There,' Mikhail said. 'Some fucking sense at last.'

But Pavel wasn't finished. 'Mikhail, the Constituent still has to be shut down. They weren't armed today, but they could have been.'

'Could have! Listen to yourself. *They weren't!*'

Pavel shook his head. 'An assassination attempt against Comrade Lenin. Revolt in the Don. Comrade Trotsky leads the peace negotiations with the Germans at Brest-Litovsk. We are surrounded by enemies and we have enemies within. We are not in normal times, Mikhail.'

Mikhail refused to be placated.

'Do you know what I hear? Excuses. That's right, you're all making excuses. Do you know what this is meant to be, a festival of the oppressed? That's what Lenin called it, a carnival of the fucking oppressed. A new world, that's what we're supposed to be building here. Well, if opening fire on an unarmed demonstration is our new world, you can keep it. You can shove it up your red fucking arse!'

'Mikhail. Mikhail!'

Anishin tugged at Pavel's sleeve. 'Let him go. He'll calm down. What's he going to do? There is the revolution and there is the counter-revolution. There is no middle way. He'll make the right choice.'

Pavel tore his arm away.

'Do you know who you sound like, Vassily? You sound just like Kolya. Watch you don't turn into him.'

Without another word, Pavel marched off across the bloodstained snow. He saw a body being bundled into an ambulance, a man sitting shocked and traumatised against a wall, fingers trembling as he clutched a flag. He looked up at Pavel. 'What happened here?' he croaked.

Pavel leaned forward, resting a hand on his shoulder. 'You just lost, Citizen. You came up against the revolution and you lost.'

He found himself walking faster, trying not to dwell on the scenes. By the time he got home, he was dispirited and exhausted. Nina greeted him with an embrace.

'What's wrong?' she asked. 'You look terrible.'

'That's exactly how I feel. There was shooting.'

'Was anyone killed?'

A sullen nod. 'I think so. I saw somebody fall right before my eyes.'

'Did you open fire? Did you shoot anyone?'

'No,' Pavel replied, 'but I did nothing to stop it.'

Nina stroked back his hair. 'I heard about the trouble. They've closed the Constituent Assembly. Nadezhda called in with food. She told me all about it. One of the sailors said he was tired and asked the delegates to leave. What does it all mean?'

Pavel stroked her stomach, feeling the baby kick.

'It means the civil war has already begun, class against class. Whatever the rights or wrongs of what just happened, it comes down to this. Either we crush our enemies or they crush us. It's as simple as that.'

'And you have to go away?'

Pavel kissed her.

'Yes, I must go. I won't be here for the birth of this little one, but you've got Nadezhda to help you.'

'Promise me you will return. I would die if you fell.'
Pavel chuckled.
'I'm a bad bastard. I'll be back. I'm like a barn rat, hellishly difficult to kill. These counter-revolutionaries are going to regret the day they involved Pavel Sergeyevich in their war.'

Part two

The revolution besieged

Svetlana

She clapped her hands.

'There,' she said, 'I told you you'd do it.'

Albina was one of the oldest women in the mill, a woman who had been there since the war with Japan, but only now had she learned to read. She beamed at her success.

'Not so long ago I was reading children's primers. Now I can tackle Gorky. Get me a copy of *Capital* next!'

'Do you see, Comrades?' Svetlana declared. 'Our workers' government, our Sovnarkom, will fulfil its pledges.'

She indicated the banners behind her that read: *Down with Illiteracy!* and *Literacy is the Sword that can Conquer the Forces of Ignorance.*

'This is how we women will free ourselves of centuries of drudgery and ignorance,' Svetlana explained. 'This is the test of our revolution. What is the role of the women in it? Do they have equal rights and education? Where did women get the vote? Was it in Britain or Germany, with all their wealth? Was it in the land of Shakespeare of Goethe? No, it was here in backward Russia.'

Albina embraced her. 'It is good to have you back, if only for a short time.'

'I know, dear Albina,' Svetlana answered. 'I can't say I was happy here, working long hours for bugger-all pay and getting groped by the foremen.'

Albina dug her in the ribs.

'You spoiled their game, Svet. Remember that bastard Vulakovich? You put a stop to his monkey business?' Anna was standing next to her mother. They had worked together since she had reached womanhood, but she was ignorant of this incident.

'What happened?'

'It was just after the first revolution,' Albina explained. 'He took a real shine to your Mama, always trying to grab her boobs or shove himself against her backside. Well, Svetlana gave him a right wallop, knocked him half senseless.'

Svetlana laughed. 'Tell the whole story. I had a mallet in my hand at the time.'

Alibina's face lit up. 'He was left with a gap between his teeth you could put your fist through.'

Anna saw her mother in a new light.

'We stuck him in a wheelbarrow and paraded him round the streets. He didn't do it again.'

Anna remembered the story. She stared at her mother, wide-eyed. 'So that's how that got started. Why didn't you tell me?'

'I didn't want you worrying,' Svetlana told her. 'The one thing that made working here bearable was the comradeship.'

'You were good for us, Svet,' Albina said. 'You were strong in every struggle, a real leader, but you never let it go to your head. You never let us down.'

Svetlana reached for Anna's hand. 'Now you have my beautiful daughter to keep the family tradition going.'

'Yes, she's a good girl. A chip off the old block.'

Svetlana pretended to scowl. 'Not so much of the old, you.'

She was there to review the success of the literacy classes. Though she had only been gone a matter of weeks, everything seemed strangely unfamiliar.

'What's your niece doing now?' Albina asked. 'We haven't seen anything of Elena either since she was uprooted by the party and sent off to serve the revolution.'

'What isn't she doing?' Svetlana answered. 'She's a trouble-shooter. She is helping to establish a children's home with a friend. You remember little Raisa, don't you?'

'Yes, such a pretty girl.'

'That's right,' Svetlana said, smiling at her careful choice of the word friend. 'She is also trying to do something about the food supplies.'

A rumble of recognition went around the room.

'What we are doing here is laying the foundations of a new world,' she said, determined to impress on the other women the importance of knowledge and culture. 'Men always told you that love and children were the top and bottom of your entire lives while work dominated theirs. Well, all that is beginning to change. We have the vote. We have equal pay.'

'What about equality in the bedroom?' came a voice at the back, setting off a torrent of laughter. 'The old bugger back home still doesn't know what it takes to make me scream.'

'It's more scream with laughter with my old man,' another said.

Svetlana waited for the ribald shouts to subside then she assumed her role of party organiser. 'Hasn't it always been freedom for the man and subjugation for the woman, Comrades? Well, our workers' state is trying to end your bondage: nurseries, schools, communal laundries and canteens.'

'All welcome,' one woman observed, 'but they need to improve the food. The gruel they fed us last night was like canal water.'

Svetlana nodded. 'We know there are problems with its quality, but we face sabotages forced on us by the bourgeoisie. They're to blame for the continuing food shortages.'

'When is it going to improve, that's what we want to know,' Albina said, earning agreement from the other women. 'You can't work on an empty stomach.'

'We have to consolidate the revolution,' Svetlana told them, sensing their impatience. 'This will be our hardest winter. There is counter-revolution in the Don and in the Ukraine. There is sabotage in the cities and there are plots to assassinate our leaders. We are under siege.'

'I thought the Bolsheviks were promising to perform miracles,' somebody shouted.

'Give them a chance,' came a reply. 'We don't even have five loaves and two fishes.'

'Comrades,' Svetlana said softly, 'my dearest friends, think of everything we have been through together, war, strikes, two revolutions. A country brought low by four years of war and conflict doesn't get back on its feet overnight.'

'We're not naive,' Albina said, 'we have endured all that together, but when do we get some respite?'

'The news from abroad is good,' Svetlana answered. 'There are strikes and the soldiers are fraternising on the various fronts. Soon, our comrades overseas will come to our aid.'

That stimulated yet another protest. 'The news isn't that good. People say it's only a matter of time before the Germans resume their advance on Petrograd.'

'Not all Germans are the same,' Svetlana answered. 'The workers are on our side. They want peace. Look across the water to Finland. The red flag is raised at the Workers' House in Helsinki. Revolt is stirring across Europe. We must hold on. The world socialist revolution has begun.'

There was a renewed ripple of applause, but it was cautious. Svetlana detected a change taking place. There was a time when her words would have been cheered to the echo, but her former workmates were being worn down by the daily grind of survival. Finally, she made her excuses, embraced Anna and started the long walk to the main gates.

'I will see you out,' Albina told her.

'Is something wrong?' Svetlana asked as they walked through the silent mill.

'I can't pull the wool over your eyes, can I?' Albina said. 'Look around you, Svet. We're short of fuel and raw materials. We're only working a few hours a day. Some of the girls are saying the bosses are holding up supplies on purpose.'

'Have you reported it?'

'We do nothing but report it. It's the same all over the Vyborg. Some of the girls are spending half their time scavenging for food, fuel, winter clothing for the kids. I tell you, we're not workers any more. We're just survivors. Why, we've got comrades saying they will have to go back to the village if things don't change, just so they can put food in their bellies. We're talking about taking over the mill and running it ourselves, but how do we organise the raw materials, Svet? This can't go on much longer without real trouble.'

Svetlana nodded wearily. 'I know the stories.'

Albina's mood had turned gloomy. 'Do you remember how it was before the revolution? Do you remember the day we saw those two women waiting in line for bread? There was one loaf left. They fought over it, fought in the street, tearing at one another while the passing bourgeois laughed and placed bets on who would win.'

'Yes, I remember.'

'And I remember what you did Svetlana. You pulled them apart, broke the loaf in half and lectured them, not just those two women, but the whole street. A real Solomon you were.'

Her face was glowing at the memory.

'Oh, I wish I had a voice like yours, so rich and strong. You said socialism was about sharing all that the world had equally between all who lived on its surface. You pointed out the bourgeois laughing and told the working women to turn their rage on the thieving scum who caused the shortages with their wars.'

She threw out her arms, as if she had an audience.

'That's right. You called those bourgeois bastards scum right to their faces. I thought the Pharaohs were going to drag you off to a cell at the Kresty prison, but they didn't raise a finger. We should have known then. It was one little sign that February was coming.'

Svetlana wrinkled her nose. 'I did what a worker-Bolshevik should do. I tried to raise the class consciousness of the workers.'

'This is my point, Svet,' Albina said earnestly. 'I can't go back to those times when the bosses called the shots. I am old. It would break my heart to see my Peter forced back under the yolk, my worker comrades at each other's throats again. We have had solidarity, Svet. It must not be broken.'

'I will fight for the revolution with all my heart,' Svetlana answered. 'You know it's true.'

'Raise it with the party, the Soviets, anybody you can,' Albina told her. 'It isn't critical yet, but we can't go through another winter like this one.'

'I know, Albina. We all know.'

Albina linked Svetlana's arm. 'There's something else. There is bad blood about the way those demonstrators were shot. Twenty-one dead, Svetlana. We can't defend such actions. At the Obukhov plant, they have replaced the Bolshevik delegates with Mensheviks and SRs. Eight thousand workers in attendance and only a hundred voted against. Things can turn quickly, Svet.'

'What the Red Guards did was an act of criminal stupidity. The Party will learn from its mistakes.'

'It better had,' Albina said, 'or we won't be in power long. It isn't just the Obukhov. At the Siemens-Shuckert factory, they voted to recall the Red Guards. They said they had acted like the old Gendarmes. This is serious.' She changed the subject. 'How's your Volodya? He's a handsome lad.'

A lump rose in Svetlana's throat. 'He's going south to fight the counter-revolution. He volunteered.'

'You can't hold the young back, Svet. You've got to give them their head.' She reminded Svetlana where Volodya got his temperament from. 'You instilled the will to fight in your kids.'

The two women embraced and Svetlana stepped into the street. Albina's footsteps died away in the chill and Svetlana wandered towards the Neva, depression weighing her down. Kolya, her Kolya, was one of the men who ordered the shooting of the twenty-one unarmed demonstrators. She was on her way back to her office when there was a scream. A man was being dragged to a car as it stood, engine running, by the side of the road. Passers-by were stopping to watch. The screams were coming from the man's wife.

'Let him go. Please let him go. He didn't mean it.'

Two leather-jacketed Chekists were manhandling their prisoner into the vehicle. He was struggling and kicking. One of the Chekists punched him. He went limp. Nonetheless, another punch came his way. There were more screams of protest from the wife standing on the pavement, quite distraught.

'Stop that!' Svetlana shouted. 'Can't you see he's had enough?'

The Chekist turned. 'What business is it of yours, you nosy cow?'

Svetlana was furious. 'I work for the Commissariat of Education. I am a Bolshevik of many years' standing. What about you? You don't look old enough to be in long trousers.'

Stung, the young Chekist defended himself.

'I joined immediately after the October revolution.'

'*After* the revolution. Doesn't that say it all? Now you go calling another comrade names, one who helped bring down the autocracy. I should drag you to the river and wash your filthy mouth out.'

That's when she heard a familiar voice.

'She'd do it too. Be a good boy and say sorry.'

The Chekist reddened before giving Svetlana a mumbled apology. He didn't want to get the wrong side of his superior officer.

'You'd do well to listen to the comrade. She's giving you good advice. There's no need to rough him up. Just make the arrest.'

Kolya made his way down the steps. 'Hello, Svetlana.'

It was their first meeting since their fateful encounter on a frozen street corner of the Nevsky Prospect. Svetlana might have expected him to be shame-faced, but he appeared unconcerned by her sudden appearance, cocky even. She was the one who felt vulnerable.

'It's been a while, Kolya.' She watched the Chekists climbing into the car either side of their prisoner. 'What's happening here?'

'Never heard of looting the looters?' Kolya asked. 'The local Soviet told this bourgeois clown they were moving two families into his house. He's got plenty of empty rooms and they've got nowhere to live. You should have heard the commotion.'

'He put up a fight?'

'He said we would move rootless scum into his home over his dead body. That's what he calls the poor, Svetlana, 'rootless scum.' I asked him if he would rather they died on the street, of cold and malnutrition. Do you know what he said? That's all they're good for.'

'So he is under arrest?'

Kolya brushed back his hair. 'He will face a revolutionary tribunal. He can answer to the people.'

At this moment, Svetlana felt a tug on her arm.

'You're a woman,' the desperate wife pleaded. 'You will have more sympathy than these brutes. Don't let them hurt my husband. All he did was try to defend our home.'

'He assaulted an officer of the Cheka,' Svetlana told her. 'I saw him lash out.'

'And did you see the lump on my poor husband's head? One of these animals rammed his face into the wall. I saw him do it.' She pointed at one of the Chekists in the car. 'That pig on the right.'

Svetlana saw the look in Kolya's eyes and took the woman to one side. 'You must listen to me. Families like yours with enough space must take in their fair share of needy families.'

The woman attempted a protest, but Svetlana silenced her with a wave. 'If you don't want this to get worse, you will listen to me and you will take in every word. In an argument between you and state security there is only one winner. I advise you to accept these families.'

'But what about my husband?'

'I will do what I can, but he must show no more defiance. He is making it hard on himself.'

The woman nodded helplessly and plodded back to the house.

'What did you say to her?' Kolya asks.

'I told her not to put up any more resistance.'

'Good advice.'

Though it was only a month since she had seen him last, Svetlana was aware of a change in Kolya.

'Can I ask you a favour?' she asked. 'For old time's' sake?'

The reply was brusque and to the point. 'Name it.'

'Tell your men to go easy on him. Return him to his family unharmed.'

Kolya folded his arms, a broad smile lighting his features.

'What's this, Svetlana? Going soft on me?'

She held his gaze unflinchingly. 'I am asking you to be humane. This is a personal favour.'

He spent a few moments considering it.

'Very well,' he said. 'We weren't going to hurt the idiot anyway, just scare the shit out of him.'

'So you will let him go?'

Kolya rapped on the car window and the prisoner stumbled gratefully to his wife.

'Is this what the Cheka does?' Svetlana asked. 'I thought you would have bigger fish to fry.'

'We deal with counter-revolution,' Kolya answered. 'It's early days.'

'Well, thank you for granting my request,' Svetlana said, 'though I don't think the arrest was justified to start with.'

'Same old Svetlana,' Kolya said. 'Hard to please.' He reached out to touch her, but she backed away. 'I'm not forgiven then?'

'What do you think? Kolya, you're an unfeeling shit. You probably always were, but I was blind to your failings.'

He looked her up and down in a way that made her feel quite naked. 'Klara sends her love.'

With that, Kolya climbed into the car and drove off. Svetlana let the breath shudder out of her.

'Do you know him?' the wife asked, watching the vehicle turn the corner.

'Yes,' Svetlana replies. 'I know him.'

'Thank you for what you did.'

Svetlana nodded. 'Just tell your husband to control his temper. There isn't much sympathy for people who have money and property. He must accept the new order. There is no future in causing trouble.'

Svetlana was still thinking about the incident as she hung up her coat and looked around her cramped office. Outside, in the corridor, Anishin was pinning a notice up.

'What's this?' she asked, leaning against the doorjamb.

'Proclamation of the formation of the Red Socialist Army,' Anishin told her. 'I hear Volodya has already signed up.'

Svetlana's eyes welled with tears. 'He is so young, Vassily, and idealistic.'

'He'll be in good hands,' Anishin said. 'Pavel Kirilenko commands his unit.'

She heard the familiar thickness in his voice whenever she was near. He was different with her. In the company of the other staff, he could be business-like, even abrupt.

'You were at your old mill today, weren't you?'

'That's right,' Svetlana told him. 'Times are hard. Production is down. There isn't enough work for everyone.' She glanced at the proclamation. 'We need a speedy end to the war, Vassily, or I don't know how our revolution will survive.'

Anishin was in complete agreement. 'I was saying the same to Comrade Lunacharsky only this morning. Without revolutions among the Central Powers, we are finished.'

She watched him. It was over a month since she had been to bed with a man. When she found out about Kolya, she was crushed, staring into the mirror with self-hatred, willing the years to fall away so her face was unlined like the features of that stupid, little tramp Klara. She took a step forward so that she was so close to Anishin she could feel his heat, smell the tobacco smoke on his clothes.

'Do you still feel the same, Vassily?' she asked. 'About me? Do you want to get me into bed?'

He seemed shocked at the question.

'You know I want you. I always have.'

She fancied she could hear the quickening of his pulse.

'Tell me when you are about to leave,' she said. 'I will come home with you.'

Then she turned, quickly, letting her body brush his just for a moment.

Abram

He scrambled into the sleeping corner of the mean, peasant hut, skin crawling with terror. He knew this moment. He had known it all his life, as long as he had had conscious thought. Was there a Jew in all Russia who didn't know the colours, sounds, scents and visceral horror of the progromists hunting their victims? Outside the weathered, unpainted wooden walls there were mounted men. The thunder of scores of hooves shook the ground. Abram's mind was racing as he tried to think of a way out. He saw the icon in the corner and smiled grimly through his fear. The peasant who lived here was probably as much of an antisemite as those bastards outside. Disturbed by the White Guards, a cockroach scuttled over Abram's hand as he lay flat on the ground, stomach pressed to the cold, earthen floor.

'Run, you little prick,' he hissed under his breath. 'Looks like you'll live longer than I will.'

His eyes searched the gloomy interior of the hut. There were *bast* shoes made from birch bark, some cooking utensils, a sheepskin hat and bugger all else. There was one way in and one way out.

'I'm fucked.'

A shadow passed across the door. Hooves thumped just a few yards away.

'Where is he? Tell me or I'll cut your nose off, you devious old fool. What are you hiding him for? He's just a Jew-Bolshevik. Did he pay you?'

There was a yelp of pain. The Whites were beating the old *muzhik*, torturing an eighty-year-old man without hesitation.

'Typical Jew-Communist. How much did he pay you, you avaricious, old fucker?'

'Please, your honour....'

'Oh, it's your honour now, is it?'

This time, Abram heard the blow, the moist crunch of bone against teeth, followed by a long, keening moan.

'Why the hell are you resisting, old man? What turned a Kuban peasant into a fucking Jew-lover?'

Then there was the shout of defiance that would cost the old man his life.

'Do you want to know?'

Abram could hear the old man spitting out blood.

'Shall I tell you why I hide the Reds?'

There was a sickening thud and another groan, but it didn't stop him speaking. Abram wanted to rush out and put a stop to it, but what good would it do? Sacrificing himself wasn't going to make the Whites spare poor old Klim. He was dead the moment he refused to point out Abram's hiding place.

'I'm no Bolshevik. I don't even know what they stand for. Here's what I know, your fucking honour, your fucking thieving, burning, whoring honour. The Bolsheviks promised us land and you give us war and hunger. That's why I hide the Reds. You know what, I'd do it again.'

Abram heard the roar of a Mauser pistol and a barked command.

'Go door to door. Tear the whole place apart. There's a reward for the Red scum, double if you take him alive. Burn the entire village if that's what it takes, but find him.'

Women's screams ripped the air at the threat to burn the village. They were accompanied by the sound of sobbing children. I brought this down on their heads, Abram thought. It's my fault the old man is dead. I should have stayed in Ekaterinodar. I might have stood a better chance. Now I'm trapped like a rat in a sack.

'Shit!'He could hear footsteps approaching. Suddenly, there was a loud cracking noise behind him. His heart leapt, pounding against his ribcage like a hammer. Somebody was wrenching a plank aside. A face appeared. It was Klim's granddaughter and only living relative, Irina.

'This way,' she whispered.

She had managed to wrench off a second plank then a third. Babbling his gratitude, Abram squirmed through the gap and crawled on his belly after her. Together, they pressed themselves to the wall of the next hut.

'It's up to you now,' she said. 'There's nothing more I can do.'

'Thank you, thank you,' he stammered, seizing her hands and kissing them. 'I am so sorry for the misfortune I have brought upon your village.'

'Our misfortune was to have been born poor,' Irina told him. 'Good luck.'

She got to her feet, brushed the dirt from her skirt and started to walk towards the centre of the village. That's when the rider appeared.

'Got you, you Jew-bastard.'

The Guard twisted in his saddle and put a bullet between Irina's eyes.

'That's what you get for hiding him, you Yid-loving bitch.'

Abram froze for a moment. He knew Irina's mother had died in childbirth, her father and brothers fighting the Austrians. Now she was gone.

'Bastard!'

He rushed at the Guard, screaming. He had hold of the man's leg, trying to wrench him out of his saddle. The Mauser pistol flew from the Guard's grasp and landed in the snow with a thump.

'You should have shot me, not her. What's my life worth now anyway?'

The Cossack was trying to draw his sabre. Abram clung on for dear life, grasping the rider's leg with one hand and clamping the other over the hilt of the sword. The horse was turning in a circle, stamping and kicking up powdery snow. Alerted to the struggle, the Cossack's comrades were already moving towards them. Abram glimpsed the Mauser and flung himself backwards, wrapping his fingers round the pistol grip. The first shot tore open the rider's eye socket. The second was a warning to the oncoming horsemen.

Abram's gaze swept the vast blanket of snow beyond the village. There was no hiding place. He was going to die on that deceptively innocent, white counterpane. Hooves were now crunching through the virgin snow towards him. In a moment, he would be surrounded. Abram came to a decision and put the barrel to his temple. He wasn't going to give the swine the pleasure of hearing a Jew scream for mercy. He would not betray his comrades. This Jewish revolutionary was going to die with honour. But before he could squeeze the trigger, hot lead raked the snow. Men and horses screamed. Bodies thumped into the knee-high drifts.

'Reds!'

For the first time, Abram could see the attackers. They had come sweeping into the village from the West. He saw motley uniforms, two machine guns mounted on carts. The sight of an ammunition belt being fed into a Maxim was enough of a warning for him to scramble for cover behind the nearest hut. Another round spat up scarlet-tinted blood. Now there were Red Guards racing towards their enemies, long coats brushing the surface of the snow, boots labouring forward with difficulty. The firefight was short-lived. The element of surprise had given the Reds the edge.

'Sound the retreat!' The White commander pulled together the tattered remnants of his company and led them away to the east. Abram rolled onto his back, staring up at the snow-heavy clouds and the watery yellow sun.

'You lucky fucker,' he gasped.

Then there was a Red Guard blocking his light.

'Who are you?' he demanded.

The Red saw the Mauser.

'Throw the gun to one side.'

Abram obeyed without hesitation, raising his arms. 'I'm Abram Goldfarb. Communist.'

'You're a Jew?'

Abram grinned. 'Can't fool you, can I, Comrade?'

The response was a suspicious frown. 'Are you taking the piss?'

Abram realised he was not out of the woods yet. 'No, I swear. I mean no disrespect, Comrade. My father calls me a godless Bolshevik, but yes, I am a Jew.'

The Red held out his hand and pulled Abram to his feet.

'You don't want to fall into the hands of that lot,' he said, nodding in the direction of the retreating Whites. 'They blame every Jew living for the curse of Bolshevism.'

'Are you a Communist, Comrade?'

'Do you think I'd be in this fucking wilderness if I wasn't?'

Abram walked to the spot where Irina lay dead in the snow. Already, there were women gathering around the body.

'I'm sorry,' he said. 'I brought this terror to your village.'

Nobody spoke. They were dumb with loss.

'I'm sorry,' he repeated, before turning back to his rescuer. 'What's your name, Comrade? Where are you from?'

'My name is Mikhail Vasilievich Luzhin. My family are from the Volga, but I am garrisoned in Peter.'

'You're a long way from home, Petrograder.'

They were joined by a second man, taller and more powerfully built than the first, lean, broad-shouldered and sharp-eyed. Though he wore no badges of rank – they had all been abolished – Abram knew that this was the commander of the unit. Mikhail introduced him.

'Meet Pavel Kirilenko, officer in command.'

Abram shook Pavel's hand. 'I owe you my life, Comrade. I just wish you could have been here five minutes earlier. Klim and Irina would still be alive.'

'Ten minutes later,' Pavel reminded him, 'and you and the whole lot of them would be dead. They would have raped the women first. War's shit, Comrade.' He looked Abram up and down, what there was of him. He was skinny, and no more than five foot four.

'You look more like a scarecrow than a revolutionary.'

Abram treated that to a rueful smile. 'Communists come in many shapes and sizes.'

Pavel was curious about the Red fugitive. 'What did you do before all this kicked off, student, teacher?'

Abram chuckled. 'Jews are all students and teachers, is that right? Maybe you think I'm a money-lender, or better, a tailor.'

Pavel flicked an enquiring glance at Mikhail. 'Is he bollocking me over something?'

Abram laughed. 'I would never denigrate the man who saved my life.' He looked around at the vast, snow-blanketed landscape. 'What are you doing here?'

'We're on our way to reinforce Ekaterinodar, wherever the fuck that is.'

Abram gestured at the vastness around them. 'Yet you fetch up in a village four hours' ride away. Why?'

'I could ask you the same question,' Pavel reminded him.

Abram nodded. 'Fair enough. I'll tell you my tale. I'm not a student or a tailor. I am an engineer.'

'Metalworker, you mean?'

That earned Pavel an indulgent smile. 'I help to design and install machinery.'

'Here?'

'No, in England. I have family there. I came home the moment news of the February revolution broke though. I joined the Bolsheviks in April.

I was in Rostov when the revolution began. I had to get out when the Whites occupied the city. The plan was to return to Moscow, but the Whites kept advancing.'

Pavel considered the isolated location.

'So you ended up here?''

Abram's arms flapped at his side like the wings of a penguin.

'Yes,' he confirmed. 'I ended up here. It's a long story if you have the time.'

'Hardly,' Pavel said. 'The Whites might just regroup and I don't want these guys facing a cavalry charge. Few have any military experience.'

Abram got the message. 'Then I will be brief. The villagers were good and brave and hid a Communist from the White patrols. They would have put out my eyes and cut off my tongue.' His voice croaked with emotion. 'But not before they had tortured the names of my comrades in Ekaterinodar out of me.'

Pavel lit a cigarette. 'Well, you're safe now. Cigarette?'

Abram grimaced. 'I don't smoke. Indulge me, Comrade, but that doesn't smell like tobacco. What's that odour, nettles?'

Mikhail rested a hand on Abram's shoulder. 'We've no idea what's in these smokes, but a cigarette takes the edge of your hunger.' He glanced at the peasants. 'I was hoping they would feed us, but with two dead on the snow, I don't think that's likely, do you?'

'You have a point,' Abram said. 'Anyway, I have told you how I got here. What about you?'

'The Whites attacked our train. We drove them off. I suppose they thought we would carry on into Ekaterinodar, but we don't like anybody taking the piss. We decided to halt the train for a while and get even.'

Suddenly, there was excitement etched on Abram's features. 'You've got a train?'

'That's right,' Pavel confirmed. 'It won't get you back to Moscow, but this time you can help defend Ekaterinodar from the Whites. I can promise you plenty of action.'

Abram nodded. 'Put a gun in my hand and I will kill as many of the progromists as fortune grants me strength to butcher.'

The village women were cleaning the blood from Irina's face.

'It looks like you've got a grudge to settle, Abram Goldfarb.'

'I've always got a grudge to settle, Comrade. One time, a big Ukrainian antisemite called me a *zhyd*. I kicked the fuck out of him.'

'*You* did?' Mikhail said, slightly incredulously.

'What, you think I can't fight?'

'Can you?'

'He was bigger than me.' He demonstrated with his hand. 'This much bigger. I punched him in his dirty, antisemitic mouth. He punched me in the face. Twice. I went down with him on top of me. He put his arm round my throat and I started to see darkness.'

'But you still won?'

'He relaxed for a moment, thought he'd won. I sank my teeth into him and held on.'

Mikhail stared deep into Abram's eyes and saw the truth of the story, the little man's desperate struggle for pride and self.

'He tried to get away, but I went after him, smashed his fat, pogromist head into the wall. Then I stamped on him until he didn't get up again.'

Mikhail and Pavel were equally impressed.

'How badly did you hurt him?'

Abram's attention was drawn to the villagers once more.

'You think I care what happened to the piece of shit?' Abram held up his own arm and pulled back his sleeve. 'Look out for a big Ukrainian with bite marks here and a face like a cow's arse. If you ever meet him, give him a beating from Abram Goldfarb.'

Done with his story, Abram thought about trying to apologise again. He started to approach the villagers, but Pavel held him back by the sleeve.

'I'm a *muzhik* myself, Abram. Let them grieve in their own way.'

Half an hour later, Abram was scrambling gratefully into one of the train's shabby carriages.

'It's not much,' Pavel told him, 'but it's got us here from Peter.'

'Only just,' put in a fresh-faced fighter

He flapped his greatcoat, exhibiting the bullet hole just above the hem.

Aram whistled. 'That's what you call a close shave.'

'You're telling me.' The kid offered Abram an outstretched hand. 'I'm Volodya.'

'See this young idiot,' Mikhail snorted. 'He could have stayed home and worked in the Putilov, but no, he has to volunteer to risk his fool neck fighting the Kornilovites. What it is to be young, angry and stupid.'

'Don't give me that,' Volodya countered. 'You and Pavel volunteered too, same as all the men here.'

'Did I say we weren't all fucking idiots too?' Mikhail answered. 'For the world socialist revolution. Victory or death.' He pulled out a filthy handkerchief and blew. 'Or some such shite.'

Abram glanced at Pavel.

'Is he always like this?'

Pavel leaned his forehead against the window and watched the snow-covered land.

'Yes, pretty much. Mikhail Vasilievich likes to make out he's a cynical kind of bastard, but he's first into the fray every time.'

'What about you?' Abram asked.

'Yes, I've got a death wish same as him.'

Abram swung round to face Volodya.

'Victory or death,' Volodya told him. 'Victory or fucking death. Do you know the difference between Mikhail and me and this guy?'

There was a brief shrug from Abram.

'The big man here is about to be a daddy.'

'Is that right?' Abram asked.

Pavel nodded. 'Nina could give birth any day now.'

This struck Abram as perverse. What makes a man leave his wife at such a critical moment to risk everything on the battlefield over a thousand miles from home?

'Yet you come here?'

Pavel grunted. 'The socialist fatherland is in danger. It's a life and death struggle.'

Abram left it at that, but there had to be more to it.

A lot more.

Raisa

Peter in peril!

The revolution besieged!

Raisa could barely breathe in the claustrophobic fug of the hall. Revolutionary banners were hanging, but few paid attention to them. Slogans that had once attracted a curious crowd had become part of the furniture. Raisa wanted to escape. There was too much talk. There were too many raised voices and pointing fingers, but this was proletarian democracy in all its fury and indignation. The arguments that were tearing the de facto government Sovnarkom apart were raging here too, at the heart of the Vyborg. Svetlana was on her feet. She gestured at the supporters of revolutionary war.

'I wish to address my remarks to the 'Lefts,'' she shouted above the hubbub, her tongue rasping the word across the room as if it was the worst insult in the world. She left nobody in any doubt that she really meant 'fake Lefts.'

'You call upon the proletariat to mount revolutionary war, war to the gates of Helskini, Berlin, Vienna.' She was fighting to be heard against the constant barracking. 'Why not Paris, London...New York?'

Shouts of 'Yes!', 'To the gates of New York!', 'World socialist revolution!'

'There you have it,' Svetlana retorted. 'The world socialist revolution. Yes, that's the aim that drives us all forward, Comrades, me, you, every one of us. We know....' She brandished both of her fists before her. 'We know that in Vienna and Berlin, Budapest in London, there is the power to defeat the imperialists.'

Somebody shouted out: 'But...', mocking Svetlana. 'We all know you are going to contradict yourself any minute now.'

'*But*,' Svetlana declared fiercely, heavy emphasis on the word, 'yes, Comrades, there is a but. This is my question to every one of you who is straining at the leash for permanent war. Is the world revolution ready to break out at every moment, to be summoned by our will alone? Don't be children! Don't be fools!'

Her eyes blazed with fury.

'Where does our authority with the masses of the people lie? It is in our Peace Decree. That's it! Don't fool yourselves. At the moment, it is not the German revolution that is sweeping forward, but the German offensive. Exhausted, demoralised, the Russian soldier abandons his weapons and walks from the battlefield. In the Ukraine, our Red Guards face Petlyura. In the Don and the Kuban, the heroes of the revolution rush to face Kornilov, Kaledin, Alekseev.'

Suddenly, all sides applauded the Red Guard offensive against the Whites, but Svetlana didn't content herself with praising the Red Army.

'Sovnarkom has issued a proclamation, the Socialist Fatherland in Danger. What do you think that means? The Germans are at the gates, better armed than us, in hard steel and morale. Japan and America, England and France are looking covetously at revolutionary Russia, ready to strip it of resources. They are arming our domestic enemies so they can strangle our revolution in the cradle.'

There was a shout over to her left. Where else? 'The proletariat will repel them.'

It earned thunderous applause from one section of the audience. Svetlana swung round, trembling with indignation. She recognised the heckler, a handsome, bearded young man. She searched her memory, but she couldn't pluck out a name.

'I am a proletarian woman,' she retaliated. 'Since I was a child, I have toiled in the mill. I gave birth to my children behind a filthy curtain while the machines roared just yards away. I returned to my former place of work recently. Do you know what I found? The machines are silent most of the day. The workers forage for food, fuel and clothing. Their sons are a thousand miles away, fighting the counter-revolution.'

At the thought of Volodya, her voice began to break, but she chose not to personalise her speech.

'We are exhausted, Comrades. Party membership is falling across red Petrograd. The Mensheviks are getting a hearing again. The needs of the workers' state are draining the mills and factories of the best Communists. Just keeping things going means we are all becoming either bureaucrats or soldiers.'

'Or thieves!'

'Yes, or thieves. With resources as thin as this, do you really think we can throw the Germans into the sea?'

Shouts of 'yes, yes, with our revolutionary will!'

Raisa could remain seated no longer. Heart pounding, she was on her feet beside Svetlana.

'Comrade Svetlana would never say it herself,' Raisa began, benefitting from a lull in the barracking as Svetlana slumped into her seat, 'but her own son Volodya is in the Kuban, rifle in hand, fighting the White Armies.' Pavel's face invaded her mind for a moment then she ploughed on. 'Our revolution's survival hangs by a thread. I work for the Commissariat of People's Welfare. We are taking children off the street, finding them food and shelter. Production in the factories is down. Food rations are cut.'

Shouts of: 'We know!'

'Yes,' Raisa cried. 'You *know*. Yet some of you want your revolutionary war so you can parade around with your chests puffed out.'

Some of the men started whistling their derision.

'Do you really think you are fooling the German High Command with your tricks? You risk German boots on the streets of red Petrograd and all for a slogan. We need respite. We need a breathing space. I believe, oh, I believe with all my heart that the workers of the Central Powers will join us in revolutionary civil war with the capitalists.'

'So let's have it,' somebody bawled, 'let's have it here and now.'

'Then what?' Raisa cried, her voice raw and breaking as she fought to be heard. 'Be honest. Are we ready? Do you want another Paris Commune? Do you want your children looking down at your bullet-riddled corpses in their serried rows of coffins?' She beat her chest. 'I know what it is to be one of the wretched of the Earth. I was one of the unattended, one of the *besprizornye*.' In her mind's eye, she saw the revolution drowned in blood, a German jackboot stamping on a screaming face and she knew she had to share something she had hidden from all those most precious to her. 'I was a child and men abused me. I was homeless and I did things, shameful things, just to survive.'

At that, the barracking abated and glances were exchanged.

'Maybe some of you have similar stories. Then maybe you will understand the fire that burns inside me. I will not be a victim any more. I will not be crushed just because you 'Lefts' want to posture and let the German troops crush our revolution. Revolutionary war is just words, empty words. Comrades, we need time. We have to have a breathing space.'

She sat down to applause and simultaneous shouts of protest from the Left Communists. She was trembling and tears spilled down her cheeks. Svetlana crushed her shoulders in a fierce embrace.

'That took courage, dearest Raisa. Wait until I tell Elena what you did here.' She pointed out the young heckler. 'Is that Grigory?'

Raisa remembered him from the battle at Pulkovo Heights. 'The one who took you to Kolya's safe house? Yes, that's him.'

'I hardly recognised him with all that facial hair,' Svetlana said.

It was true. He was almost unrecognisable with his thick beard and leather cap pulled over his brow.

Despite Raisa's speech, and Svetlana's, the debate raged on for over an hour, swinging first one way then the other. There were three positions, for Lenin and an immediate peace, for Bukharin and revolutionary war and for Trotsky and delay. Grigory was on his feet, pressing the case for war.

'Look at what the Germans are demanding,' he yelled. 'We would lose the Ukraine. They would take our coal, our iron, the ability to feed ourselves from the great bread basket of our territory. We would be humiliated before the whole world. How could we inspire the workers of the world to revolution if we flinched like cowards before the imperialist war machine, tell me that.'

He gestured in the direction of Svetlana and Raisa.

'These comrades use personal anecdotes to blackmail us into surrender. Haven't we all got stories of sacrifice? We don't all parade them like shrouds. The Communists have no family but the revolution. Forget these personal stories however much they tug the heart strings and put the good of all at the centre of your thinking.'

Blackmail! Raisa was tempted to march across the room and slap Grigory across his face. Sacrifice! He was a student whose parents were teachers and living in relative safety.

'Sovnarkom must not accept Germany's peace terms. Comrades, we must fight to the last drop of our blood.'

His fiery speech produced uproar. Raisa felt as if she had exposed her heart to no purpose.

'Fine words from a petit bourgeois,' she retorted, 'you want to fight to the last drop of somebody else's blood, more like.'

Suddenly, Grigory was screaming at her, demanding she withdraw the slur.

Finally, Anishin took the floor. He lacked the passion of Svetlana and Raisa, but everyone in the hall knew him. He was patient and methodical, his voice weathering the protests of the Left Communists.

'Comrades,' he said, 'There can be no more delay. We must not wait. If we are to deal with counter-revolution in the south, we must halt the threat from the German Army.' He addressed Grigory's objections. 'Will there be concessions? Absolutely. Will they make us scream with pain? Yes, without doubt.' He played his trump card. 'Without the driving revolutionary will of Comrade Lenin, would there have even been an insurrection? Just cast your mind back. Think what our party was saying before he returned from Zurich. Would October have happened without his April Theses? Comrade Grigory, Lenin armed the revolution.' Grigory was ready with a riposte. Scrambling to his feet, he bawled his answer.

'And he disarms it now!'

Anishin ignored the taunt. 'This is what Lenin has to say on the matter: we must save the revolution in Russia as a bridgehead of the world revolution. We must do this at any cost. I move that the question be put.'

To the frustration of everyone, the vote was indecisive and the rowdy meeting broke up without any resolution. The crowd spilled onto the street, still arguing. Even an appeal to the authority of Comrade Lenin had failed to win the day. Anishin called Raisa over. His eyes were sympathetic, but she wondered whether she was not somehow diminished in his eyes by her confession.

'That took great courage,' he told her.

Raisa felt utterly defeated. She had stripped herself bare before the Party comrades and still they wouldn't listen.

'It didn't convince the meeting.'

'It convinced some of them,' Anishin told her. 'It slowed the advance of these bloody Utopians. There were more votes for our side than ever before. What more do we have to do to convince them? The German Army has taken Pskov, less than three hundred kilometres from here. This is all posturing.'

'The Left SRs are also for revolutionary war,' Svetlana added, before expressing her frustration in a cry of rage. 'Shit! Shit, shit, shit.'

Raisa understood her outburst. Volodya was far away, fighting for the survival of beleaguered October and here, in its birthplace, there were comrades demanding the Red Socialist Army fight on three fronts at once.

'Our fighters don't even have proper uniforms,' she groaned. 'They have little training, only their courage and revolutionary determination.'

Anishin took her in his arms and Svetlana pressed her face to his chest to hide the bitter tears. It was the first time Raisa had seen Anishin show any intimacy towards Svetlana. The moment made her want to be with her own lover.

'I have to go,' she said. 'Elena is alone with the children.'

'Do you have no other help?' Svetlana asked, pulling away from Anishin. 'I thought the Commissariat was going to get you some staff.'

'Our people are spread thin,' Raisa said.

That drew a sympathetic nod from Svetlana. 'You do so much, Raisa, and you are little more than a child yourself.'

'I am seventeen,' Raisa said, 'as old as the century. I can manage.'

Svetlana pulled her close and kissed her on the forehead. 'I am sure you can.'

Raisa was about to go when Grigory approached. Svetlana greeted him with some suspicion, but made an effort to be welcoming.

'I didn't recognise you with the beard. What's this, Grigory, revolutionary style? Are you trying to look like Comrade Bukharin?'

Grigory blushed. She had obviously touched a nerve.

'How's Kolya?' he asked. 'I hear he is with the Cheka.'

At the mention of Kolya's name, Anishin looked uncomfortable.

'I ended the relationship, Comrade Grigory.' She said bluntly. 'I found him untrustworthy. Like a snake.'

Grigory was taken aback by the venom in her voice. His face betrayed a burning curiosity as he wondered what Kolya did, but he didn't say another word on the subject.

'I wanted to say...'

'What, no hard feelings? Comrade Grigory, we are Communists. We have the argument. We come to a majority decision. We treat one another with mutual respect.'

'Unfortunately, there was no majority decision,' Grigory observed pointedly. He glanced sideways at Raisa who was yet to speak. 'It became somewhat personal.'

Raisa knew what is expected of her. For the good of the party, she had to respond to Grigory and end the discussion without rancour. In any case, she was desperate to return home to the arms of her beloved Elena.

'I took no offence, Comrade,' she answered, in clipped, neutral tones.

'Thank you,' Grigory said. 'Then I will be on my way.'

She waited until he was out of sight and nudged Svetlana. 'Took no offence? Like fuck!'

A tram was about to depart. She raced to catch it and stumbled into an elderly woman, apologising profusely as they scrambled on board. The tram clattered off on the rails, sparks showering from the cables. The old woman smiled.

'Don't you worry, my dear. I'm a tough, old bird. You have to be in these hard times.'

Her words drew the attention of a workman in a faded blue smock. 'Truer words were never spoken. Peace, bread and land, they said. Well, my family is hungry and the Germans are approaching. What the fuck did we fight two revolutions for?' He realised he had sworn. 'Apologies for my language, Comrades.'

'I have heard worse,' the old woman said, 'and I dare say the same goes for this little creature. War makes people coarse.'

She glanced at the worker then winked at Raisa. 'I was pretty like you once. Hard work and half a dozen children took their toll. Now I worry about my grandchildren. Have some fun if you can. You keep your looks, my dear. Life is short.' She nudged Raisa. 'Here's my stop. Have a good life.'

Raisa watched her shuffling through the crush. 'Yes, you too.'

The old woman skidded as she stepped down on the icy pavement and only managed to keep her footing with the help of a convenient lamp post. She saw Raisa watching and gave her a cheery wave before plodding off through the gloom. In spite of herself, Raisa felt a film of tears blurring her vision. She realised that the worker had his gaze on her.

'Is something wrong?' He laughed. 'Besides the shit of just living.'

'No,' Raisa told him. 'Nothing's wrong.'

She abandoned the tram one step before her own. She would break down in tears if one more person spoke to her.

'You've got to pull yourself together,' she announced to the icy Neva. 'What are you, some empty-headed bourgeois girl?'

Snow was beginning to fall, dancing about against the velvety, northern sky like apple blossom. Suddenly, everything was in flux. There was an impish wind tossing the snow and litter around, pinching her cheeks and stinging her eyes. Where everything had been damp and static moments earlier, now it was restless and wild.

'Have some fun?' she said, remembering the *babushka's* words. 'Have some fucking fun!' She shouted at the stars. 'Do you hear that? We've got bayonets at our throats and hunger at the door. We've got counter-revolution and sabotage and kids without families or homes.'

She threw out her hands, fingers flared, and spun wildly in imitation of the Cossack *Gopak*, kicking her heels and flailing her arms. She imagined music and colour and life. She imagined blazing fires and laughter.

'Everywhere there are enemies,' she cried 'In every corner, there is the shadow of death. Well, fuck it. I choose revolution. I choose life.'

She realised she was being watched, a pair of drowsy Red Guards following her movements with bleary eyes as they stood by a brazier.

'You know what you need to do, Comrades,' she shouted. 'Go and have some fun!'

'Chance would be a fine thing,' one of them grumbled.

The second laughed. 'Bring that sexy little butt over here and we can have some fun together.'

'Dream on, Comrade,' Raisa shouted as she raced off down the street, light and fast as a deer. 'I've got somebody waiting for me.'

She burst through the boarding house door – she still called it a boarding house in spite of its new designation as a home for abandoned children – and was immediately mobbed by her charges. She saw Elena emerging from the living room, looking at her wit's end.

Dina was standing at the back of the swarm of children.

'Comrade Dina!' she announced in her most authoritative voice.

Dina picked up the thread, standing to attention and saluting. 'Yes, Comrade Raisa. I await your orders.'

'I appoint you Commissar of Ready for Bed.'

This produced a chorus of plaintive wailing.

'Oh no,' Raisa told them. 'Comrade Elena has just been demoted for letting you stay up way beyond your bedtime. She is the Commissar for No Authority Whatsoever. Isn't that right, Comrade Dina?'

'Absolutely right,' Dina agreed. 'Room one, line up.'

Half a dozen children grudgingly obeyed.

'Room two, line up.'

Another half a dozen shuffled into unruly ranks.

'And room three.'

'Now march!'

Raisa pulled Dina close and hugged her. 'Your hair is growing.'

Dina frowned. 'It is, but you already knew that. You only saw me three hours ago.'

Is that all it is, Raisa thought. Three short hours, yet it feels as if days have slipped by.

'Well, you are looking very pretty,' Raisa told her. 'I just wanted you to know.'

Dina was wearing a bewildered expression. What had got into Raisa?

'You really should have helped Elena,' Raisa scolded. 'You know how she struggles to keep order.'

Dina grinned. 'I like seeing her flounder. She doesn't have any idea, you know.'

The child was older than her years.

'Well, you shouldn't just let her struggle,' Raisa told her. 'You are almost thirteen. It is time you took some responsibility.'

Dina clearly had something up her sleeve.

'I'll do it,' she said, 'on one condition.'

Raisa laughed out loud. 'Oh, so you're bargaining now!'

'Of course,' Dina told her, 'like a good Communist should.'

Raisa sat on the second stair and Dina sat beside her, snuggling close.

'I think I should stay up later than the others, seeing as I am in a position of authority.'

Raisa planted a kiss on her cheek. 'Of course. There is an extra mattress against the wall on the landing. It is for you and you alone as supervisor of our wild tribe.'

Dina winked and let her in on a secret. 'I have already laid it out on the floor.'

Raisa caught Elena's eye and winked.

'You've got half an hour, Dina, then it's up to bed.'

Once Dina was safely tucked up in bed, Raisa patted the stair. 'Sit here with me.'

Elena joined her lover. 'I take it we won the vote.'

'No, it was a stalemate. The Lefts still want their revolutionary war. They would throw away the whole revolution on a whim.'

Elena was clearly confused. 'So why are you in such a carefree mood?'

Raisa rested her cheek on Elena's shoulder, earning the expected caress along her throat, the warm brush of fond lips on her own.

'We are alive, my love. Twenty children are saved. The revolution lives.'

Elena parted Raisa's lips with her own, easing her tongue inside Raisa's mouth. Raisa felt the warm, melting feeling Elena's kisses always produced in her. It was Elena who ended the kiss.

'I'm not cut out for childcare, you know,' she said. 'Put me in front of five hundred unruly factory women and I am a warrior chieftain. Put me in charge of a unit of the Red Guard and I will storm any fortress. But this...I just don't have the patience. Maybe I don't have a feminine side.'

Raisa smiled. 'Of course you have, just not a mothering instinct. I don't think we will be doing this for long.'

'How's that?'

'It's something Svetlana said this evening. The party is drawing up a proposal to put to us. Anishin will be in on the meeting.'

Elena frowned. 'That sounds ominous. I will ask Aunty Svetlana what they've got in mind.'

'She said not to,' Raisa answered. 'She said it would be wrong to divulge details before everything is ready, even to family members.'

'What can it be?'

'I have no idea, but we wouldn't have to talk to the pair of them together unless they had something important to say.'

Suddenly, Elena squirmed with pleasure at her lover's touch. 'What are you doing?'

Raise had started unbuttoning the crisp, white blouse that Elena had fastened to the chin.

'What do you think?'

Elena trapped Raisa's fingers for a moment. 'What if the children see us?'

Raisa was not to be deterred. Her fingers stole inside Elena's blouse.

'You look like a secretary.'

'Anishin's orders,' Elena said.

Already, Raisa was exploring inside Elena's under garments.

'Forget about Anishin until tomorrow,' she said. 'Before that, we have a whole night ahead of us. I want your undivided attention.'

Aroused by Raisa's touch, Elena had become dreamy.

'Let's go to bed.'

Kolya

The proclamations had been posted across the city for several days now. He read the peeling poster on the wall outside the Cheka headquarters on Gorokhovaya Street: *In order to save our exhausted and depleted country from the miseries of a new war we made the supreme sacrifice and notified the Germans of our readiness to accept their conditions of peace.*

Kolya removed his spectacles and cleaned them with a rag. He had heard from several sources that his old friend and comrade Grigory was siding with the Left Communists. Kolya had some sympathy with their point of view. It fitted in with his idea of pure revolutionary zeal, a blood sacrifice to save the honour of the revolution. Even Dzerzhinsky was unconvinced by Lenin's desperate desire to rush through a peace treaty with the Germans. He focussed on the now familiar words: *The Socialist Republic of Soviets is in the gravest danger.*

This was the sentence that had signalled a great change in the city. With the German Army at the gates of red Petrograd, Lenin had ordered that Sovnarkom move to Moscow, away from imminent danger. The appeal to defend the revolution told Kolya that the Cheka's work was about to become more significant. For weeks, he had done little more than investigate individuals of little real importance. The paragraph ended with a nod in the direction of international revolution: *Until the German proletariat rises and is victorious, it is the sacred duty of the workers and peasants of Russia to defend the Republic of Soviets against the bourgeois-imperialist hordes.* He heard the scrape of boots and turned. He was staring into the face of Peters, his immediate superior, accompanied by a man with swept-back, wiry hair and pince-nez glasses, he looked like the classic revolutionary intellectual.

'Who better to defend the Republic of Soviets than the Cheka?' said Peters.

'My thoughts precisely, Comrade Peters,' Kolya said.

'This proclamation has put the cat among the pigeons and no mistake,' Peters grunted. 'The Latvian Rifle Regiment is shipping out to meet the German offensive.' He grinned. 'You know that I am Latvian, I assume.'

'Yes.'

'We Latvians do our duty, unlike some of these bloody false Communists. There are regiments pledging to die for the revolution just so long as they can do it sitting on their arses here in Peter.' He laughed scornfully. 'If the Germans set foot in the city, we will all be standing in front of a firing squad.'

'Yes, Comrade Peters.'

'Well, by *we*, I mean *you*, of course.'

Peters had a brutal sense of humour. His office was already cleared. He was accompanying comrade Dzerzhinsky to the relative safety of Moscow. Their replacement was due any day. Kolya glanced at the man with the pince-nez glasses.

'Many people are on their way out of Peter these days,' Peters said.

Kolya nodded. 'I came past the Finland Station on the way over. People are trying to get out of the city.'

'Do you know Comrade Uritsky?' Peters said, finally introducing his colleague. 'Moisei Solomonovich is the new head of the Petrograd Cheka.'

Kolya offered his hand to Uritsky.

'It will be a privilege to work under your command, Comrade,' he said.

'It is good to meet you, Kolya,' Uritsky said warmly.

'We can't stand here gassing all day,' Peters said. 'There's work to do. You don't need to come into the building, Kolya. There's a truck waiting for you with half a dozen men. We've got armed gangs breaking into houses and workers ransacking the factory stores. I can hardly blame them. The poor bastards haven't been paid in weeks. On top of that, Comrade Polukarov tells us that there is a citywide conspiracy to overthrow the Soviet government.'

'I know,' Kolya replied. 'These bomb scares are a worry.'

'We're in for more than scares,' Peters snorted. 'We've got our work cut out, whether we're in Moscow or Petrograd. There is a list of locations with your driver.'

This came as a surprise to Kolya. He was expecting files, photographs of faces, information on suspects' movements. Now all they were giving him were addresses.

'What am I supposed to do?'

Peters seemed unimpressed by the question. Kolya sensed the displeasure and shifted his feet uneasily.

'Bring some kind of order, if you can, Kolya. You may know that one of Comrade Lenin's favourite words is initiative.'

Kolya was now wishing he had kept his mouth shut.

'If there is anybody acting suspiciously, arrest them. You must have seen the latest circular. Crack down on counter-revolutionaries, speculators, thugs, hooligans, saboteurs and other parasites.' He held out a meaty palm. 'That gives you plenty to go on.' Peters strode towards the front door of No 2 Gorokhovaya Street, with Uritsky by his side. 'Oh, if the Germans arrive, shoot the fuckers.'

Kolya stared.'I beg your pardon.'

'Comrade,' Peters said pityingly, 'that was a joke.'

Not for the first time, Kolya felt the back of his neck burn. Peters must think me wet behind the ears, he thought.

'Yes,' he said. 'Of course.'

He found the truck just around the corner, engine idling. He clambered into the passenger seat next to the driver and ran his eye down the list of locations.

'You won't find anything happening there,' the driver said.

'How's that?'

'Somebody inside Gorokhovaya is tipping people off. Anybody running a scam is being warned in advance. Trust nobody.'

'So what do you suggest?'

The driver winked and held out a small notebook. 'Some of us like to take things into our own hands.'

Kolya reached for the book, but the driver withheld it.

'In exchange, you put in a word with Comrade Peters. I'm capable of a lot more than driving. I could do with one of those leather coats.'

That made Kolya laugh out loud. He recognised people who could be useful to him and this man had the kind of street knowledge and low cunning that could increase his reputation.

'What's your name, Comrade?'

'I'm Leonid Akhmetov.'

'Nikolai Markov.'

Leonid released the handbrake and the truck pulled away from the kerb. He handed over the notebook.'I know who you are.' He leaned his arm out of the open window. 'Is it true that the Left SRs heckled Lenin at the Soviet Executive for signing the peace treaty?'

Kolya nodded. 'So I hear. There were shouts of traitor and Judas. I'm told Communists joined in.'

Leonid squinted against the rush of the wind from the open window.

'Why don't you wind it up?' Kolya asked.

'I like fresh air,' Leonid answered. 'See, if I was in charge of the Cheka, if some twat called my leader Judas I'd have him up against the wall.'

'Seriously? You'd shoot him outright?'

'Too fucking right.'

Kolya grinned and shook his head. 'You don't shoot people for what they say.'

'You're too soft, Comrade. You call somebody Judas today and you end up putting a bullet in his brain tomorrow. If you want to fight a war wearing kid gloves, that's your look-out. Now me, if I get into a scrap, the other guy isn't getting a chance to do me in. I'm not giving him a way to come back at me, if you get my drift.'

Kolya considered the driver's high, flat forehead, his broken nose and pockmarked skin. He might as well have had the words Hard Life tattooed on his face.

'Your hands aren't as clean as you make out anyway, Comrade,' Leonid drawled.

'Meaning?'

'I've been finding out a bit about you. Shutting down anti-Bolshevik papers, ordering the shooting of protestors outside the Tauride, it seems you're not averse to a bit of repression, yourself.'

'I'll have to keep an eye on you, Leonid,' Kolya said. 'What's the first location?'

'Engineering plant,' Leonid says. 'Just outside the city.'

He told Kolya the name.

'I've run Workers' Circles in this factory. What's going on there?'

'Tell you what, Kolya, my friend, let's make it a surprise.'

Leonid glanced over his shoulder and the Red Guards in the back rocked with laughter.

'A pleasant one?' Kolya asked.

'Just a surprise.'

Leonid was enjoying himself.

A short drive south took them to the vicinity of the factory where Leonid pulled over. Kolya frowned.

'This isn't the main gate.'

103

'It isn't what's happening at the main gates that will interest you, Comrade Kolya.'

Leaving the truck around the corner, Leonid jumped down and the entire unit of six men jogged along the wall on the far side of the plant, some way from the main gate. Leonid stopped suddenly and tugged at Kolya's jacket.

'Take a look down there.'

Kolya peered into the mist and saw shadowy figures moving back and forth.

'What are they doing?'

'Remember this conspiracy Comrade Polukarov has been talking about? I think we just found one head of the hydra. The factory has got naval engineers in, plating up an armoured train to send to the Don and the Kuban. The last train got pretty badly shot up. These bastards are sabotaging the war effort, taking away components.'

'How do you know all this?'

Leonid tapped his nose with his finger. 'Some of us have got cousins working in the stores. They know when things are going missing.'

'This cousin of yours,' Kolya said 'He's a Communist, I assume.'

Leonid shakes his head. 'Weasel? Don't make me laugh. He's the sole member of the Weasel Party. He expects a reward. You scratch my back, I'll scratch yours.'

'You call your cousin Weasel?'

'Right.

'I know I shouldn't ask,' Kolya says, 'but why Weasel?'

'He's a fucking weasel – but he's our Weasel. He doesn't like Bolsheviks, Communists, whichever name you're using now, but he can't stand anything to do with the autocracy and anybody who wants to bring it back. He also hates his family going hungry, so you see him right and he'll use his contacts to feed us more information.'

Kolya unclipped the leather holster containing his Browning pistol. 'Let's go and have a word with these saboteurs.'

He waved three of the men forward, indicating an arc out to the left. They nodded and moved low through the murk. Satisfied that any escape route was covered, Kolya made his approach.

'Do you have business here, Citizens?' he asked, blindsiding them.

A hand moved to a hip, but Kolya had the Browning trained on the would-be resister.

'I wouldn't touch that if I were you.'

Behind the saboteur, his Red Guards had their rifle stocks securely lodged against their shoulders, eyes squinting down the barrel. Kolya moved forward, examining two boxes on the ground in front of the saboteurs. One of them had just become aware of the Red Guards outflanking him to the rear.

'Shit.'

'Shit is, I think, the correct response,' Kolya said. 'You, my friend, are in it up to your neck.' He indicated the snow-covered ground with his pistol. 'Deposit any weapons there. Leonid, pat them down.'

He was going through the boxes. One contained tools, the other various components filched from the factory. Ashen faces greeted Kolya as he rummaged through the various parts that had been removed from the machinery.

'I can explain...'

'No,' Kolya said. 'You can shut the fuck up. You will be interrogated at Gorokhovaya.' He turned to Leonid. 'Pick me up here in a couple of hours.'

The saboteurs started to protest. 'Comrades....'

Kolya barked a command, his voice almost metallic. 'Be quiet.' He marched forward. 'I could have you shot right here, right now and nobody would lift a finger. The Cheka has the absolute trust of the people. Do you understand me?'

He noted the hurried nods and smiled with satisfaction.

'Get them out of my sight.'

While Leonid and the Guards marched the four men away, Kolya wandered through the rear gate. There was no security whatsoever, just an anxious-looking worker in blue overalls staring at him from an open doorway.

'Were you expecting somebody else?' Kolya demanded. 'Name?'

The man was twitchy, but he gave it.

'Ionov.'

Kolya pulled out his notepad and scribbled the name onto a fresh page.

'Well, Citizen Ionov, it looks like you have some questions to answer.'

Ionov went to speak, but Kolya silenced him with the wag of his forefinger.

'Later,' he said, 'at Gorokhovaya. Now, I would like you to direct me to the appropriate manager.'

There was a surprise awaiting Kolya in the office.

'Svetlana!'

She was not alone. Anishin stood and instinctively placed his hand on the back of Svetlana's chair. Raisa and Elena were also there.

'Quite a Communist delegation,' Kolya remarked, recovering from the shock of the unexpected reunion.

For the first time, he registered the presence of a stocky, balding man in his late forties.

'Nagorny,' he stammered nervously. 'Pyotr Ivanovich Nagorny. I am delighted to meet you,'

'Citizen Nagorny,' Kolya said, taking a seat. 'Maybe you would like to explain this happy coincidence.'

He watched the exchange of glances between Anishin and Svetlana, the proximity of dull, colourless Vassily's hand to her shoulder, the tension in both faces. Raisa and Elena were sitting close together, quite the little, lovebirds. Love indeed was all around.

Clearing his throat, Nagorny began to explain.

'I am a junior manager, you understand. The Comrade Director has an appointment in the city.' He ran the tip of his tongue nervously over fat, wet lips. 'I was assigned the duty of showing the delegation around the plant.'

Kolya pulled together what he knew about his comrade Communists. He was struggling to understand what could have brought them all together here, in one of the largest engineering concerns in the region.

'No time like the present,' Kolya said. 'Do you mind if I tag along?'

Nagorny glanced nervously at Ionov as he stood, hand gripping the door handle wishfully.

'Of course. This way.'

Ionov seemed about to make his escape, but Kolya rested a hand on his bony shoulder and whispered in his ear.

'I have not forgotten about you, Citizen. You will wait for me here.'

Nagorny led the party through a cavernous hall. Before them stood a locomotive. In a second section, plating was being secured to a second-class carriage. In yet another section, a platform was being bolted to a flatbed.

'An armoured train,' Kolya said, walking around the rolling stock. 'Very impressive.'

'It is something of a rushed job,' Nagorny admitted. 'It will transport reinforcements to the Ukraine or the Don, wherever they are needed to suppress the counter-revolution.'

He glanced at his other visitors, wondering how much to divulge. Anishin took over the explanations.

'The Whites shot up the first train we sent. Fortunately, it made its way through to Ekaterinodar without any casualties beyond a few splinters. It was felt that continuing to transport our fighting men without any significant protection was foolhardy.' He ran his hand over the steel plating. 'Hence the armoury.'

'It is all very commendable,' Kolya said, 'but tell me, does this stuff have anything to do with the operating of the train?'

He produced one of the components he had found in the box outside. Instantly, sweat stood out on Nagorny's brow and he began to rush out a hurried response.'Where did you find it? I can't imagine how it came to be in your possession. I will initiate a most thorough inquiry.'

'There is no need for that,' Kolya advised him. 'The Cheka will be carrying out its own investigation. Sabotage and counter-revolution are part of our remit.'

At this news, the blood drained from Nagorny's flaccid features.

'I am confused about one thing, Citizen Nagorny.' He brandished the component. 'You haven't asked where I got it.'

By now, Nagorny was agitated to the point of panic. Kolya allowed enough time for Nagorny to attempt some form of rushed explanation then he interrupted the manager in full flow.

'There is a box outside the gates. Have an employee bring it in.' Pointedly, he added. 'Make sure it isn't Citizen Ionov.'

'Of course, of course.' Nagorny scurried away.

Kolya was not done. The presence of four comrades working in different Commissariats had piqued his interest, not least because Svetlana's haunting features still crept regularly into his mind in unguarded moments.

'I have one question, Comrades. Why does it take four of you to inspect one armoured train?'Svetlana did the explanations.

'You may as well know, Kolya. Raisa and Elena will be part of the detachment travelling south. They are both excellent agitators. Raisa has a gift for public speaking. They are trained in first aid and they are excellent shots. Most importantly, they have the complete trust of the Party.'

'And you expect the men to obey them?'

'We are Communists, Kolya. Women are men's equals in our new Russia. Several women have become outstanding Red Guards.'

Kolya chose his next words carefully, acutely aware of Anishin's presence next to Svetlana.

'No man is your equal, Svetlana.'

He enjoyed the way Anishin bristled, but resisted the urge to give Kolya a hiding.

Kolya was intrigued by the party's decision. 'The last I heard, Comrade Raisa, you were the saviour of the street children, young mother of the *besprizornye*.'

'Children must receive an education,' Raisa explained. 'Svetlana is arranging for the boarding hou...the home to be renovated so that there will be a school room. Svetlana and her daughter Anna will be in personal charge.'

Kolya noticed Nagorny making his way back. Leonid had just arrived and was carrying the box of components.

'I will have a word with Citizen Nagorny then I must be off. The hydra of counter-revolution has many heads.'

He had gone several yards when Svetlana called after him.

'So you are the man who will sever them?'

Kolya half-turned.

'Surely you know the answer. I will do my revolutionary duty.'

Pavel

'Here's the thing, Comrades,' Pavel told the huddle of men before him as they squatted next to the halted train. 'We're not the only people with problems. We are an army of soldiers without officers.'

Volodya raised his hand as if he was still a kid. 'Aren't you an officer?'

Pavel indicated his men. 'These idiots elected me.'

There was a nod from Mikhail. 'That's right. We did.'

Pavel decided it was all right to continue. 'We are an army of soldiers without officers. Kornilov's troops are an army of officers without soldiers. Just imagine it, every puffed-up little fucker who wants to be a colonel or a major has got to take orders. I don't envy the man that's got to keep a lid on all the petty jealousies.'

'Don't talk about officers to me,' Mikhail grumbled. 'We should fuck them right off.'

Volodya sprang to his feet and snapped into a salute. 'I am Officer KrapOnHisMen. I love the revolution.' He put a finger to his lips and leaned forward conspiratorially. 'I actually love the Tsar, but don't tell anybody.'

There was a ripple of laughter at Volodya's antics, but Pavel waved for him to sit down.

'Volodya's a bit of a clown, Comrades, but he's got a point. Our problem is that most of us don't have a clue about military strategy and tactics. We're poorly clothed and poorly armed and most of us wish we were back in Peter.'

'I wish I was home in bed with my wife,' said one man. 'She gets lonely without me.'

'She won't be lonely for long,' came the reply. 'Some likely lad will see to that.'

'Fuck you!'

'Settle down, Comrades,' Pavel said. 'We all wish we were somewhere else instead of freezing our bollocks off down here.'

'All you've done is talk about problems,' came a voice from the back. 'So what's the good news?'

'Scratch a self-proclaimed democratic White,' Pavel answered, 'and you've got a Tsarist counter-revolutionary who thinks workers should hang from every lamp post. They think the peasants should accept their lot and grovel at the masters' feet. Half the buggers want to go out and slaughter every Jew they can find. Isn't that right, Abram?'

Abram squinted through the smoke, keeping his counsel, but he did nothing to contradict his commander.

'We will meet a lot of people who are suspicious of us,' Pavel continued, 'but they are bloody terrified of the generals.' He warmed his hands in front of the fire. 'The peasants want an *end* to the landlords. They know the Whites will *restore* them. That, Comrades, is to our advantage. It will tell over time.'

Mikhail shuffled closer to the fire. 'Over time, Pavel Sergeyevich. How many of us poor bastards will be dead before our advantage starts to tell?'

'You're not going to get any heroic speechifying from me, lads,' Pavel answered. 'I'm a dumb *muzhik* like those poor buggers we met yesterday. I call it the way I see it. Not all of us are going to get through this, but more of us will make it back to Peter if we stick together. You elected me your commissar. That's as far as democracy goes.'

He punched home his point by clenching his fist and raising it before his face.

'You've heard the stories. We've had Red Guards outnumbering the enemy and the soft buggers ran away at the first setback for lack of leadership. Well, I've got a wife, and a kid on the way. I've got something to lose and no cowardly shithouse is going to stop me going home to see if I'm father to a boy or a girl.' This struck home in the hearts of men with families. 'We're not having a vote every time we mount an attack and if you try to run away I'll put a bullet up your arse. Is that clear?'

Mikhail had his gaze trained on the trembling dusk. The snows were beginning to retreat. He asked the question that had been bothering him since the skirmish with the Whites.

'Where's the Front in this war anyway?'

'This is a different kind of war,' Abram put in. 'Do you know why they tried to shoot up your train?' Faces turned to him. 'The railway line is the Front. Every factory where a worker organises is the Front. Every village where the peasants seize the land or burn down the manor, that's the Front too. Do you want to know where the Whites are?' His hand swept a broad arc in the air.' Well, they're behind you. They're ahead of you. So far, this is a conflict without static trenches and artillery batteries. Welcome to class war.'

'How do you know so much?' Mikhail asked.

'I've lived this crap for weeks. I was organising among the factory workers when the Whites came. I saw how the proletarians regrouped the moment the Whites rode out. I've ate, slept and drunk the class war for the last three months.'

Pavel listened intently to Abram. This man had a huge advantage over any of them. He knew Rostov, Taganrog, Novocherkassk and Ekaterinodar. He knew the Don and the Kuban. Most of all, he had more to fight for than most of the men under Pavel's command. His name was known and the Whites would mutilate him and bury him alive if they could. In Abram's case it really was victory or death.

'Have you got anything else to tell us?'

Abram took his cap off and scratched his head.

'Don't go running away with the idea that every Cossack is against you. If that were true, you might as well pack up and head off north.'

In the thoughtful silence that followed, it struck Pavel that he and Abram had something in common. They could command an audience.

'The class war is at play here as much as anywhere else,' said Abram. 'Those bastards you ran into yesterday, they were the sons of the rich. There are plenty of poor Cossacks who would happily put a bullet in their brains.' He watched the moon roll out from behind the clouds. 'That's not the only split. See, some of the young boys have been taking it up the arse from the officer class for three years now. They see the same men wearing white armbands and they are in no rush to serve.'

Volodya thumped Pavel's shoulder. 'Do you hear this guy? Maybe we should have another election and put him in command.'

Pavel was ready with an answer.

'Believe me, Volodya, I have no great yearning to be in charge of you bunch of hairy-arsed morons, but right now I'm the best you've got.'

Volodya grinned and held up his hands. 'Only joking, Comrade.'

'Yes, well you're going to joke yourself into a thick ear in a minute.' Pavel got to his feet. 'Try to snatch some sleep. We reach Ekaterinodar tomorrow.'

He intercepted Volodya on his way back to the train.

'Where are you going? You're on first watch.'

Volodya paused, hooked his rifle strap over his shoulder and perched sulkily on a barrel.

'Mama said you'd take care of me.'

'I will,' Pavel told him, 'but you're not getting any special privileges just because you're Svetlana's son. First watch and no dozing off. Those Whites might still be creeping around.'

He set off towards the locomotive.

'Where are you going?' Abram asked.

'I'm reconnoitring the area to put my mind at rest,' Pavel told him. 'I don't want any nasty surprises in the night. You could say we're in bandit country now.'

Abram stood up.

'Do you mind if I tag along?'

Pavel was glad of the company. He liked a man who was a proven survivor. It was like having a good luck charm hanging round your neck.

'You said something to the men that didn't quite ring true.'

Abram rubbed his nose and turned.

'And what was that?'

'The Whites came. The Whites left. The workers regrouped.' Pavel looked Abram in the eye. 'I'm starting to get a picture of what's going on beyond Petrograd and there's got to be more to it than that. Call my cynical, but I don't see these White scum giving the Red workers a kiss on both cheeks and buggering off.'

The two men were standing against a backdrop of melting snow under an enormous, empty black sky. Their breath frosted as they talked, trust growing between them.

'There's a lot more. I didn't want to spook the guys.'

'You're not going to spook me.'

'Fine, I'll tell you what happened, but keep it to yourself. The workers' committee armed the town, but they were ill-prepared and there weren't enough weapons to go around. The Whites took the place by storm.'

Pavel knew where this was going.

'There were reprisals?'

Abram relived the horror in his mind.

'Too fucking right. It was a massacre. The Whites marched twelve Red workers out into the town square. They cut off their noses and put out their eyes. They made their wives and kids watch. Pavel Sergeyevich, the scum we are up against are fucking sadists. This is no accident. Kornilov says he would see three quarters of all Russians perish to defeat Bolshevism.'

The scene unfolded in Pavel's imagination.

'You witnessed this personally?'

'That's right,' Abram answered. 'Before the Whites overran the town, some of the men who later died found me a hiding place. I got to watch from a window. Nobody gave me away.' His voice broke off. 'Too many good people have died to keep me alive.' He took a step forward. 'I want a promise from you, Pavel Sergeyevich.'

'Name it.'

'When we fight for Ekaterinodar, we will be facing some of the same filth that killed my comrades, that slaughtered Klim and Irina. Promise me that you will show them no mercy.'

'No quarter asked,' Pavel answered, 'no quarter given. Class against class, right to the end.'

Abram embraced his commander.

'For this pledge,' he growled, eyes glittering, 'I will give my life if need be.'

Pavel patted his back.

'Let's hope that won't be necessary. Isn't there a toast? To life.'

Abram smiled.

'There is. *L'chaim.*'

Dawn was breaking when they saw the bridge. There were dark figures silhouetted on the riverbank.

'Whites or Reds?' Mikhail wondered out loud.

'We'll soon find out,' was Pavel's answer. 'They could be trying to stop us reaching Ekaterinodar.'

Abram had commandeered one of the few pairs of binoculars. 'There are red flags. They're ours....as long as it isn't a trap.'

On the far side of the bridge there was a small town, not much of a place at all, just a few houses, a grain store, some outbuildings. As the train moved closer to the bridge, the first sounds of gunfire could be heard. Pavel sent a message forward for the driver to reduce speed. Presently somebody approached from the straggle of Red Guards around the bridge. As the locomotive came to a halt in a hiss of steam, the representative of the unit scrambled on board.

'You're a sight for sore eyes,' he told them. 'The Whites are holed up in those buildings and they've got us pinned down on this side of the river.'

'Where are you from?'

'Stavropol.' He saw the blank looks. 'Couple of hundred miles. Look, we've been held at this fucking bridge for an hour. Half our guys just threw down their guns and pissed off. They only joined up to get a warm coat and something in their bellies. No stomach for a fight.'

'What about you?'

'The guys that are left will do what it takes. Bring the train across the bridge. We'll use it as cover.'

He was about to go when Pavel called him back.

'Hey, Stavropol,' he shouted. 'What do we call you?'

'Nikita?'

'Nikita what?'

'Does it matter?'

The train was halfway across the bridge, belching steam, when a hail of bullets hammered against the sides of the carriages. What little plating had been attached now seemed scant protection.

'Holy shit!' Mikhail bawled, throwing himself to the floor. 'What the fuck are they using to shoot at us?'

Pavel was at the window, squinting through the clouds of steam. He had a feeling the driver was doing this on purpose to give them extra cover.

'Machine gun posts,' he shouted over the guttural barking of the machine guns. 'One over to the left. One by the warehouse.'

He was dodging his head back and forth, trying to get a glimpse of the enemy positions. Muzzle flashes alerted him to one emplacement. The locomotive was almost over the bridge. He scrambled to the door, ducking low and leaned out, lurching back inside as more machine gun fire ricocheted against the walls.

'Hey, Nikita, can you skirt round to the left? Give us some covering fire'

'What are you going to do?'

Pavel had his eye on the warehouse. The gunner was more experienced. He was laying down fire with far more accuracy than the emplacement to the left.

'See that fucker in the warehouse? We're taking him out.'

Nikita waved his men forward to filter out btween the huts and piles of logs along the sidings. He watched as the deadly blizzard of hot lead pursued the scampering Guards through the barely-adequate cover. A blood-spray signalled the death of one of the youngest Reds, but there was no time to mourn. His body lay sprawled where he fell. From their hiding places in the sidings, the unit returned fire.

'This is it.' Pavel chose his men, pointing them out one by one. 'On my command.'

'What about me?' Volodya protested.

Pavel weighed up his options. This was Svetlana's son, proud, headstrong, fiery. Try to leave him behind in the train and he would probably chase after them anyway and get his fool head blown off.

'OK, you too, Volodya, but no heroics. You keep your head down and do exactly as I say. Got it?'

Volodya was offended. 'You're not saying that to anybody else.'

'Your Mama kept you away from the cadet rising and the fight at Pulkovo. You're a virgin.'

Volodya grinned. 'There are two beautiful women in the Vyborg who'll testify otherwise.'

'Stop boasting,' Mikhail told him sourly, 'and don't do anything to put the rest of us in danger or, believe me, I'll make sure you won't be fit to be with a woman ever again.'

The steam had just billowed over to the right of the train.

'With me!'

Machine guns raking the sidings with fire, Pavel worked his way around the back of the warehouse, flanked by Abram and Mikhail. The stammer of the nearest gun was deafening as they approached.

'If I know guns,' Pavel hissed, 'and I do know guns, that Maxim is starting to overheat. We wait for a break in the fire and we go in.' He twisted round to see who was closest. 'Mikhail, Abram, see the far wall? Those planks look rotten to me. Kick your way in and come at them from behind. Volodya, we're going to get their attention. We're aiming for the coal pile.'

'We're meant to use that for cover? There's nothing of it.'

Pavel shrugged. 'It's all we've got.'

He raised his arm, waiting for the Maxim to choke. Suddenly, there was a moment's respite and his hand came down.

'Go!'

They reached the coal pile just as the Maxim opened up again. Coal dust sprayed their faces.

'Single shots at intervals,' Pavel ordered. 'There's no point wasting ammunition.' An outbreak of screaming to the left, machine gun fire ripping along the wall of the warehouse.

'Fuck me if Nikita didn't storm his machine gun nest. He's targeting them with their own weapon.'

It seemed the gunner in the warehouse was in two minds – prioritise the captured Maxim to his right or the riflemen in front of him? As it turned out, the question was academic. Abram appeared, ghostly pale in the gloom of the warehouse. His first shot took out the gunner. His second killed the feeder.

'Clear those buildings,' Pavel ordered. 'Keep your wits about you. There may be more Whites hiding.'

It was over. Nikita's unit killed two and took four prisoners in a brief mopping up operation.

'On the ground,' he yelled. 'Put your arms out. That's right, make the sign of the cross.'

Pavel laughed.

'Are you taking the piss?'

The train disgorged the rest of the Petrograders. They started sweeping the outbuildings.

'Right,' Pavel said, perching on the coal pile, 'you can get on your knees. Keep your hands behind your necks. Volodya, frisk them.'

Volodya shouldered his rifle and patted down the Whites. Three were young men, Volodya's age. It was the older White Guard who interested Pavel.

'I only got the briefest glimpse of the bastard that shot the villagers,' snarled Abram. 'He was riding away at the head of his men at the time.'

He scrutinised the older man.

'Do you know me?' he asked.

The head-shake failed to satisfy Pavel.

'Let's try another one. We fumigated a village of White scum, fifteen, twenty versts from here.' He gave its name. 'Recognise it?'

He saw the way the White's right eye twitched. 'Am I onto something,' Pavel wondered, 'did he just have a tic?'

'No,' the White drawled through a dry throat. 'Never heard of it.'

'Are you sure about that? You see, you're looking pretty nervous to me.'

The White kept his gaze steady. 'I'm positive.'

Abram was still in the warehouse, unaware of Pavel's suspicions. The latest recruit to the unit seemed to find something really funny.

'Hey, Pavel Sergeyevich, do you know what happened to Mikhail here?'

Mikhail limped into view, a rueful look on his face. There was blood on his trousers.

'He only got his foot stuck when he put his boot through the planks.'

Mikhail grimaced. 'It's not funny. Hurts like fuck.'

Pavel was less interested in his comrades' horseplay than the identity of the machine-gunner in front of him.

'Are you a good rider?' he asked. 'You see, the guy I'm looking for was a really able horseman. He knew his stuff.' He scanned the buildings in front of him. 'Are there any horses?'

'We saw some tethered in the woods back there,' Nikita informed him.

Now Pavel had eyes back on his man. 'There's somebody I'd like you to meet.'

There was that tic again. 'Abram, take a look at this guy.'

He saw the way Abram frowned then the change of expression as the new addition to the unit saw the man kneeling by the coal pile.

'Recognise him?'

'It's the fucker who shot Klim.'

'Are you sure?'

Abram walked over to the White and leaned forward.

'It's him.'

'Look closely. Are you absolutely sure?'

'I can make sure,' Abram answered. 'I only glimpsed him briefly, but I had to listen to him taunting Klim before he shot him. I will never forget the voice of the thug who killed the old man.' He pulled something from his jacket. 'See this?'

He dangled a Star of David in front of the killer's face.

'It's called the *Magen David*. Maybe you would like to kiss it.'

The killer blinked twice. 'What?'

'You've got a choice. You kiss it, or I cut your balls off before I kill you.'

The killer went to kiss the object, but Abram pulled it back. 'I wouldn't let your greasy, pogromist lips pollute it, you scumbag. My mother gave it to me.' He glanced at Pavel. 'Do you want me to make doubly sure?'

Pavel nodded. Very deliberately, Abram spelt out what he wanted to hear.

'Say *Jew-lover*. That's what Klim's killer said.'

Urine had started to stain the White's groin. 'I don't....'

'Say it,' Abram said. 'Say Jew-lover. If I recognise the voice of the man who killed Klim, I'll put you out of your misery. One shot. Merciful. Of course, I might not recognise it. In that case, you're our prisoner. It's worth a shot, don't you think?' He glanced at the stream of urine. 'Take your time, we can wait till you've finished pissing yourself.'

The White Guard was trembling.

'So are you ready? Say Jew-lover.'

The White had started to sob.

'Oh, what is this?' Abram groaned, rolling his eyes. 'You're crying like a fucking baby. Say it!'

The words bubbled up through tears and snot. 'Jew-lover.'

Abram turned hard, dead eyes his way. 'Move to one side.'

The White tried to stand.

'Oh no, you stay on your knees, you murdering bastard.'

There was a comic waddle away from his comrades.

'If you are religious, you can say something to your God before you die.'

A shake of the head. Abram pulled out his pistol. A shot rang out and the White fell face forward in an isolated patch of snow, staining it scarlet. Abram considered the body for a moment then he seemed to think of something.

'There were two different killers,' he announced. 'The one who killed Irina was a younger guy.'

That produced a wail of terror from one of the surviving Whites.

'I was under orders,' he screamed. 'I didn't want to do it.'

Abram walked across and stood in front of him. 'To think I nearly missed you. So what was that excuse again? Did a big boy tell you to do it?'

117

He stared down at a face smeared with tears and snot. The pistol roared again and there was a second body crumpled on the frozen ground. Now the Reds were clustered around the remaining prisoners. One was sobbing, head sagging. The final man held his head erect, azure eyes staring vacantly across the steppe.

'What do we do with these two?' Volodya asked.

Pavel lit a cigarette. 'They come with us to Ekaterinodar. – You lost a man, Nikita. Shall we bury him?'

Nikita laughed humourlessly. 'I'd like to see you dig a grave in this frozen earth. The bodies go in the river. We'll weight them down.'

While Nikita's men consigned the three bodies to the waters, the machine guns were loaded on the train. Pavel inspected the horses.

'Do you know about horseflesh?' Volodya asked.

'I grew up with horses,' Pavel told him. 'We'll take them with us. This is going to be a mobile war. We have to counter the White cavalry.' He rested a hand on Volodya's shoulder. 'Your first firefight. You just lost your cherry. How does it feel?'

Volodya considered his reply for a moment.

'I nearly threw up when that machine gun opened up. Is that pathetic?'

'No,' Pavel told him. 'It's human.'

Raisa

'Once there was a warrior-chieftain. She knew what it was like to be poor, to live on the streets with only the sky for a roof above her head.'

Iskra wrapped her painfully thin arms found Raisa's legs and gazed up at her, listening intently. 'Is the warrior-chieftain you?'

'When I tell a story,' Raisa answered, 'I always include myself as the hero.'

'So the hero is beautiful?'

'Of course she is! She is beautiful and wise. She has long, blond hair and vivid, blue eyes, just like me, and anybody who says otherwise goes to bed early.'

Raisa continued her tale, watching the faces of the children before her, children she had to let down in the cruellest fashion.

'She found a way to build a home for herself and many children like her and she loved them all dearly. She loved them so much she thought her heart would break.'

Iskra turned to the others. 'See, it is Raisa.'

Raisa continued her tale. 'At first, she thought life would always be this way, the warrior-chieftain, her friends and her new family of lost children, but the war came. The land she thought was free began to shrink and shrink. Many warlords encircled her beloved homeland. It was time to fight.'

Dina was looking steadily at Raisa, with clear, aware eyes. Raisa fought the lump in her throat and struggled on.

'Sometimes you must take up the sword and fight for what you believe. The warrior-chieftain got the summons to arms and said goodbye to her young friends, leaving them in the care of people, good people, who would love them.'

Iskra's chin was on the taut platform made by Raisa's skirt. 'Is there a happy ending? Does the warrior-chieftain come home?'

'She comes home, my little spark. Yes, she comes home.'

Dina was the one who spoke for all the others. 'When do you go, Raisa? What is going to happen to us?'

Elena's hand closed round Raisa's, reassuring her.

'You know that I would never abandon you,' Raisa told the twenty children gathered in Mrs Kuznetsova's old parlour. 'This is your home. Aunty Svetlana and Aunty Anna will take care of you.'

Dina was suspicious. 'Svetlana is always busy.'

'She will make time to keep things here just as they are,' Raisa answered. 'This is my promise to you.'

Dina's pale eyes seemed to have lost the ability to blink. The ensuing silence lasted an age. The clock ticked. The wind soughed. Somewhere in the distance a foghorn brayed on the river. Eventually, Dina, her hair getting long and lustrous now, rose to her feet.

'It's time for bed,' she said. 'Group one.'

Raisa saw how Dina's authority had grown. She had divided the children into regiments and they retired to bed without a murmur of protest.

'Group two.'

More bare feet pattering off to bed.

'Group three.'

'Dina,' Raisa said, reaching out a hand, 'can we talk?'

Dina withheld her hand and followed the final group up the stairs. 'Your mind is made up, Comrade Raisa. There is nothing more to say.'

Once the children had gone, Raisa slumped against Elena, dissolving into tears.

'Did you see the disappointment in their faces?' she sobbed. 'Dina in particular hates me.'

Elena's warmth enveloped her. Familiar, loving hands stroked her and lifted her chin.

'She will never hate you, Raisa. Wasn't it Svetlana and Anna who first brought Dina to your attention? She knows the children are in good hands. It's a big change. Give her time.'

Raisa nodded and let her lover wipe her tears away with the gentlest of touches.

'She is right about Svetlana. She never stops. There is the Commissariat of Education, her work in the factories of the Vyborg and now this extra burden.'

'Anna will devote herself to the children,' Elena said. 'Raisa, you said it yourself in your little folk tale. The noose is tightening around Petrograd. The imperialist states are arming the Whites. Requisitioning units scour the villages for grain. You read the letter from Pavel. Half the Red Guard units abandon the battlefield because nobody has any experience of military leadership. The Front needs dedicated communists to stiffen the backbone of our soldiers.'

'Will they listen to the likes of us, a pair of women?'

Elena responded with her usual flinty stare when anyone expressed a doubt.

'My love, we will make them listen.'

Raisa offered her face for a kiss. 'What would I do without you?'

Elena gave a throaty, mocking laugh. 'You would have the whole of the bed to yourself. You're always complaining I take up more than half the space.'

The smile slowly drained from Raisa's features as she remembered the way Dina was, so serious, her face so lacking in expression. In all these weeks, Raisa had never been able to get Dina to talk about what happened to her while she was surviving on the streets, but it was there in her eyes, in the way she sometimes brooded for hours on end. They had an unspoken link, a bond made from shared pain. Raisa wondered what it would take to give it voice. Now that she had told the children she had to go away, the chance of Dina sharing her story seemed further away than ever.

Presently, Raisa squirmed free of Elena's arms.

'I am going to look in on them,' she said.

She checked on Groups One and Two, but it was the room where Dina was sleeping that drew her. She eased the door open and watched the sleeping forms. There was one child who was wide awake. In her single mattress, apart from the others, Dina was lying on her side, pale, fixed stare penetrating the gloom. Raisa wondered if she should say something or approach Dina and give her a reassuring hug. In the event, Dina watched her for a moment, then rolled over, swaddling herself in the blankets. With a heavy heart, Raisa made her way to the room where Elena was undressing for bed.

'She was wide awake,' she reported.

'Dina?' Elena answered. 'It is a big change. She adores you.'

'I think she is learning to hate me.'

Elena approached. 'She doesn't hate you, my love. Nobody could hate you.'

She laid a carpet of kisses on Raisa's forehead and cheeks, nuzzled the lobes of her ears, found her mouth and prised open soft lips with her tongue. Soon, she was lying on top of Raisa, small breasts brushing her lover's chest and stomach. Her mouth was hungry, searching ever lower until Raisa's back arched and she found some measure of solace in the sensations rushing through her.

When their passion was spent and Elena slept, arm tossed casually across her lover, Raisa stared at the gap in the curtains. Beyond this little sanctuary there was terror and war. Even red Peter, birthplace of the revolution, was menaced by the Germans and the Whites. Most of all, though winter had passed, the city was threatened by hunger. The great Putilov Works, one of the pistons of the October revolution, was growing restless, desperate for an end to rations that could barely sustain the workers.

'Tomorrow I will be transported into Hell.'

Next to her, disturbed by her voice, Elena stirred. Raisa's fingers stole along her lover's arm, chilled in the dead hours of the night. At least she would enter the gates of Hell protected by her angel.

Svetlana was there at first light, Anna and Anishin flanking her like guard dogs. She was known to the children and soon had them clinging to her skirts. There was just one child who kept her distance. Dina thought that she had just turned thirteen, though she found it hard to remember the exact date of her birthday. She drifted, like a lost soul, as Raisa and Elena completed their packing. Everything went into one easily portable canvas bag. Each of the women had a rifle, a holstered pistol and a first aid bag. It was a little over six months since they had rushed to Pulkovo Heights, similarly equipped. Already, it felt like a lifetime ago. It was time to leave. Raisa embraced every child in turn, whispering a special message to each one. Iskra clung to her the longest, pleading with her to stay, but Raisa had to peel away the little girl's fingers and step away from her. If she stayed a moment longer, a flood of tears would let her down.

'What about you, Dina?' she asked. 'You're not too old for a hug, are you?'

Dina approached reluctantly, eyes averted. The embrace was stiff and distant, with Dina turning her face to one side. To this hurt and frightened child-woman, the parting was a betrayal. Raisa felt the distance between them like a branding iron.

'Forgive me, Dina,' she whispered. 'I will return. Please don't make this any harder than it already is. My soul is torn in two.'

There was no answer from Dina, who drew back, stood before Svetlana and announced to the other children in a loud, clear voice that their school day was about to begin with Maths.

'It's time we were on our way,' Elena advised.

Raisa clung to the moment then followed her lover out of the door. Svetlana and Anna saw them off. Some of the children jostled in the doorway. The tiniest, Iskra, took her place at Svetana's side, watching the departure, eyes brimming with tears.

'I hope your stomach ache gets better,' Iskra said.

Raisa frowned. 'I don't have a stomach ache.'

'Yes, you do,' Iskra insisted. 'I heard you last night through the bedroom wall. You were moaning really loudly.'

Raisa's eyes widened. As her cheeks reddened, Svetlana howled with laughter.

'Oh, *that* stomach ache. I'm sorry I kept you awake.'

Of Dina there was no sign. Finally, Anishin embraced Svetlana and kissed her on the lips.

'We will think of you every day,' Svetlana tells her new man and her comrade-sisters as they walk to the tram stop. 'The children sill sing songs about you.'

'Keep walking,' Raisa whispered to Elena, hoping Anishin hadn't heard. 'I tell you, if I look back, my legs will give way beneath me.'

The tram that took the trio to the marshalling yards was so densely packed she could barely breathe. She smelled tobacco, sweat and resignation. This was a city that clung on to life in the hope that victory would come soon and relax the cruel band of steel that was crushing it. The flags and banners they saw on their journey were tattered and faded. Raisa knew blood had been draining from the revolution for months. Only renewed Red triumphs could bring their October back to life.

Within the hour, they were walking the length of the armoured train. The description was flattering. There was some armour plating, but the work had been done in haste. It was hard to imagine that it would afford much protection to the scores of Red Guards, soldiers and sailors who were boarding with their belongings. There were two machine guns. Raisa wondered about the freight cars, imagining what weaponry lurked inside. The last time she had seen the train, it had been little more than a stripped-down hulk. now it would be her home for many months to come.

'Make your way to the second carriage down from the locomotive,' Anishin told them. 'That is where we will house the propaganda and medical units.'

'Which are we, propaganda or medicine?' Elena asked.

Anishin grinned. 'Both.' When nobody laughed, he said: 'We have few resources. I mean it. Both.'

The carriage had a printing press, a telegraph station, a radio transmitter, and a large bookcase filled with revolutionary literature. There were two mattresses on the floor, amid bound bundles of leaflets and pamphlets.

'This is revolutionary war,' Elena remarked. 'The word is as important as the rifle.' As she passed Raisa, she allowed her fingers to trail across her lover's back. '*Two* mattresses. We are the only women on board. They obviously think we are just good friends.'

She realised that Raisa hadn't heard a single word.

'You're thinking about Dina, aren't you?'

Tears spilled down Raisa's cheeks.

'She pretends she is tough. She is the most vulnerable of them all. She has seen more than any of them. '

Elena adopted a brusque, business-like manner. The last thing Raisa needed now was a friend who encouraged the emotional side of her nature.

'Raisa, my love, she has Svetlana. She has Anna. She will be there when you come home. You must be single-minded about our mission here.'

Outside, there was a hiss of steam, the piercing whistle announcing that the train was ready for departure. Raisa busied herself cataloguing the stationery supplies and the small boxes of ammunition that were their own personal supplies. She heard Elena moving about. No matter what she did, she couldn't banish Dina from her thoughts.

'Elena, it is so hard to leave.'

'It is harder to see you go,' came the reply, but the voice wasn't Elena's, but a child's. Raisa spun round to see Dina standing before her.

Dina smiled hesitantly. 'Elena stepped outside when she saw me.' She read the question in Raisa's eyes. 'Svetlana brought me.'

'Do you forgive me?' Raisa asked.

'There is nothing to forgive. You are a revolutionary, a Communist. You are doing your duty.'

'Such an old head on young shoulders,' Raisa sighed, still thrown by Dina's sudden arrival.

'You were right about me,' Dina told her. 'Men bought me. There are always men like that. When I am old enough to carry a gun like you, I will put them against a wall. There will be no mercy.'

Raisa felt the shock of recognition. She too had had thoughts like this.

'You want revenge,' she said.

'What, do you think I should be able to scrub it from my mind,' Dina cried, 'forgive the scum who preyed on me?' Her steady gaze didn't leave Raisa for a second. 'I was so scared. They made me feel dirty. I hated myself. Don't tell me you don't relive your own shame every day.'

'You are thirteen and you sound....'

'Old?' Dina laughed. 'No, I am not old. I put this mask on, Raisa, but I cry when nobody is looking. You, more than anyone, know this.'

Raisa's fingers clawed at her face. 'I should have stayed.'

The presence of this child wounded her. Dina was a recreation of herself, a witness to what the likes of Bagrov had made her.

'Don't feel guilty,' Dina told her. 'If not for you, if not for Svetlana and Anna, my life would still be a living hell. I had forgotten what happiness was until you took me into your home.'

Then she was in Raisa's arms. Her tears flowed freely and mixed with those of her rescuer.

'Come home when the war is won, Comrade Raisa,' she declared, releasing her from the embrace and walking to the door. 'Return to Peter in triumph. I forbid you to die.'

Then she was gone, a frail, fleeing figure engulfed in billowing steam. Elena reappeared.

'Go and wave,' she said.

Raisa did as she was told, rushing to the door and waving wildly until Dina was just a ghostly figure, like a reed on a riverbank, far in the distance.

Abram

Abram was satisfied that he had found a true band of brothers. Pavel had told his men that he was their best chance of survival and he was right. In him, Abram recognised a leader of men. He saw all the necessary qualities of a good soldier: composure, courage, decisiveness, but Pavel was much more than a warrior. He had humanity and conscience. Abram had come across men who used the revolution as cover for their own ambitions or their own inadequacies. He had encountered cowards and he had had to entertain fools.

Revolutions are as much a product of imperfect human beings as any other social activity. To Pavel, revolution was a means to an end. He yearned to return to his village and a life free of oppression. Abram recognised the dream. He had never met a man or woman without demons and of course, Pavel was no exception. There was a kind of minor crisis whenever Pavel mentioned his wife and child. His voice betrayed him every time. Where there should have been joy and pride, there was guilt, even fear.

'A penny for them, Comrade Abram?' Nikita said cheerfully, striding through the pre-dawn murk.

'My thoughts?' Abram said. 'Believe me, they are not worth a kopek.'

'Pavel wants your opinion on something,' Nikita told him.

A conference of the most trusted men was underway. Pavel was haunted by stories of Red Guards melting away under fire. The transformation of these units into a true Red Army was barely underway. Pavel was discussing the consequences of that when Abram arrived.

'As far as we know, the Volunteer Army numbers over a thousand men,' he was saying. 'It could be several thousand. Intelligence is patchy. Cossacks from the *stanitsas* are swelling its ranks. Thank God for the thaw. It has reduced the roads to mud. That gives us chance a to dig in, ready for their assault on the city.'

'Still believe in God do you, Comrade?' Mikhail teased.

Pavel rolled his eyes. 'Do you know what I believe in, Mikhail Vassilievich? I believe in an easy life, food in my belly and a good woman at my side...'

Abram listened. A good woman. Pavel hadn't referred to Nina by name.

'...Oh yes,' Pavel said, 'and the world socialist revolution. Now, can you stop picking me up over every little detail and listen to what I've got to say?'

Mikhail grinned. 'I was only pulling your leg.'

Focussed on his briefing of officers and commisars, Pavel was in no mood for his friend's lousy jokes.

'Yes, like you were only pulling your cock last night so shut the fuck up and listen.' Satisfied that he had everyone's attention, he continued. 'The Kuban river is in full spate, swollen by the melted ice. There is a strong current that makes a river crossing difficult, but not impossible. That means we have a bridge to guard. It is the best place the White Army has to negotiate the river if the bridge is impassable. This bastard Kornilov plans to break into Ekaterinodar and massacre the lot of us. We're going to stop him.'

Pavel swung round.

'Any thoughts, Comrade Abram?'

Abram took a seat. 'This Kornilov, he's a hard bastard, a career soldier from the age of fifteen. He was captured by the Austrians as a prisoner of war and held for a while. Then he got his arse kicked by the Red Guards outside Petrograd and he will not like that. The way I see it, he is smarting from these defeats. He is determined to take the city to recover his reputation. He is prepared for heavy losses.'

'So it's just about pride?' Pavel asked.

'It's more than that. Ekaterinodar is strategic. He needs a victory. If he turns back, his officers' army could fall apart in petty squabbling. The alliance with the Cossacks would crumble.'

'In the first days' fighting, we lost more men than he did,' Pavel says ruefully. 'I just got an estimate from the commissars and it is enough to make your hair white.'

'We've got the better position,' Abram said. 'He has to come at us. Look, we've got solid barricades on all the bridges. Unless some fucker fouls up, he's coming across the river. If we stop them getting a foothold, we win the battle.'

Pavel approved. 'I like the sound of that. We have one more advantage and it isn't one I like to boast about. The enemy is too cocky by half. The White Guard army has got professional soldiers and we're short of numbers in that department. They mowed our comrades down yesterday, took advantage of lads who were wet behind the ears. They think we're going to be a pushover again today. They think we'll break and run when we see them disembarking. We're going to prove them wrong.' He gave his final instructions. 'We double the numbers defending the bridge and mass on the eastern bank of the river. If they penetrate the first line of defence, drive them north. I've got a little surprise waiting. Let's see what these Whites are made of when they meet real resistance.'

Dawn was lightening the sky when there was the first movement on the far bank. Pavel reached for binoculars.

'Decoy boats,' he notes. 'Lay down some gunfire.'

'What do you want to shoot at decoys for?' Abram asked. 'It's a waste of ammunition.'

'Let them think they've got us fooled. You can call it a double bluff.'

'Crafty bugger, aren't you?'

'Oh yes.'

As gunfire greeted daybreak, Pavel inspected his machine gun emplacements.

'Keep your heads down, lads,' he said. 'We don't want them seeing the reception party too early.'

'It certainly sounds as if you know what you're doing,' Abram said, accompanying Pavel as he returned to higher ground to oversee the defence of the eastern bank.

'Appearances can be deceptive,' Pavel reminded him.

He scanned the river with the binoculars and picked out the first two boats, brimming with men.

'Take aim,' he ordered. 'On my command.'

The passage of the boats was painfully slow, but soon they were in range, strung out across the river, already too many to deter from landing.

'Fire!'

The throaty, metallic roar of the machine guns filled the air, bullets singing, spitting into the surface of the water, raking the sides of the tiny, fragile vessels. Screams tore the dawn and men tumbled into the dark waters. The Maxims kept up the deadly fire until Pavel called a halt.

'That should scare them off,' Nikita murmured.

'Don't you believe it,' Pavel told him. 'This isn't a small-scale skirmish like the one in the railway sidings. What we are looking at here is a major assault. The size of the offensive means the decisive battle will be on land. Be ready.'

He looked over his shoulder and saw a score of Red Guards scrambling down the bank to get closer to the action.

'What the hell are they doing?' He started waving his arms. 'Get back behind cover.'

Pavel sprinted towards the Guards, waving with one hand and firing in the direction of the river with his pistol.

'Fall back!'

His warning was too late. Half a dozen men went down under accurate rifle fire from the river. First blood to the Whites.

'That,' Pavel said grimly, sickened at the unnecessary slaughter, 'is why we need military discipline in the ranks.'

There were launches and paddle steamers approaching the length of the bank, White Guards massing ready to wade ashore.

'They've concentrated their attack here,' Pavel observed. 'Get a message down the line. We're stretched.'

Already, scores of the enemy were jumping out of their transports and slithering onto the bank. The Reds' machine guns were roaring, but the enemy were too numerous, their forward progress too well-drilled. Already, some of the Reds, fresh from the factory bench, were looking to lay down their weapons and flee.

'Throw away that rifle,' Pavel told one man, 'and I'll shoot your fucking balls off. Now pick it up and stay in position.'

Abram voiced his support. 'They need a reminder like that, Comrade. Why should somebody who has spent the last few years turning out armoured casings be expected to have nerves of steel on the battlefield?'

Pavel nodded to acknowledge the backing. 'We'll remind the fuckers. Any man who runs gets a bullet.'

He checked he had a response from the ranks, but his mind was already racing towards the next manoeuvre.

'Abram, get some men over to the left before the bastards overrun those machine gun posts.'

Abram had a dozen men at his disposal. They skidded down the greasy bank, ready to confront the White assault. In kneeling positions, designed to give the enemy less of a target, they opened fire.

'Steady,' Abram yelled, seeing wild, purposeless firing. 'Pick your man, take a breath, fire.'

The Whites were in the process of setting up a machine gun post of their own to counter the defensive fire.

'Get that fucking gun,' he yelled.

The enemy gunners were trained soldiers. They had the weapon up and ready within moments. Any minute now, they would be laying down deadly fire, possibly turning the tide of battle. Abram pulled the pin on his grenade.

'Down!'

It exploded in the middle of the Whites. Among the bodies, he could see that the gunner was still standing. Without a moment's hesitation, he sprinted forward and put a bullet between the man's eyes with his revolver. Sliding across the mud, he swung the Maxim round and started mowing down the White attackers. The entire enemy force was swinging away to the north. It was as if Pavel was inviting them into the city.

'What the fuck? Why isn't he telling us to put up more resistance?'

Suddenly, Pavel was standing, etched against the brightening sky, arm raised.

'He's got to be crazy. He's a sitting duck out in the open like that.'

'Who's he signalling to?'

'Buggered if I know,' Nikita said.

That's when the first shell landed in the middle of the advancing Whites. Men screamed. Earth sprayed, rising like crows from the woods. Dozens of enemy fighters were now falling over themselves in panic, trying to retreat from the ambush.

'That Pavel's a devious swine,' Abram said. 'He kept quiet about the artillery.'

Nikita's face was lit by a smile of triumph. 'Now we know what his little surprise was.'

Dirt, debris, shrapnel, rocks the size of a man's first were tearing into the Whites.

Bodies flew like dummies. The artillery barrage continued, as deafening as it was deadly.

'Use the artillery fire as cover,' Abram shouted. 'Move that machine gun forward. We're driving these bastards into the river.'

Mikhail emerged from the fog of battle. 'Pavel says the artillery barrage will end in two minutes. The moment it does, we counter-attack.'

'I hope they've spent all their ammunition,' Abram told him, 'or we're going to take heavy casualties.'

The roar and whistles of the falling shells ended. A moment of shocked silence.

'Charge!'

The Reds were sweeping forward in large numbers, many falling as the retreating Whites put up a robust defence, but all the momentum was with the men swarming down from the top of the bank. Already, the White Volunteer Army attackers were tumbling exhausted and demoralised into their vessels. Some of the boats cast off before they were even half full. Abandoned soldiers floundered in the shallows to be finished off by the Red Guards. The shallows had turned scarlet. There was a paddle steamer, heavily laden with defeated men, trying to get away to the west.

'Target that boat,' Abram yelled. 'Every man we spare is a killer to come back and bump us off tomorrow.'

Withering fire from the Maxims cleared the deck of soldiers. Under a watery sun, the expanse of red river grew. About fifty Whites, left behind in the panic, were putting up a reckless defence further up the bank. Pavel appeared in time to lead the attack on their beleaguered position. The riflemen encircled the Whites, preventing their retreat. Machine guns were being dragged into place. There was another metallic roar and the Whites fell like wheat under a scythe.

'Call that war?' Nikita said, watching the merciless destruction. 'It's murder. They're sitting ducks in the water.'

'You've never experienced a pogrom,' Abram told him. 'When you've seen how these scum act when they've got innocent people at their mercy, you'll forget about pity.'

With the isolated group annihilated, the full power of the Red guns was trained on the boats fleeing back across the river. At least three were put out of action, every man on board riddled with bullets. Wild cheering rose.

'You'd think we'd just driven Napoleon from the gates of Moscow,' Nikita said.

'Let them have their moment,' Pavel told him wearily. 'It might just be the first time these men have gone into a proper battle and stood their ground. They think they can win again.'

A few days later, Abram woke to wild cheering.

'What's this about?' he asked, rolling over to see Mikhail talking to Nikita.

He was on his feet, buttoning his shirt.

'Well, are you going to let me in on your little secret?'

Mikhail was the one to break the news.

'It's Kornilov. We got the old bugger a few days ago. It turns out he was watching the battle unfold from a farmhouse on the heights. The swine is so arrogant, he perches himself up on a ridge, a perfect target for our shelling.'

Abram was stunned. 'Are you sure about this?'

'Kornilov's death is verified, Comrade. The enemy tried to keep it quiet, but rumours started immediately. I won't be shedding any tears. Do you know what Kornilov told his men?'

Abram nodded. 'I know exactly what he said: 'The greater the terror, the greater our victories."

'Says it all, don't you think? Well, good riddance to the old swine. Now we're up against Kornilovites without Kornilov. They're finished.'

The tramp of boots announced the unit commander.

'Don't be so sure,' Pavel told them. 'Kornilov's death might just have done our enemies a favour.'

Mikhail seemed bewildered. 'How do you work that out, Pavel Sergeyevich?'

Pavel was eating *kvass* from a bowl. 'Kornilov was an arrogant piece of work. He brooked no opposition. If it had been up to him, the Whites would have attacked again and again. We would have broken them here, at Ekaterinodar. Leadership passes to Denikin now. When the rest of the Russian Army was pissing off home, he led a successful offensive in Romania. That means he's nobody's fool. Unlike Kornilov, he might just be able to recognise a lost cause.'

'So he will surrender?'

'For Christ's sake, Mikhail, do you listen to anything I say? No, he won't surrender. Even as we speak, he is beating a tactical retreat. If our generals have any nous, we will go after him and smash his forces before he can regroup.'

Abram had been listening carefully, following the conversation without interruption. Finally, he leaned forward.

'So the war could end here?'

Pavel didn't want to commit himself. 'I'm just an officer commanding a disorganised bunch of Red Guards, but I think we could smash one of their armies.'

'And if we let him go?'

Pavel finished his breakfast and put the bowl down.

'If we let him go, we're bigger fools than the Whites take us for. This Denikin, he strikes me as the kind of butcher who will bury us Reds alive for fun. As for the Jews, men like Denikin have been slaughtering them for generations.'

'And a red Jew?' Abram asked pointedly.

Pavel picked up his bowl again and patted Abram on the shoulder as he headed back to the field kitchen. 'Nothing down for you, mate. You'd better fight hard or you're going to die horribly.'

Abram sat brooding for a few minutes, chewing over Pavel's brutal truths.

'Are you all right?' Mikhail asked.

'Never better,' Abram told him.

'So why the long silence?'

Abram stretched. 'I was just thinking about what Pavel said. Looks like I'd better kill a few more Whites before they kill me.'

Before long, the order came down the line to get into marching formation.

'Where are we going?'

'Into the city. There's a victory parade'

'Victory? So what's happened to Denikin?'

'He's fucked off with most of his army. They've found Kornilov. Some village called Elizavetskinskaya.'

Abram folded his arms across his chest and waited for an explanation. Nikita was unforthcoming so Mikhail was the one who offered the information.

'This is a White general, the would-be butcher of Petrograd. Kornilov is symbolic.'

Abram still didn't get it. In fact, the Reds' intention didn't become plain until they arrived in the heart of the city. A procession was underway with red banners flying and workers' contingents to the fore. A military band was playing revolutionary songs.

'What are we celebrating?' Abram wondered out loud. 'We've won nothing. The Volunteer Army's still intact. Shouldn't we be pursuing Denikin?'

Nobody had an answer until a discouraged-looking Pavel made his appearance.

'Just look at the stupid bastards,' he grumbled. 'We're supposed to be fighting a war and we decide to hold a carnival instead. They're big fucking kids.'

'Didn't we hold this city?' Nikita asked, loathe to dismiss the impact of the victory.

'When you win a victory,' Pavel riposted, 'you press home your advantage. We could have smashed the Whites. Instead, we've got this farce.'

Grudgingly, they fell in step with the procession, ending up in a large square. There was cheering and applause. Presently, smoke started to climb into the sky and drift away to the east. The celebrations grew wilder and more prolonged. Abram had an inkling what the crowd were doing, but he asked anyway.

'What's burning?'

Pavel spat on the floor and sat heavily on a low wall. 'I'll tell you what's burning, Comrade. They've set light to Kornilov's carcass.' He rested his arms on his knees. 'That's right. We lose hundreds of men in the defence of Ekaterinodar so what do we do next? We dig up a corpse and make a bonfire out of it. It's mediaeval, is what it is. We must have shit for brains.'

The stench of burning flesh reached them. Abram wondered what this grisly bacchanalia had got to do with the revolution. Did his Red comrades die for this? Pavel was beside him. He examined the proud, round face and saw something he never expected. Were those tears?

'Remember this day,' Pavel told his men. 'We could have chased Denikin's army down. We could have turned the tide of the war.'

He pointed an accusing finger at the senior officers watching the spectacle in the square, frustration written into every inch of his face.

'We're going to pay for this.'

Kolya

He had an office now, and there was an unexpected visitor. He held the door for Svetlana as she stepped inside and took a seat. With her back to him, she sat upright, proud as ever, but uncomfortable in the surroundings of the Cheka headquarters. He took his time walking round to his seat behind his desk. The sight of her hair, her neck and shoulders, still inflamed his senses. Svetlana half-turned to see what he was doing.

'What can I do for you?' he said as he settled into his chair. Her brown eyes were deep with discomfort.

'I wouldn't come if I wasn't desperate.'

A desperate woman and a man in a position of power. Kolya found the prospect intriguing.

'Go on,' he said.

'I need food for the children.'

Kolya leaned back in his seat.

'Are you sure you have come to the right department?' he asked. 'I can point you in the direction of the grain requisitioning detachments.'

'Oh, cut the bullshit, Kolya,' Svetlana snapped. 'We both know the Cheka has a hand in everything these days. You can pull a few strings.'

Kolya scraped his chair back as he stood, and walked to the window – a silhouette to Svetlana, he said over his shoulder:

'Why would I do that, Svetlana?'

'The children are on the verge of starvation. I can't stand to see them like this.'

Kolya turned and picked up some sheets of paper.

'I have these from the Commissariat for Food Supply.' He started to read from the telegrams. *"We have no bread. Situation hopeless. Hunger is everywhere.' 'Food situation close to catastrophe.' 'No shipments of grain for two weeks. Workers collapsing at their machines.'* Shall I go on?'

Svetlana had her hands on her lap and she was picking at her nails.

'In December,' Kolya said, 'Workers' rations were a thousand calories. Now it is down to 700. There is typhus in the city. The Whites are a threat, but the spectre of famine is deadly.'

'I know the situation,' Svetlana answered in a low, dead voice. 'You have been protecting some of the grain detachments, Kolya. You supervise the road blocks. You arrest the bagmen. You must…'

Her voice broke. Kolya watched her shoulders trembling for a moment then he came round the desk and offered her a handkerchief. While she dabbed her eyes, he knelt beside her.

'Are you asking for special privileges, Svetlana?'

He reached across and rested a hand on her shoulder before slowly tracing a line across her throat, then downwards into the V of her neckline. Svetlana clamped her hand on his.

'Don't you touch me, Kolya. I am not your fucking whore to be bought for a loaf of bread.'

Kola took his hand away and returned to his desk.

'We were good together, Svetlana.'

'Then you screwed it up.' Svetlana tossed the handkerchief onto the desk. 'How is she, your Klara?'

Kolya chuckled. 'She is very well. There is something of an irony here, my dear Svetlana. Klara has given up whoring, you see. She has a job now. Would you like to know where?'

Svetlana's eyes were hard. 'I'm sure you're going to tell me.'

'She's at the People's Commissariat for Food Supplies,' Kolya said, triumphant. 'What do you think of that?'

Svetlana rose abruptly. 'I think this was a bad idea. I should never have come.'

She started for the door, then paused. 'I loved you, Kolya. I can't believe what you've become.'

Kolya felt the sting of her words, felt it more than she could imagine, but he hid it well. He was the heartless Chekist.

'What have I become, Svetlana?'

She turned slowly and folded her arms. 'You just tried to buy me.'

'Did I?' Kolya asked. 'I don't remember that. I touched you, the way I used to when we were together. Don't tell me you don't still have feelings for me. I know you do. I felt it in the way your flesh responded.'

For a moment, Svetlana was lost for words as she stared at Kolya. His face was expressionless.

'I betrayed you, Svetlana, but I would cast Klara aside for you this moment if you were to give me any encouragement.'

The only sound in the room was the tick of the clock and the gurgle of the radiator. Kolya rested a hand on the phone on his desk. 'I could give Klara a call this moment. Feeding twenty hungry children doesn't sound too difficult, even in these difficult times.'

'In return for what, Kolya?'

His fingers ran along the receiver.

'In return for what?' she repeated.

'When I lie in bed at night,' Kolya told her, 'it is your hair I smell, the warmth of your body I feel. Do you remember our time together?'

'Of course I do!'

He leaned forward. 'I mean really remember it? When you lie awake at night, do you feel my heartbeat against yours? Do you feel my lips brush your own?'

Svetlana had heard enough. 'Kolya, you disgust me.'

There was still no flicker of expression in his lean features. 'We both know that isn't true. When I touched you, I felt your need.' Her lips parted to protest. 'No, don't deny it. You are far too honest for that.' He sipped from a glass of water. 'How's Anishin? Have you heard from him?'

'I have had a letter,' Svetlana answered, unsure how much to say.

'Where is the train now?'

'They have been sent to the Volga. The Czech Legion is threatening to cut the railway line, but you don't need telling any of this. It is common knowledge.'

'How is Vassily?' Kolya asked. 'Do you miss his sparkling conversation?'

Svetlana glared at him.

'Do you miss his fevered kisses, the way his fingers explore the secrets of your body?'

In her summer dress and kerchief, Svetlana was every bit as beautiful as when he first met her, maybe more so. Could suffering actually enhance a woman's beauty?

'Stop it!' she cried. 'I'm leaving.'

'Wouldn't you like me to call Klara?' Kolya asked. 'Do you really want to return to those begging bowl eyes with nothing to give them? She has access to bread, butter, cheese, sausage, all the things a growing child needs.'

Kolya saw a shadow at the frosted glass pane in the door. It was bound to be Leonid. His timing was unfortunate.

'Wait!' he shouted at the blurry form outside.

He approached Svetlana and saw the wariness in her gaze. 'I have hurt you. I know that, but my feelings are true. I can't bear to see us at one another's throats.'

'You just tried to buy me, you bastard.'

'I am in despair,' Kolya answered. 'I miss what we had. Forgive me, my beloved Svetlana. I am no monster. You will have your supply of food for the children's home. I will make it happen.'

'In exchange for what?' Svetlana demanded.

'In exchange for nothing,' Kolya answered. 'You are incorruptible, Svetlana. I know that.'

He watched her expression soften.

'You will really send the food? The children are living skeletons.'

'It will be with you this very day. There is still room for some flexibility.' He faltered. 'A little. This is children we are discussing, after all.'

The wary look didn't leave Svetlana's eyes.

'Thank you, Kolya.'

'You know your way out, don't you?' he asked. 'I have someone waiting to come in.'

Svetlana nodded and opened the door, passing Leonid as she walked down the corridor. Leonid followed her with his eyes.

'Good-looking woman,' he said. 'Is she a friend of yours?'

'We were together once,' Kolya said distractedly.

'I tell you,' Leonid said, 'if I had a woman like that, I would never let her go.'

Kolya frowned him into silence and led the way inside. Leonid closed the door behind them.

'Did you follow up on our friend Nagorny?'

Leonid watched Kolya taking his seat and planted himself on the wooden chair. 'The guy is bent. He was flogging parts to another factory. He was making himself some pocket money, nothing more than that. What do we do about him?'

'Have you informed the Soviet and the trade unions?'

Leonid nodded. 'Of course.'

Kolya glanced at the file. 'I'll leave the case open for another month. If no other parts go missing, we can call it closed.'

He saw something in Leonid's slab-like face.

'Do you have something to say, Leonid?'

'Only this, treat these bastards with kid gloves and they will keep on filching stuff.'

Kolya tended to trust Leonid's instincts, but sometimes he was too eager to employ brute force.

'You don't think Nagorny's learned his lesson?'

'He'll behave himself for a few weeks,' Leonid answered, 'then you watch him get up to his old tricks. He likes the good life, does our moon-faced friend and he isn't going to go without if he can help it. Think about it, Kolya. The Red forces are in retreat everywhere. We've got hunger in the city, typhus, cholera. The peasants are hiding grain. The only way you do well these days is to steal. He'll do it again, you mark my words. He's a greedy, little shit. You don't carry that much lard around by living on average rations.'

'Don't you trust anyone, Leonid?'

Leonid pulled a face. 'Not a fucking one, Comrade. If you want this revolution to succeed, you're not going to make it happen by playing games, like him along the corridor.'

'By that, I assume you mean Comrade Uritsky,' Kolya said, struck once again by Leonid's indifference to authority.

'Look at these directives,' Leonid grumbled. 'Guidelines to control the way the Cheka does searches. Strict regulation of searches to root out fake and corrupt Chekists.'

'The Cheka must be above criticism,' Kolya said. 'Its actions must be transparent and accountable.'

'That's the main concern, is it?' Leonid asked. 'I've heard you sing a different tune. Dzerzhinsky and Peters knew what was needed before they buggered off to Moscow. They'd have used the iron fist against the likes of this Nagorny. I'll tell you what to do with all these speculators and counter-revolutionaries, stick them in front of a firing squad.'

Kolya gave him an indulgent smile. 'Comrade Uritsky has expressly refused to sanction shootings. He says it is better to act against violence and economic sabotage than to unleash indiscriminate terror.'

'Well, more fool him,' Leonid growled. 'Do you remember the order he sent out about people hoarding guns and bombs? You're got three days to hand them in, he says. Three days to hide them from the Chekists is more like it.'

'Comrade…'

Leonid cut Kolya off, shoving his face forward.

'Listen to me, Kolya,' he snarled. 'You and comrade Uritsky, you're cut from the same cloth. You both went to university and got your heads turned by what you read in your fucking books. Well, old Leonid learned his politics on the street, fighting hard bastards who'd razor you as soon as look. This is class war, Comrade. There are no half-measures in something like this. Go easy on your enemies and you're signing your own death warrant.'

'Of course, force is necessary,' Kolya responded. 'I handled the Constituent rebels and I didn't use kid gloves, but you have to have rules.'

'Rules!' Leonid's jaw was set. 'This isn't a chess game.' He looked towards the door.

'Look what the White Finns did across the water just two months ago.'

'I know about the massacre,' Kolya said.

'Twenty thousand dead,' Kolya. 'Seventy thousand held as prisoners. Women and children used as hostages. Reds executed without trial. The reactionaries know exactly what it takes to win a war. We need to toughen the fuck up. It's something I tell my kids, get your retaliation in first.'

Kolya was wondering why he was on the back foot. 'When I joined the Cheka, I said I would use any means necessary.'

'Saying it is one thing,' Leonid told him. 'It's what you're willing to do about it that matters. Let me put it to you in words any man on the street would understand. You like that woman, don't you?'

Kolya saw Leonid searching for a name. 'Svetlana.'

'Right, Svetlana. Best piece of ass I've seen today.'

Kolya went to say something, but Leonid waved his protests away. 'Fine, so you think I should speak *delicately*. She's an angel, comrade, a flesh and blood angel. Say some bastard came sniffing round her, what would you do to keep her?'

'Leonid, I....'

'There you go. You don't know, do you? Me, I'd batter the filthy dog senseless and drag her off to bed to remind her who she's meant to go home to every night.'

'I'm sure you would, Leonid, but we're different people. Besides, Svetlana and I are no longer together.'

'You wish you were though, don't you, Comrade? I bet you dream about her every night. If I had a woman like that, I would never let her go.'

Kolya looked into Leonid's knowing eyes for a few moments, then he managed a forced laugh.

'You're a rogue, Leonid Ivanovich.'

'Call me what you like, Kolya,' Leonid countered. 'I hang onto my woman.'

The uncomfortable silence that followed was broken by the sound of running feet in the corridor. A fist hammered on the door, which flew open.

'Comrade Uritsky,' Kolya said, 'what's wrong?'

Uritsky's face was taut and pale.

'It's Volodarsky,' he said. 'He's been shot. Shot dead.'

'What happened?' Kolya asked, shaken.

'Moisei went to the Obukhovsky Works on the order of Zinoviev. He was trying to quell discontent about food rations and other issues stirred up by the SRs and Mensheviks.'

'Do we know who did it?' he asked, as they headed outside.

'A workman under the influence of the SRs.' He fumbled in his pocket for a piece of paper. 'He has been apprehended with some other men. His name is Grigory Ivanovich Semyonov, a member of Central Battle Unit of the Socialist-Revolutionary Party.'

'I will drive,' Leonid said.

Uritsky nodded. As he strode ahead, Leonid turned to Kolya.

'Still think you can behead the counter-revolution by playing according to the rules?'

Svetlana

The city conference of the Petrograd Bolsheviks gathered under a cloud. She entered the hall and found a corner where she could prepare her thoughts. Her head was spinning after days of factory meetings, most of them rowdy and increasingly hostile. It was the assembly at her old mill that had left her depressed and close to tears. Anna found her leaning against the wall.

'Are you all right, Mama?' she asked, concerned. 'You look exhausted.'

Svetlana stroked her daughter's cheek. 'What are you doing here? Who is watching the children?'

'Nina is there with Nadezhda.'

'Nina Kirilenko? Pavel's wife?'

'Yes, she brought the baby for the children to see. Oh, Roman is such a fine little boy. I can see his father in him.'

Svetlana thought of the many red Petrograders dispersed across Russia, fighting the counter-revolution, her own son, handsome, roguish Volodya among them.

'I wonder if Pavel even knows he has a son.'

She realised that she hadn't been to see Nina since the birth. 'How is she?'

'She is quite weak,' Anna said, 'and painfully thin. I think the baby is draining her of all her strength.'

'You still haven't told me why you're here. Is something wrong? Is it Voldoya?'

Anna smiled. 'Nothing is wrong. He has sent you a letter, that's all. I thought you would want to see it. Mama, he is well and he has good comrades who look out for him. There are Pavel and Mikhail of course, but he has made a close friend called Abram.'

'Did he say when he would be home?' Svetlana asked. 'Is he going to get any leave?'

'He says the Volunteer Army and the Cossacks are rallying their forces for a counter-attack. There is no prospect of leave.'

'Is there anything else?' Svetlana asked. 'You're quite sure that's all he has to say?'

'I am not hiding anything from you, Mama,' Anna told her cheerfully. 'I just wanted to put your mind at rest about Volodya. I'd better get back.'

Svetlana embraced her daughter. 'Did the supplies come?'

'Yes, the food arrives like clockwork,' Anna answered. 'Whoever you talked to at the Commissariat, it did the trick. Iskra is finally putting on some weight.' She frowned. 'Is something wrong?'

Svetlana's shoulders were sagging. There was an air of defeat about her.

'I was at the mill,' she said. 'The things they shouted at me. They blamed me for the food shortages and the typhus. Albina has torn up her Party card. She isn't the only one.'

'Don't they understand what's happening in the country?' Anna said.

Svetlana was sobbing. 'All they know is that there is no end to hunger and disease. I promised them things would get better and they think I lied to them. You promised peace and bread, they shouted and all we get is war and hunger. Do you know what somebody shouted from the back? Soviets without Bolsheviks.'

Anna wiped the tears from her mother's face.

'Please don't,' she said. 'I can't stand to see you like this.'

'Ignore me,' Svetlana said, fighting the sobs. 'I am an old fool.'

'Mama, you're not old.'

'So why am I so tired? Some days...I don't want to open my eyes.'

Anna held her mother for several moments before releasing her. 'I have to go back to the home, Mama. Will you be all right?'

Svetlana forced a smile. 'Of course. Ignore me. I am being an idiot.'

Anna took a few steps, gave Svetlana an encouraging smile and went on her way, leaving her mother to read Volodya's letter. It was short. A typical boy's letter, Svetlana thought. Finally, she tucked it into her skirt pocket and took her seat. Zinoviev was speaking as President of the Executive Committee of the Northern Commune. She stared at the touslehaired figure and prayed for some news that would lift her spirits. There was none. What did she expect? Some comrades called Zinoviev Lenin's biggest mistake.

'Comrades,' he was saying, 'the situation is difficult.'

His comment earned exasperated shakes of the head from some members of his audience.

'Our revolution is isolated. The Whites have drowned the Finnish revolution in blood. We have dire food shortages.'

The delegates' faces were grim. Nobody was in any doubt about the seriousness of the situation. Zinoviev carried on, oblivious to the impatient reactions of some delegates.

'The Petrograd party organisations are in a dire situation,' he was saying. 'Membership has fallen from 36,000 in February of this year to 13,472. Many comrades are engulfed in government work, many more are fighting at the shifting Fronts in the war with the White Guards. They have lost all contact with their Party organisation.'

Svetlana thought about Volodya out there on the Kuban steppe.

'Worse still,' Zinoviev said, 'hundreds, maybe thousands of the new members who have joined since October are opportunists, even out and out criminals.'

Every word struck home. Svetlana remembered the thug she had met in Kolya's office. Men like him scared her – and she didn't scare easily. At the end of Zinoviev's address, speaker after speaker laid out the problems red Petrograd was facing. One speaker struck a chord.

'Comrades,' she said, 'we must be honest with ourselves. Our revolution is clinging to life by a thread. We have just come through workers' protests against food shortages and unemployment. The great factories that were once the backbone of the revolution are empty places. Peter has lost a million of its people as they flee the city just to survive. As if that isn't enough, Moscow demands more and more of our best cadres to help staff the workers' state. We can't go on like this.'

The audience clapped her words, but the applause was sporadic and lacked enthusiasm. Little wonder, Svetlana thought, who would want to clap at a funeral? She remembered the children's official rations. To live for two days, you had fifty grams of bread and five herrings. Without Kolya's additional help, she couldn't imagine what state the children's health would be in. When the session ended, Svetlana made her way to the back of the hall. It was almost as if her feet were treading water. She had little sense of moving at all. The faces around her danced garishly.

'Are you all right, Comrade?' came a familiar voice.

'Comrade Stahl,' Svetlana said. 'I didn't see you there.'

'Come and sit down,' Stahl said, finding her a chair. 'You were swaying. I thought you were going to faint.'

Svetlana's senses cleared a little.

'Was I? I don't know...sometimes I forego my rations to give a little more to the children.'

'Ah yes,' Stahl said. 'The children's home. Comrade Kollontai told me you had taken the project under your wing. How are you managing?'

Svetlana was vaguely aware of Stahl snapping her fingers at somebody.

'It is difficult,' she said. 'We struggle to find enough food and the children keep coming. There is a second home now, you know.'

'You give your food away to the children, you say?' Stahl said. 'How often do you eat?'

'I don't know,' Svetlana said. 'Sometimes it's just once a day.'

Then she was aware of a plate being set in front of her. There was sausage and some bread.

'You must eat,' Stahl said.

'I don't want any special treatment,' Svetlana protested. 'The Communists share the privations of the workers.'

'We have done that,' Stahl said. 'We take the wage of the average worker. We eat their rations. What then? What happens to red Russia if its leaders faint for want of nourishment. Comrade Lenin says that in such critical circumstances, we must have extra rations.'

Svetlana went to protest again.

'You will eat what is put in front of you,' Stahl insisted. 'What good are you to the revolution if you make yourself ill? Comrade, those children need you.'

Slowly, still with some reluctance, Svetlana began to eat. Once she had finished, Stahl had some tea brought over.

'Are you feeling better?' she asked.

'Yes, much better.'

Svetlana dissolved into tears again.

'I feel as if I am betraying the people,' she moaned.

'What, by eating a little bread and sausage?' Stahl laughed. 'It is hardly luxury.'

'You said that Lenin favoured preferential treatment for party officials,' Svetlana said.

'You should know that Comrade Lenin is incorruptible,' Stahl replied. 'He lives in three small rooms in the Kremlin. We are talking about modest extra rations, not luxury.'

'All the same…'

'All the same, the workers' state must not die because its cadres collapse at their posts.'

Stahl was insistent. Svetlana was still sipping her hot, sweet tea when Stahl patted her arm.

'There is someone here who is concerned about you.'

Svetlana looked up and saw Kolya watching her with concern. She tried to shove him away, furious that he dared come near.

'You are unwell,' he said. 'I will take you home.'

'No,' she answered. 'I am quite recovered. It was just a moment's dizziness.'

'Nonsense,' Kolya insisted. 'You are not yourself, Svetlana. You are the strongest person I know. I don't like seeing you like this.'

Svetlana's mind was in a spin. Kolya was poison. He had betrayed her, tried to blackmail her.

'I will go home and get some sleep. There is so much to do.'

She rose to her feet, careful not to stumble.

'There,' she said. 'I'm fine. Don't fuss.'

Stahl was walking away, talking to another delegate. Svetlana wanted to call her back, anything to escape Kolya's stifling presence.

'I went without any breakfast then I was late so I skipped lunch. Kolya…'

'You might fool the others,' Kolya told her. 'I know you too well. This isn't the first time you have fainted, is it?'

'I am not the only Petrograder to go without food,' she insisted.

She leaned forward, whispering in his ear.

'I want nothing to do with you. Have you forgotten the way you talked to me in your office?'

This was a different Kolya, indulgent, caring, but which was the genuine article?

'I still love you, Svetlana,' he told her.

His words produced an indignant reaction.

'No!'

She shot to her feet and made for the door. Blinking as she burst out into the summer sunlight. she walked two blocks before stopping to lean against the railings and gaze out across the river. What struck her was the emptiness, the streets missing people, the sky where barely a single chimney smoked, a place haunted by its departed citizens.

'Is it just a few months since October?' she murmured.

'Nine months,' came a voice behind her, 'the time it takes to make a new life.'

Svetlana turned. 'I told you not to follow me.'

The sunlight was on Kolya's face. He looked the way he had when she first met him.

'But you are not the same person,' she said.

Her words produced a frown.

'You don't believe that.'

'Why did you do it?' she asked, pain invading her voice. 'Why her? Why that whore?'

'You judge Klara harshly,' Kolya said, 'yet you love Raisa as if she were your second daughter. They both had to sell themselves to survive.'

'You can't compare Raisa to that creature!'

'Can't I?' Kolya said. 'You should talk to Klara. I was fooled to begin with, drawn into believing her little act. Her story and Raisa's are not so different.'

Svetlana hesitated. 'It isn't Klara I blame. It's you.'

'I can't argue with that,' Kolya answered. 'I know my imperfections far better than you do.'

'You do nothing to fight your demons,' Svetlana retorted. 'You give in to them.' She searched for the words. 'You nourish them.'

He approached her, resting his arms on the railings.

'Do you mind?'

Svetlana said nothing to deter him so he gazed across the river next to her.

'I do, you know,' he said. 'I do fight my demons. When I first arrived at Gorokhovaya, I was eager to cleanse the world of counter-revolutionaries by any means necessary. Do you know, I was actually angry because we weren't using firing squads.'

Svetlana let him talk.

'Comrade Uritsky has changed my way of thinking.'

'How's that?'

'I looked up to my leaders. Peters was the daring robber, Dzerzhinsky the pure revolutionary. Iron Felix could do no wrong.'

Svetlana turned to listen.

'I suppose you know that comrade Uritsky opposes summary shootings,' he said.

'I do.'

'He is even willing to admit that there is corruption at Gorokhovaya. Several times recently, he has come into conflict with Dzerzhinsky.' She realised she was hearing his debates with himself. He went on to speak of Uritsky by his first name and patronymic. 'Moisei Solomonovich has even said the abolition of the Cheka might be a good thing. It risks becoming a law unto itself.'

'Do you agree with him?'

Kolya gripped the railings until his knuckles whitened. 'I don't know, Svetlana. Moscow could be right. Uritsky is too cautious. Maybe he is too soft to root out counter-revolution.'

'You like him, don't you?'

Kolya nodded. 'I feared Peters and Dzerzhinsky, feared and respected them. Comrade Uritsky is…approachable.'

Svetlana could feel her old feelings for Kolya returning. Much as she wanted to resist them, she yearned to hold him.

'Maybe he brings out the human in you,' she said.

Kolya nodded. 'Maybe you're right. Now, can I give you that lift?'

The wind whipped Svetlana's hair about. On impulse, Kolya reached out and swept it from her face.

'Can you forgive me?'

She eased his hands from her face but kept hold of them. She shook her head. 'No. I can't believe you have the balls to ask.' She saw the look of surprise in his eyes and laughed. 'You really are an arrogant pup, aren't you?' She made him wait for an explanation, before continuing. 'In spite of everything, I find it hard to resist you.'

'So I can take you home?'

'You will wait around the corner from the home while I go inside to check on things.' She averted her gaze. 'I don't want Anna seeing you.'

'And after that?'

What am I doing, she wondered.

'We can't go back to my room. Your appearance would have tongues wagging. It would be around the party within hours.'

Kolya decided it was time to spring his surprise.

'Klara doesn't know it, but I have the use of my old room at Mrs Turisheva's.'

Svetlana considered him, wondering what he used it for.

'How's that?'

'The old trout has gone back to her village. She no longer has an income in Peter.' He saw her looking at him. 'I don't use it for secret trysts, if that's what you're thinking. I have only slept with two women in my life, you and Klara.'

Svetlana wanted to walk away from him, forget the longing that was growing in her breast, but she had needs and they were not only physical. Kolya had left a hole in her life that nothing, not her family, not Raisa, not the party could fill.

An hour later, Kolya was leading the way up familiar stairs. Svetlana hesitated, glancing at the light under Mrs Turisheva's door.

'Who lives there?'

'He has just moved in. You've seen him, that day at Gorokhovaya. He's a driver for the Cheka, name of Leonid.'

Svetlana recalled the brutish-looking man whose eyes had followed her with a little too much interest.

'Is the whole building inhabited by Chekists?'

Kolya turned the key in the lock. 'Does that bother you?'

She shook her head. 'No.'

She followed him inside and wandered around the room, running her finger over dusty surfaces.

'How long has this room been empty?' she asked.

'Only a few days,' Kolya said. 'It's been aired and I have changed the sheets.'

Svetlana's head snapped round.

'No, no,' he said quickly. 'There was no premediated plan to get you in the sack.' He hesitated. 'I was going to move in with Klara. I'm not good at this, am I?'

Svetlana shook her head, a slight smile on her lips. 'You're terrible.'

She started to unbutton his shirt.

'But not so bad you want to walk away?' Kolya asked.

Svetlana ran her fingernails down his chest, digging them into his flesh until he winced.

'I must be mad,' she said, 'truly insane.'

Then her hand was inside his trousers, squeezing his cock. Kolya closed his eyes for a moment then he was undressing her. He considered her naked form.

'You're thinner.'

'Is that a bad thing?'

He continued to examine her, trailing his gaze lazily over her breasts, stomach, the untidy triangle of public hair.

'Stop it,' she said. 'You're treating me like horse flesh.' She laughed, possibly at her own weakness. 'It's time to ride the old mare again.'

Kolya guided her onto the bed and started to place kisses along a line from her throat to her navel.

'Don't talk about yourself that way. I love you, Svetlana.'

'You love screwing me. It's different.'

'I've missed you,' he said. 'I've missed you so much.'

They kissed, gently, tenderly to begin with, then with heat and passion. She parted her legs and gave a shudder as he entered her. Then they were together. Instinctively, she sank her nails into his back and tore at his skin.

'Are you punishing me?' he asked, gritting his teeth as he looked down at her.

'I'm reminding you I am no lovelorn fool to be used and tossed to one side. I demand respect, Kolya.'

There was a fondness and predictability to their lovemaking. He enjoyed her changing expressions as their bodies moved together. When they were done, she asked the predictable, timeless question.

'What does this mean?'

He rolled away from her.

'We fucked. Does it mean anything?'

She was on her side now, frowning at him. Suddenly, she burst out laughing, her whole body trembling. She pinched her lips, trying to control herself, then laughed out loud again.

'What's come over you?' he demanded.

'The roles are reversed,' she said. 'There's your little scorpion, Klara, waiting for you...'

Kolya's eyes widened. 'How do you know my nickname for her?'

'You just said it to me, while we were screwing. I dug my nails into you and you complained about my sting.'

'Shit, I need to be more careful.'

Svetlana seemed to find the whole thing amusing. 'It didn't take much of a guess where it came from.' She buried her face in his shoulder. 'Klara's the wife and I'm the mistress. Fancy that.'

'Does it worry you?' Kolya asked.

Svetlana thought for a moment.

'No. Fuck it. We're all consenting adults.'

'What about Anishin? He hasn't given his consent to this.'

Svetlana's face clouded. She hadn't given Vassily a moment's thought before climbing into bed with Kolya.

'I feel bad about cheating on Vassily. He deserves better.'

Kolya rubbed Svetlana's buttocks. 'He doesn't excite you though, does he?'

She met his words with a scowl. 'He's a good man, a good, honest man and that's more than you will ever be, you pig.'

Kolya had a smug smile on his face. 'I notice you didn't contradict me. Look me in the eye and tell me he excites you.'

Svetlana slapped him.

'You love yourself too much, Kolya.'

He wrapped his arms round her.
'You're right, but I might just love you more.'

Part Three

Children of the revolution

Raisa

Steam rolled over the fields. The locomotive lay beached among the waving, golden wastes like a great, black whale. Here and there, the Red soldiers sat, cleaning their rifles, smoking or digesting the news from Moscow. The oppressive August heat haze distorted the distant trees, the endless horizon. One of the men, a gangling nineteen-year-old called Konstantin, turned to look at Raisa as she sat in the open door of the carriage.

'You're our political officer, Comrade Raisa. What's this news from Moscow?'

Raisa met his stare. She knew he was sweet on her. She had to negotiate his interest every day. It was easier to shake off the clouds of midges than to escape Konstantin's attention.

'The Left SRs have committed political suicide,' she answered, happy to have their conversation restricted to politics. 'Think about it. Why would they assassinate the German Ambassador?'

The murder of Count Mirbach had been the main topic of conversation all morning, ever since the news first broke.

'These SRs have always used terror, haven't they?' Konstantin asked, clearly delighted to have Raisa's undivided attention. 'Maria Spiridonova spent years in Siberia for shooting some landowner.'

Raisa dismissed the idea that it was all about the SRs' innate obsession with terror. 'But to what purpose, Comrade? Why kill a German diplomat? There can only be one reason. They are trying to provoke us into revolutionary war with Germany. They do nothing but bleat about our shameful peace.'

Konstantin spat on the ground. 'That's just what we need, another enemy to fight. Do you know what one of the lads told me? There are twenty governments in Russia and only one of them is Bolshevik.'

'That sounds about right,' Raisa said, swatting away a darting dragonfly. 'The revolution is under siege.'

'Well, the SRs got their arses kicked, didn't they?'

He didn't take his eyes off her. Raisa's neck was burning with discomfort. This was all she needed, a lovesick soldier trailing round after her.

'That's one way of putting it,' she said. 'Hundreds of members arrested, a dozen of their leaders shot, the party out of government. You wonder what Spiridonova was thinking. She is a hero of the revolution, but she destroys the SRs' credibility in a moment of madness.'

Konstantin got up, stamping the dust from his boots, and wandered over.

'Well,' he said, 'they've blown it now. They're finished as a party. Does this help the Communists or not?'

One or two of the other soldiers were watching with interest. Konstantin wasn't the only man with his eye on Raisa. Men, even Bolsheviks, could be such dogs.

'It's hard to say,' she answered. 'We have lost our coalition partner in government, but at least we don't have to worry about a stab in the back any more.' She squinted as she looked up at Konstantin with the sun behind him. 'We Communists are holding the line on behalf of the workers and peasants.'

An older man snorted. Oleg Konnov was the kind of man who saw the worst in every situation, a perennial grumbler. Raisa had taken an instant dislike to him from the moment he joined the train at Vladimir.

'Good luck with that,' he said. 'There are bugger all workers left in the factories. Half the plants in Peter are idle. As for the peasants, they're too busy hiding grain or turning it into hooch to listen to political speeches.'

'We are beset by enemies,' Raisa reminded him. 'England, France, Japan, America arm the counter-revolutionaries. The most class-conscious workers are at the Front, fighting the enemy. What would you have us do, Oleg, surrender?'

Oleg's face was sullen.

'What's the matter, Comrade Sourpuss?' one of the men said, slapping him with his cap. 'Don't you like taking political lectures from a woman?'

Oleg flapped irritably at his tormentor, but he was on the defensive.

'All I'm saying is it's a rum kind of workers' and peasants' state when the workers are out of work or going back to their villages and the peasants are butchering Bolsheviks who come to steal their grain.'

'The cities are starving,' Raisa said. 'What would you have us do? Famine and disease is threatening the very survival of Soviet power. We in the Red Army are the custodians of the world revolution.'

It was hard to be natural in the middle of a crowd of men obviously wondering what she looked like naked. The lounging soldiers were watching the confrontation with interest.

'There you go with your fancy words as usual,' Oleg said. He waved at the broad expanse of wheat fields. 'We're a long way from the world fucking revolution out here. Do you know what I can see, horse shit and grass.'

'Leave her be,' Konstantin said irritably.

Oleg shook his head. 'Just listen to the kid. There's only one reason he's hanging round young Raisa. The soft bastard wants to get his leg over.'

Livid with rage, Konstantin stamped across the ground and cuffed Oleg across the head.

'Apologise!'

Oleg was on his feet in an instant, fists clenched. Before blows could be exchanged, Anishin had made his appearance, alerted to the raised voices.

'What's the meaning of this?'

Silence followed.

'I asked you a question, Comrade Konnov.'

'It's all right, Vassily,' Raisa said. 'It's just a misunderstanding.'

Oleg wasn't in any mood to let it drop.

'Misunderstanding, my arse!' he said, pointing at Konstantin. 'This piece of shit raised his hand to me. His mouth is going to get him....'

He never got to finish his sentence. There was a loud crack that sent the crows flapping into the limpid sky, cawing in panic. There was a puff of scarlet and Oleg fell face first in the dust, stone dead. All eyes turned to the open plain where, out of the trembling heat, there emerged scores of horsemen. Their mounts whinnied. Sabres hissed from scabbards and loud roars broke the lazy silence. The earth shook under the drumming hooves. Already, the Red fighters were scrambling for cover, snatching up their weapons as they went. Under an azure sky, death had arrived.

'Fuck!'

'Cavalry!' Anishin roared. 'Take your positions.'

Elena arrived behind Raisa, assessing the decision with a single glance.

'With me, Raisa. We're nearest the gun.'

Together, they sprinted to the next carriage down and pulled the bolts, releasing the panels that disguised the mounted Maxim. Small arms fire ricocheted around them.

'Good job they're on horseback,' Elena said. 'They're firing wild.'

She took up position as gunner, legs splayed out before her. Raisa fed the belt into the gun. Within moments, the barrel was spitting death into the galloping riders, tearing men from the saddle. Anishin and Konstantin lay in the dust, pumping out rounds at the thundering cavalry. The engagement lasted just a few minutes. By the end of it, a dozen Whites and two Reds lay dead. The Whites peeled away, in headlong retreat. Some of the Reds set off in pursuit, vanishing into the rippling grass before giving up and trudging back to the train. Konstantin shielded his eyes against the bright sunlight.

'Look at the lousy cowards,' he scoffed. 'They ran like women.'

At that, Elena stepped away from the Maxim, jumped down from the train and stabbed him in the chest with her forefinger.

'Watch your mouth, you ignorant shit! If it wasn't for two women using their heads and getting that Maxim barking, there would be a lot more of you bastards lying dead.'

Some of the other soldiers were laughing at the spectacle of the fiery Elena shaming a man who towered over her.

'That's telling you, Konstantin.'

'My apologies, Comrade,' growled Konstantin, neck red as beetroot.

Anishin looked down at Oleg's body and the other casualty of the skirmish.

'Who was on duty?' he snarled. 'Somebody's responsible for this fuck-up. They should never have been able to catch us napping like that.' He looked around. 'Well, who's responsible?'

Konstantin had his head down. 'It was me.'

'So what were you doing instead of keeping your eyes on that fucking landscape?'

'He was chatting up Raisa,' somebody said.

Anishin planted himself in front of Konstantin. 'Is this true? You're supposed to be keeping look-out and you're chasing a piece of skirt?'

There was a nod of admission. 'I am sorry, Comrade.'

'I should put a bullet in your brain, but I need every gun I can muster.'

He removed his cap and wiped the sweat from his brow.

'From now on, lover boy, think about the gun in your hands, not the cock in your pants, you stupid fucker. Your carelessness cost two comrades their lives.'

Anishin gestured to Raisa 'Can I have a word?'

She followed him into the propaganda office, still smarting about being referred to as a piece of skirt..

'Vassily,' she started, embarking on her protest.

Anishin cut her off instantly. 'I can't have you distracting the men, Raisa.'

Raisa was outraged. 'I didn't distract him! I did nothing to encourage him. I was answering questions about the SR revolt.'

Behind them, Elena's eyes were blazing.

Anishin was unmoved: 'I appointed you to the position of political officer to guide the men, not to take their attention off their duties.'

Raisa's eyes stung at the unfairness of the accusation.

Elena broke in, her voice high with outrage. 'Konstantin hangs round her with his tongue hanging out and you yell at Raisa. This is bollocks, Vassily.'

Anishin shook his head. 'It was a risk appointing women as political officers, especially when you're both so young. You made an impression, but that belongs to yesterday. Either you shape up or there will be a change of personnel.'

Elena opened her mouth to protest, but Raisa warned her off with a glare. Anishin ploughed on.

'Make sure nothing like this happens again, either of you.' The tension started to slip from his face. 'Sit down, please.'

He walked to the door and barked out some names. Soon, there were half a dozen of them sitting around the table. Anishin unfolded a map.

'Kazan has fallen,' he said 'Half the defenders simply threw down their weapons and deserted. The entire Front is collapsing for lack of military leadership. I have had word that Comrade Trotsky's armoured train is on the way from Moscow to stiffen resistance.'

A murmur went around the table. If the Commissar of War himself was on the way then the situation must be critical.

'Red troops are retreating from Simbirsk.'

'In other words,' Elena said, 'if we fall back any further, we're fucked.'

There were frowns at a woman talking in such terms. Elena returned their looks defiantly.

'Crudely put,' Anishin said, 'but accurate. We have to hold the line and retake Kazan. This will be a battle of strategic importance. I have been appointed military commissar for this unit. We will join the Red forces outside the city. There will be no further retreat. We win here or we die here. Is that understood?'

There were nods around the table.

'Good. Elena, get some men together to bury the bodies.'

'Just ours, or theirs too?'

'Fuck the Whites. Leave the bastards to the crows.'

'Did you hear the hairy-arsed sods?' Elena raged. 'We save their skin and they talk about us as if we're a pair of cheap...'

Her voice trailed off.

'Cheap whores?' Raisa said, finishing her sentence for her. 'Is that what you were going to say?'

Elena approached Raisa and took her hands. 'Raisa, I should tear out my tongue.'

'It just goes to show, doesn't it?' Raisa murmured frostily. 'It isn't only the men who enter the world of tomorrow with the ideas of the past. I expected better of you.'

'Raisa,' Elena said, 'you know I would never intentionally hurt you.'

Raisa slid her hands from those of her lover. She listened to the now-familiar sounds of the train.

'We'll be departing soon.'

Elena was still not forgiven for her verbal stumble. Raisa was in no mood to build bridges, her mind full of Anishin's rebuke. She busied herself, securing weapons, sorting leaflets, boxing ammunition. Finally, she looked up from her chores, deciding it was time to forgive.

'I didn't mean to shout at you.'

Elena nodded. 'We're all exhausted.' There were tears in her eyes. 'We're in retreat everywhere. I can't go home defeated. I *won't*.'

'We're not soldiers, my love. None of us are. Those boys out there, they might have guns, but their hands shake with terror every time the Whites attack us. Even our own commissar is just a plain factory hand. Did you see him when the Whites attacked? He didn't even think to deploy the machine guns. He doesn't have a fucking clue.'

It was airless in the heat of the closed compartment. Raisa tugged at her blouse where it was sticking to her skin.

'They say Trotsky is appointing Tsarist officers to positions in the Red Army. Do you think we can trust them? I don't want a bullet in my back. What if they betray us?'

'Fuck knows,' Raisa snorted. 'It's the job of the commissars to blow their brains out if they do.' She smiled. 'Listen to us. When did we start cursing like field hands?' She looked around. 'Have you seen Vassily?'

'Konstantin's lapse of concentration has got him worried,' Elena explained. 'He is manning the Maxim in case the Whites come back.'

Elena shook her head. 'It's a bit late now.'

The long plaintive whistle of the locomotive announced imminent departure. On impulse, Raisa rushed to Elena and planted a kiss on her lips. Her hand was soon kneading the small of her lover's back. Her fingers slid under Elena's blouse. She felt Elena stiffen and she turned just in time to see Konstantin retreating from the carriage, face twisted in disgust.

'Shit!'

She pursued him, catching up with him on the way into the machine-gun carriage.

'Konstantin…'

'What, you're a fucking dyke?'

'Please don't use that word.'

'What word do you want me to use? Lesbo? Shit, I liked you.'

'You can still like me. I'm the same person.'

Konstantin laughed scornfully. 'Are you taking the piss? What I just saw, it's sick. It's unnatural.'

Raisa tried to reassert her authority. 'Comrade, by order of Sovnarkom, homosexuality has been legalised.'

'Homosexual? That's men. This, it's… What do you even do?'

Raisa took hold of his sleeve. 'Konstantin…'

He shrugged her away. 'Get the fuck off me, you weird bitch.'

She released her hold and watched him making his way down the train. Just once, he looked back, utter contempt written on his face. She returned to the office and slumped in a chair. The train started to roll.

'We should have been more careful,' she said. 'We just made an enemy.'

Kolya

He recognised the voice as he hurried down the long corridor of the Astoria, now known to many as the Cheka Hotel because of its proximity to Gorokhovaya. Turning the door handle, he slipped inside. Grigory was on his feet, pointing at Uritsky.

'You talk, Comrade, of due process. You wish to apply the rules of bourgeois legality to the revolution. The voice of the workers of red Peter, expressed through the Petersburg Committee, demands a program of mass terror.'

Uritsky was making notes, his eyes averted from his accuser. Behind Grigory, Zinoviev watched impassively.

'The hydra of counter-revolution,' Grigory thundered, 'has many heads.'

He started to count them off on his fingers.

'German, France, America, Japan, Krasnov, Denikin, Kaledin and they are only our external enemies. What of the SRs who assassinated Comrade Volodarsky or the Mensheviks who rush to join governments that rise in rebellion against the Soviet order? The workers demand blood for blood.'

When Grigory was finally done, Uritsky looked up. In calm, measured tones, he countered the demands for retaliation.

'Comrades, if we go down the route of indiscriminate slaughter, it could prove counter-productive.'

This caused barracking from some in the room, especially those around Grigory.

'We need proof of the activities of counter-revolutionaries.' He thumped the words home, his index finger and forefinger on the table. 'There is no surer way to reduce popular support for our revolution than unwarranted or unjust repression. If we are convicted in the eyes of the masses of indiscriminate terror, we will be stained by the blood of the innocents.'

This drove Grigory into a fury. 'If we fail to deal with the conspiracies of our enemies, we will drown in blood ourselves. Only this week, a conspiracy was unearthed to kill Comrade Zinoviev sitting here among us. There was a time when the revolution released its enemies on a promise of good behaviour. Krasnov ran straight from detention to join our enemies. The age of innocence is over. That time for leniency is past.'

Uritsky struggled to control the ever angrier debate in the room.

'I am not afraid of firm action,' he argued. 'Did we not execute conspirators from the Military Academy?'

'Six counter-revolutionaries. What good do you think that will do?'

As the meeting broke up, Kolya made his way to Uritsky's side.

'The tide is against me, Kolya,' Uritksy confided. 'I believe you know this hothead Grigory.'

Kolya nodded. 'We are friends. We marched together many times in the early days of the revolution.'

'He has talent as an orator,' Uritsky said, 'but he is too much the firebrand.' He shook his head. 'Did you see Zinoviev? He could have taken my side. He didn't say a word in my defence.'

Kolya saw a man under pressure.

'I could have done with you by my side today, Kolya. Why were you late?'

'I'm sorry, Moisei Solomonovich,' Kolya said. 'It was this case. I lost track of the time.'

'Ah, the engineering plant. You have a problem with the arrests?'

Kolya has a file in his hand. 'Leonid has overstepped the mark again. I was assured that the case against Nagorny and Ionov had been closed. They were making money, not actively sabotaging the revolution.'

'And that is not the case?'

'Leonid has arrested them. I want you to sign off their release.'

Uritsky nodded. 'Of course. So Leonid is ignoring your orders?'

'He is a law unto himself, a complete loose cannon.'

Uritsky shuffled together his papers. 'We will have a meeting at Ghorkovaya and make clear the chain of command.' He took a deep breath. 'Something I did not reveal in the meeting was that there were other shootings. Four of those executed were former Cheka commissars. Corruption is rotting confidence in the commission from within, Kolya. From now on, any whiff of corruption will result in the most severe punishments. Did you know that some of the roadblock patrols have been taking food from the bagmen only to consume it themselves?'

Kolya felt suddenly uncomfortable. Imagine if Moisei Solomonovich knew he was helping divert supplies to the children's home.

'I am going to the Commissariat. I will see you at Gorokhovaya later.'

Kolya was about to leave himself when Grigory perched on the table next to him.

'I thought you wanted to be the sword of revolution, Kolya,' he said

'You seem to be after that mantle, Grigory,' Kolya retorted.

'Signing the peace treaty hasn't stopped the war, has it?'

Kolya sighed. 'Let's not go over old ground.'

That produced a chuckle from Grigory. 'Fair enough. How's Klara?'

'She's well.'

'And Svetlana?' Grigory asked.

Kolya stared.

'That's right,' Grigory said. 'I know all about your little secret. After all, Leonid lives in the same building as you. He has a loose tongue.'

'So you know him?' Kolya said.

'I do,' Grigory replied. 'I make it my business to know men of talent.'

He held out his hand and Kolya shook it.

'I was disappointed to see you siding with Comrade Uritsky,' Grigory said. 'He is a compromiser, Kolya. Soft hearts don't make revolutions. I thought you knew that.'

Kolya watched him go. Soft hearts, he said. Is that me? Leonid seemed to think so.

'Well, that's a turn up,' Kolya murmured in the now empty room. 'The pure revolutionary has become a pragmatist.'

He heard footsteps and the swish of material. A maid was standing in the doorway.

'May I clear the room, Comrade?' she asked.

'Of course,' Kolya said. 'I was just leaving.'

It was a ten-minute walk to Gorokhovaya so Kolya had left his car. He enjoyed the walk through the sunlit streets. The thought that he had mellowed amused him.

'Talking to you, Grigory,' he murmured as he walked, 'is like looking into a mirror and seeing one aspect of myself.'

He was halfway down Bolshaya Morskaya when he heard a loud report and screaming. He felt a sudden tug in his chest and started to run. Someone shot! It came from the direction of Palace Square. He pushed through a gathering crowd.

'What is it?' he demanded.

Seeing the Chekist, the onlookers parted and Kolya saw the sight he had been half-expecting. Uritsky was lying sprawled on the ground, Blood was pooling around his stricken form. The people attending him saw Kolya watching, the obvious question in his eyes.

'There is nothing we can do for him, Comrade. He is dead.'

Two days later, Kolya was walking away from Uritsky's funeral. He passed Zinoviev, talking to Molotov. For a former member of the Military Revolutionary Committee, this bespectacled man in the shabby raincoat was quite unremarkable. A scarlet party banner fluttered behind them. Everyone present that day knew that the world had turned. Events in Moscow had transformed everything and Dzerzhinsky had just arrived back in Peter to deal with the crisis. Leonid was approaching.

'Still think we can treat the revolution with kid gloves?' he asked.

Kolya spoke in a dull voice. 'I never did.'

'Could have fooled me,' Leonid said. He glanced at the party leaders. 'First Uritsky then Lenin. These terrorist bastards are taking the piss.'

The news from Moscow had alerted everyone present to the gravity of the situation. Lenin, the mastermind of October, lay in the Kremlin, seriously wounded.

'I heard he was dying,' Leonid said matter-of-factly. 'Have you got any news?'

'Comrade Lenin is alive,' Kolya said. 'There is a bullet lodged in his neck.'

'I hope they got the bastard responsible,' Leonid said.

'It was a Socialist Revolutionary,' Kolya said. 'Fania Kaplan. She opened fire as Comrade Lenin left the Mikhelson iron foundry.'

Kolya found Leonid's flat, hard face impossible to read.

'Well, I hope they put her against a wall.'

'Is that your answer to everything, Leonid?'

'It would be a good, fucking start,' Leonid answered in his gravelly voice. 'You're not telling me the assassin's still alive?'

'So I believe,' Kolya replied. 'She is under arrest.'

Leonid shook his head. 'What does it take for this revolution to get serious, Kolya? Three leading Communists shot down in cold blood. We need firing squads. Lots of them.'

Kolya treated Leonid's words with some coldness. 'I seem to remember you wanted firing squads before any of these assassinations took place.'

Leonid's expression was unchanging. 'A few more firing squads and maybe our Communist brothers would still be alive.' He cast a glance across the funeral cortege as it broke up. 'Anyway, I'm not here to discuss the morality of terror. Comrade Boky has called a meeting at Gorkhovaya. I'm here to drive you back.'

The meeting was packed. Boky described the details of the terror so far while Dzerzhinsky sat in a corner, listening intently.

'In response to the White terror of the counter-revolutionaries,' he said, 'we have launched Red revolutionary terror across the city. One of our main targets has been White Guard officers and SRs implicated in conspiracies against the workers' state. Our response will be proportionate and controlled.'

Kolya knew this was a reference to Zinoviev's demand for workers' justice on the street. Dzerzhinsky sat up at Boky's words, but said nothing.

'In attempting to assassinate Comrade Lenin, the enemies of October seek to behead the revolution. They will not succeed.' He deferred to the man known universally as Iron Felix. 'Do you have anything to add, Comrade?'

'Only this,' Dzerzhinsky said. 'We are not negotiating with the counter-revolution. This is not a discussion of justice or fairness. This Extraordinary Commission is not an investigation committee, nor a tribunal.' His clenched fist was in the air above his head, as if clasping a weapon. 'It is a sword wielded on behalf of the revolutionary workers and peasants. It does not put the enemy on trial, it strikes them down. Comrades of the Cheka, you must do your duty without hesitation.'

Applause filled the room. Finally, the assembled Chekists got their orders. Kolya shared his instructions with Leonid, the immediate execution of prisoners already being held in a nearby police station. As they approached the cell, Kolya sensed a certain smugness in Leonid's demeanour, as if there was some private information he and he alone knew. Keys scraped in cell doors and the prisoners stumbled into the artificial light in the corridor. Kolya stared in disbelief at the dishevelled group before him. He drew Leonid aside.

'There's got to be some mistake,' he said.

Leonid waved their instructions under his nose.

'There's no mistake, Comrade. All ten prisoners are due for execution. Here it is in black and white.'

Kolya turned and stared at the storeman Ionov and the manager Nagorny.

'They're thieves, not counter-revolutionaries. This can't be right.'

Leonid was unmoved. 'Thieves, counter-revolutionaries, saboteurs, it's all the same to me, Kolya. Our orders bear the signature of Comrade Boky.'

Kolya drew close and hissed in Leonid's ear. 'You're enjoying this.'

Leonid held his gaze.

'You need to get a grip, Comrade. My feelings are neither here nor there. Now maybe you would like to put these men back in their cells and go and waste Comrade Boky's time, ask for clemency when none will be granted. No, I tell you what, take it straight to Comrade Dzerzhinsky. I am sure he will be very patient with you.' He let that sink in. 'Me, I say we get on with it.'

It was as if a great weight had been placed on Kolya's shoulders. He caught Ionov's gaze and the storeman crumpled to his knees.

'Tell them, Comrade,' he pleaded. 'I stole some parts. That's all I did, I carried a few boxes out to a truck to make a few roubles.' He pointed at Nagorny. 'That fat fuck put me up to it. Tell them! I've got a wife and kids. I didn't do it to be rich. He's the one who squandered it on Vodka and whores. I needed the money to pay a bagman for bread.'

His eyes drifted towards Leonid then back to Kolya, desperately looking for even the slightest sign of sympathy.

'The money was to pay for food. Do you know what it's like hearing your kids whimpering with hunger? Have you even got children?'

It was Leonid who spoke.

'I've got kids. I don't steal from the workers' state, you pathetic toad.'

'You're a fucking Chekist!' Ionov screamed. 'We had one of you bastards in the cell with us, some corrupt arsehole who got caught taking back-handers.'

Before he could get out another word, Leonid was kneeling in front of him, powerful hands gripping his jaw.

'Say another word, you whining, little shit and I'll take you back in that cell and give you a good hiding before I put a bullet through you myself. I advise you to shut the fuck up.'

With that, Ionov's resistance collapsed.

'I'm sorry, I'm sorry, I was angry. I…Please have mercy.'

Leonid got to his feet and waited for Ionov's final whimpering pleading to subside. Remembering who was the one in a position of authority, he glanced sideways at Kolya.

In a dull, dead voice, Kolya gave the order.

'Take them to the courtyard.'

The prisoners were divided into two groups of six. Nagorny was in the first, Ionov in the second. Nagorny simply stood there, quivering with terror, like a goat awaiting the butcher's blade. The Chekist firing squad aimed and shot down the condemned and dragged the bodies away. With the cordite still hanging in the air, the second group was marched to the wall.

Ionov held out his hands.

'Do you call this justice? I stole some engine parts, a few fucking bits of machinery. I never talked to any White Guardists. I don't know any.'

Before he could say another word, the roar of a rifle volley silenced him. Leonid examined the bodies.

'Tough little bastard, this Ionov,' he observed. 'He's still alive. Somebody needs to put him out of his misery.' He unclipped his holster. 'It'll be down to me, I suppose.' He fixed Kolya with a stare. 'I doubt whether you've got the stomach for it, Comrade.'

Kolya scowled and drew his own pistol.

'Get out of the way.'

He peered down at Ionov's shocked, trembling face and put a bullet between his eyes. Without another word, he strode out of the courtyard and into the street. A short walk took him back to his office in Gorokhovaya. He checked that nobody was watching and shut himself into the bathroom where he vomited into the bowl. It took him a few seconds to compose himself then he washed out his mouth and splashed water on his face. He saw bloodshot eyes staring back at him.

Monsters aren't born, he thought, they're made.

Pavel

'You were right,' Abram said

He was half awake, lying on a blanket a few feet to Pavel's left.

'Right about what?'

'We should have smashed the Volunteer Army while we had them at our mercy.'

'Who gives a fuck anymore?' Pavel snorted. 'We all had a good day out watching them burn Kornilov's lousy corpse, didn't we? I mean, you don't see a general set alight every day, alive or dead.'

Abram was lying on his side, listening to Pavel's usual invective.

'I can still smell the burning flesh.'

'Gets you in the back of your throat, doesn't it?' Pavel grunted.

'You sound bitter.'

'Of course I'm fucking bitter,' Pavel said. 'We lost good men defending Ekaterinodar, friends, comrades. When you shed blood, it should be for a purpose. Now we're in full-scale retreat. Talk about snatching defeat out of the jaws of victory. Stupid bastards.'

The sky above them was mink-black and studded with stars. The night wind was whispering through the grassland, soft as a lover's voice.

'There's been so much blood spilt, Abram. Do you ever ask yourself when there's going to be a bullet with your name on it?'

'All the time,' Abram said. 'What about you?'

'I think about it every day.'

Abram let out a long breath. 'I've probably got more reason than most.'

'Because they kill Jews slowly?'

'There's that,' Abram agreed. 'They're inventive about how they kill men like me. Do you remember what I told you about that execution, the working men in the square?'

Pavel remembered every detail, how the Whites cut off noses and gouged out eyes. He would take his own life rather than be taken alive and subjected to such horror.

'Of course I remember,' he said. 'You don't forget a story like that.'

'It is always with me too,' Abram said. 'I've escaped death twice. Sometimes it keeps me awake at night. The same scene plays through my mind over and over again. Sometimes, in my mind's eye, I'm looking down at my own lifeless body…. Can I ask you a favour?'

'If I'm in a position to grant it,' Pavel replied.

'These Whites,' Abram said, 'they're mobile. They know this land. The way I see it, it's only a matter of time before they have us surrounded.'

Pavel didn't try to disabuse him. Abram wasn't alone in thinking that they were living on borrowed time. Twice in as many days they had squirmed out of the noose thrown around them by the Whites. Abram was a brave man, as courageous as anyone in the makeshift company, but there was a shake in his voice.

'If they take me…'

'We are comrades,' Pavel said, interrupting him. 'We fight together. We die together. I'm not going to leave any man behind.'

Abram smiled his appreciation, but he was in no mood to be fobbed off with a few easy slogans. 'The surviving Red units were dispersed across the open steppe, prey to the marauding Whites, Pavel Sergeyevich,' he said.

'Things don't always go the way you plan,' Pavel said. 'You get dispersed. War isn't something planned. It's chaos, sheer bloody chaos. So what's your favour?'

'I've got a reputation now among the men pursuing us,' Abram said. 'They all know the name Goldfarb. Maybe, around some camp fire, they're discussing whether to peel the skin from my body or maybe they're discussing the logistics of burying me alive. You've never seen these people when they've got an enemy at their mercy. They're sadists.'

Pavel watched the path of a shooting star across the vastness of night.

'You're in a cheerful mood,' he observed. 'I won't be asking you to give the lads an inspirational speech in the morning. What is it you want me to do?'

'I'm not interested in brave words here, Pavel. We both know it will be a miracle if we survive this mess. The Whites are everywhere, hunting down the survivors of the Red Army. They're going to slaughter us all like rabbits.' Abram made his pitch. 'Don't let them torture me. I'm not scared to die, but I can't give those fuckers the satisfaction of hearing a Jew beg for his life.'

'You're a brave man, Abram. You'll die shouting your defiance.'

Abram shook his head.

'We both know different, don't we? Every man breaks. There are no exceptions. Don't let the progromist scum humiliate me. I don't want to die with their laughter ringing in my ears.'

'So what is it you do want?' Pavel asked.

Abram sat up and warmed his hands over the dying embers of the campfire.

'I want the best shot in the unit – that's you, Comrade – to pick up his gun and point it right at my head. I want you to take one shot, deadly accurate, and blow my fucking brains out. Maybe, at the moment of my death, I'll see the flash of sunlight on the barrel and I'll know it's you.'

'See what I mean?' Pavel said. 'Cheerful.'

'Don't try to laugh it off, Pavel Sergeyevich. Just tell me you'll do it.' Abram's face was intense.

'Yes, I'll do it,' Pavel said, 'and you do it for me.'

That made Abram rock with laughter.

'The crap you talk, Pavel. I'm a lousy shot. If you're the one caught, you need to get Mikhail to do it.'

Pavel yawned. 'I was trying to be all heroic there.'

The wind picked up and fed the fire, making the embers glow more brightly.

'I know, but let's be practical, Comrade. We've got White cavalry all round us. It's a wonder we got this far. The chances of any of us making it out of this shithole alive are slim.'

For the first time, Pavel showed signs of losing patience

'Keep your voice down, for Christ's sake! I've spent the last week trying to keep up morale. The Whites smashed us to bits at Tikhoretskaya. They marched back into Ekaterinodar two weeks ago, undoing all the good work we had managed. Now they've taken Novorossysk. This is shit, Abram and do you know what's even more shit, twelve hundred miles away I have a little boy and to pile shit on shit, there's famine in Peter and I don't know if he's got enough food to grow up strong and healthy. So lay off the fucking pessimism before I take my gun and shoot you right here to save the Whites the trouble.'

Abram was staring at him, shock painted all over his face. Pavel watched the wounded look for a few moments then roared with laughter.

'I had you there for a minute, didn't I?'

Abram took some time working out how much of Pavel's tirade was true.

'You do have a kid then?'

The smile faded from Pavel's face. 'Yes, I've got a kid. He's a few months old now and I've never held him.'

'What's his name?' Abram asked

'Roman,' Pavel answered.

'It's a good name, a strong name.'

'He'll need to be strong,' Pavel said. 'This is a tough time for a little guy to come into the world.'

He buttoned his uniform jacket and pulled on his boots.

'Try to get some sleep, Abram.'

He had seen what was in Abram's heart. There would be no sleep for him. He would lie awake, staring at the sky, anticipating a painful death. Pavel had a choice, to stay there and be a sounding board for Abram's terrors or find something else to do.

'Where are you going?' Abram asked.

'I'll see to the horses. They talk more sense than you shower of bastards.'

He fed the horses they had taken from the Whites, letting his favourite nuzzle for oats.

'I wish I was like you, boy,' Pavel murmured. 'You eat, you run, your sleep, you fuck. You don't have another thing going on in your head, do you?'

The stallion shuddered.

'Got the shakes, eh? Well, me too. This could be my last dawn. If not today, it will be tomorrow.' He turned and watched the sleeping men. 'See those poor, dumb fools. They think I know what I'm doing. They see me leading the way every time we go into battle and they think I'm something special. Do you know how old I am? Twenty-one. Shit. Nobody knows their arse from their elbow at twenty-one.'

Pavel talked it all through in those early hours of the morning, his fears, his insecurity. He even explained about Nina and Raisa.

'Do you know how my Nina survives? She gets handouts at the children's home. That's right, the home Raisa founded. Nina's the mother of my child and Raisa's the only woman I've ever loved. Now here's the punchline, my equine friend. The Raisa I love has got the hots for another woman. What do you think of that? Hysterical, isn't it? I bet you're glad you're a horse. It's simpler that way. You don't know you're mortal. You just canter through life then one day – boom – you're dead.'

He leaned against a tree and watched the darkness thinning to the east. The late summer dawn was little more than a smudge of yellow. That's when he saw them, the nightmarish shapes he had been expecting, the approaching silhouettes of enemy riders. A shock, like icy water, cascaded down his spine. He peered through his binoculars, willing the apparition to be nothing more than a trick of the early morning light.

'Fuck!'

It was as if Abram had had a premonition all along. The silhouetted figures were taking on more solid form. Pavel raced for the camp, raising the alarm. The first enemy shell tore open a gouge in the earth no more than twenty yards from the sleeping men. They had light artillery covering the attack.

'To arms!' he yelled. 'They're coming.'

Within moments, half-dressed men were opening up with rifles and machine-guns. Rounds tore through the grassland, making a sound like a razor slashing cloth. The momentum of the cavalry charge took them right into the Red camp. Soon, sabres were slashing down. Pistol shots rang out. Then ferocious hand-to-hand fighting. Pavel was in the thick of it, cursing as he pulled one of the Whites off Nikita and pistol whipped him to the ground. A single shot ended the White Guard's resistance.

'Where did you come from?' Nikita panted. 'I thought you'd pissed off.'

'Lucky for you I didn't,' Pavel told him. 'Now get on your feet and start shooting.'

He heard his own words and grasped a new reality. The machine gun had been silenced. He turned, as if in slow motion, insides dissolving. The barrel of the gun was moving his way.

'They've captured the Maxim!'

Then the guttural roar of the machine gun made his warning superfluous. Blood mixed with tossed up dust and soil as men fell. Nikita had been lucky the first time. Not so the second. Hot lead ripped him apart. One after another, men jumped and jerked like puppets, then lay still. Pavel looked around him wildly. His unit was completely overwhelmed. He saw throats cut by daggers, men sliced in half by the merciless action of the machine gun. That's when his eyes settled on

Mikhail dispatching a White officer with his pistol and, behind him, Volodya covering his comrade. He was Svetlana's son, all right.

'This way,' he yelled.

The three of them scampered through rifle volleys to where the horses were tethered.

'We're running?' Volodya asked.

'The battle's lost,' Pavel said. 'We're all that's left alive.'

They wheeled their mounts and galloped into the grassland.

'Where are we going?' Mikhail demanded. Pavel rocked back in the saddle, face turned up to the sun.

'You knew this was coming. You knew,' he said.

'What?' said Volodya. Who are you talking to?'

Pavel's head cleared and he looked straight at the others.

'Did you see anyone else still alive?' he demanded. 'Anyone?'

'Fuck knows,' Mikhail replied. 'I was too busy saving my own skin to count.' He wiped the dust and sweat from his face and glanced gratefully at Volodya. 'Without this young buck at my side, I'd be fly food by now. Are you seriously going back?'

'I promised not to leave anyone behind,' Pavel answered. 'What have we got to lose? We're dead men anyway. They're bound to outflank us. With luck, they shoot us dead.'

'And if we're unlucky?'

Pavel shook his head. 'Work it out for yourself. '

'Fine,' Mikhail said. 'What's the plan?'

Pavel shook his head. 'You think I've got a plan? Comrade, that really is flattering. Here's why we're going back. I didn't see Abram alive or dead. Last night I made him a promise. If they've taken him alive, they'll gut him like a fish. They'll hold his own steaming entrails in front of his dying face. Do you want that on your conscience?'

Mikhail's breathing was troubled. Pavel knew the sound of fear. They tethered the horses and returned on foot, weaving through the long grass. Presently, they had eyes on the camp. The Whites had ten prisoners, more than they thought. Abram was one of them. The White officer was enjoying himself.

'So here's how we do this.' He waved his Browning pistol, a gift from the British. 'You see, I hate fucking Reds, but I hate the yids even more. So you boys....' He indicated Abram's comrades. 'You're going to dig yourselves a nice, big open grave. You get to go the easy way, one bullet and – thump – into the grave. Say thank you, Your Honour.'

Some of the Reds mumbled the words. One said, 'Fuck you.'

It earned him a bullet.

'Now that was just silly,' the officer said. 'Who goes jumping the gun and earning themselves an early death? Start digging boys.'

Pavel lowered himself onto his stomach and crawled forward, Mikhail and Volodya following behind

They lay under the rising sun with the heat on their backs and waited. Before long, Volodya whispered a question.

'How the fuck do we take out forty Whites with three rifles?'

Pavel wiped the sweat from his eyes. 'We don't.'

'Come again...?'

'We're all dead men' Pavel said. 'Not one of us walks away from this alive.'

'So what is this about?' Mikhail asked.

'Here's the thing,' Pavel said. 'You heard that bastard. Everybody gets a bullet, except for Abram. They're going to make his suffering last. I promised to make it short. Do you have a problem with that?'

Mikhail shook his head. 'No.'

'You?' Pavel said, glancing at Volodya.

It was the same answer from the younger man.

Finally, the graves were dug. The White officer counted four men from the line.

'Shoes off,' he said.

The order earned him a puzzled frown.

'I don't want blood ruining perfectly good boots.'

The four men stood at the edge of the pit. Shots rang out and their bodies tumbled in. The officer nodded to the remaining men. They sat on the ground, unlacing their boots with trembling fingers and made their way to the pit. More shots. More bodies.

'Well, that's the overture,' the officer said. 'Now the opera begins. Let's call it The Suffering of Israel. What do you think Abram Goldfarb? Is that a good title?'

Abram licked dry lips and cleared his throat.

'Fuck you, you piece of shit.'

'He's trying to earn himself a bullet,' Pavel whispered.

'Fuck you,' Abram repeated. 'Fuck Denikin and Kaledin and the Tsar and fuck your wife and kids.'

'Brave words.' The officer turned to his men. 'Clever little bastard, isn't he? He thinks I'll get so angry I'll shoot him dead.' He approached Abram. 'Well, forget it. I've got something original in store for you. Let's see how brave you sound in half an hour.'

Pavel shoved the rifle stock tight into his shoulder. He recalled what Abram had said about the flash of light on the barrel and raised his head a little. Abram seemed to be searching the landscape for some sign of him. That's when Pavel saw it, the ghost of a smile on his friend's lips as he spotted the gleam of mercy.

'What the fuck are you smiling for?' the officer roared.

Pavel knew. Abram had spotted the tell-tale sparkle of sunlight on his rifle. His finger was on the trigger. The moment he fired, he was going to give away his location and bring the wrath of the Whites down on him and his comrades. He didn't care. He started to squeeze.

A gun barrel housed the angel of mercy.

Raisa

They left the train and set out on horseback, freeing up the main line for Trotsky's entourage. The company plodded along, slowing their pace so as not to leave the infantry behind. She could feel the hostile stares of some of the men at her back. Their Communism was no more than the frosting on a cake.

'Ignore them,' Elena advised. 'They're jealous. I get to have you and they don't.'

She glanced back and used her tongue to make an obscene gesture directed at Konstantin.

'Stop that!' Raisa snapped. 'Why do you have to wind them up?'

Elena rocked with laughter. 'I'm just telling the dumb fuck he'll never arouse you like I can.'

Raisa blushed. 'Sometimes you can be really crude. Don't make yourself as bad as them.'

She felt Elena's hand slap her thigh.

'You love me for it though, don't you?'

Raisa looked away, her thoughts travelling north west across the vast land to a little guesthouse near a river.

'Are you thinking about the kids?'

Raisa nodded. 'They live in a famished city. I worry about them every day.'

'You can trust aunty Svetlana,' Elena said. 'Anna's great with them too. Stop worrying. They're safe. We've got bigger fish to fry.'

Presently, the rolling thunder of heavy guns sounded in the distance.

'Where are we?'

'Fifteen miles from Kazan.'

'Which way?'

'West.'

They came across stragglers from a Red Army platoon. When Anishin questioned them there was a rasp of warning in his voice.

'Aren't you going the wrong way, Comrades?'

Eyes blinked with suspicion.

'How do you mean?'

Anishin leaned down from his mount. He rested his forearm on his thigh, giving them have a good view of the Nagan pistol in his hand.

'I think you know exactly what I mean, *Comrade.*' The jab of a finger indicated the distant growl of war. 'That's where the battle's taking place. Correct me if I'm wrong, but I think you're going in the opposite direction.'

That set off turned heads and a series of whispered squabbles as the deserters tried to work out the best way to avoid getting shot.

'Let me make it easy for you,' Anishin said. 'Either you turn around and join us or I line the lot of you up and put some good Red ordnance into you.'

The deserters shuffled reluctantly into line.

'Good choice,' Anishin told them. He gestured to one of the men closest to him. 'Come over here and describe the situation.'

Raisa eavesdropped on the conversation. It turned out the men were all that was left of a force defending the railway station at Chikrana. They had been overrun by White storm troops and put to flight. Anishin digested the report and gathered his augmented platoon together.

'It's like this,' he said. 'All men get scared. All men run. Who wouldn't want to save his skin? I would. You should know this though. If we run here, if we piss off and let the Whites advance, eventually the whole fucking lot of us will be dancing from lamp posts. Do you remember why we made a revolution? It was to end the war, feed the cities, give land to the peasants. We wanted a workers' and peasants' state. Well, I still want that. I'm not going to ask if you do because frankly I don't give a shit. Let's put this simply. It is me or the White scum. There is nothing in between. The lot of you look as if all you can think about is something to eat and somewhere comfortable to sleep.'

One or two men nodded.

'I'm not going to lie to you,' Anishin said. 'The whole Volga Front is in a state of collapse, but we intend to take a stand. Comrade Trotsky is expected any day. You can either join the Communists and fight back or you can have a bullet in the head. It's up to you.'

He wheeled round without another word and cantered to the front of the column.

'Why didn't you give it to them straight?' Elena said, sarcasm dripping from her tongue.

Anishin grinned ruefully.

'They've probably taken all the bullshit they can stomach,' he said. He blinked the dust from his eyes. 'I just hope Comrade Trotsky's everything people say he is. I heard him at the Cirque Moderne. He's a great orator, but has he got it in him to lead an army?'

Before long, they reached the outskirts of a small town. Elena asked an old woman the name of the place.

'This is Sviyazhsk,' came the answer.

'It's the right place,' Elena told Anishin. 'I wonder when Trotsky's going to get here.'

'The commissar in the armoured train?' the old woman said. 'He's here. He arrived yesterday.' She cackled. 'He executed a couple of officers, shot a whole bunch of soldiers too, said it was the only way to restore discipline. He's a mean fucker, that one.' Her eyes narrowed. 'Not a true Russian, if you get my drift.'

'What did she mean by that?' Raisa asked, glancing back.

Elena pulled a face. 'Another bitter, old woman who doesn't like Jews. The venom pollutes the arteries of this country, it will take generations to flush it out.'

They entered the outskirts of Sviyazhsk in late afternoon. Hundreds of soldiers were gathering.

'What's happening here, Comrade?' Raisa asked one man.

'Trotsky and Vatsetis are going to address the army.' He looked her up and down and turned to his mates. 'Look at this. First they send us fifteen-year-old kids from Moscow. Now we've got bits of girls. How old are you, for fuck's sake?'

Raisa's eyes flashed. 'I'm seventeen. I can shoot a rifle better than you can. I can handle a machine gun. I was at the battle of Pulkovo Heights and I've got twelve kills to my name in this war. So you can stick that up your fat, pink arse, *Comrade*.'

Konstantin shouted from the back. 'Tell them what else you can do.' He glanced meaningfully at Elena. 'To her.'

It was his turn to make an obscene gesture with his tongue. That earned a peal of laughter. Anishin was watching how this would develop. Raisa unclipped her holster and drew her pistol.

'Have you forgotten that I'm a political officer, Comrade Konstantin? I'm in my rights to blow your brains out for insubordination. From what that old woman said, shooting big-mouthed bastards like you is all the rage.'

She stared Konstantin down.

'Well?' she asked. 'Have you got anything else to say to me?'

The moment had passed. She holstered her gun and watched Trotsky and Vatsetis mount a hastily erected platform. She too had seen Trotsky at the Cirque Moderne. He was sporting the usual leather coat and a matching cap. Vatsetis cut a bulky figure beside him. The Latvian general had been in charge of the forces driven out of Kazan. If Raisa knew military men, he would be itching to put that right. Trotsky's speech was short and aimed at restoring morale.

'If Kazan is allowed to remain in enemy hands,' he barked, his powerful voice carrying across the crowd, 'Nizhni-Novgorod is next and, beyond that, Moscow itself. The fate of the revolution will be decided here at Sviyazshk. The honour of storming Kazan and saving the workers' state has fallen upon you.'

Raisa watched the listening soldiers. Some seemed to think it was a dubious honour.

'The retaking of Kazan means merciless revenge against the armies of the counter-revolution. Do not allow the enemy to take a step further. Tear Kazan from his hands. Drown him in the Volga!'

Among the crowd at Trotsky's back was a woman listening intently.

'Who's that?' Raisa asked.

'Don't you recognise comrade Reissner?' Elena said. 'That's Fyodor Raskolnikov's wife.'

'She's beautiful,' Raisa said.

Elena pinched her, much to Konstantin's distaste.

'If I have a rival,' she said, 'I'll have to shoot her myself, even if she is married to the hero of Kronstadt.'

Vatsetis had stepped up to have his say. Compared to Trotsky, he was a dull and plodding speaker.

'We begin the assault tomorrow,' he said. 'So you will need to get an early night. Snatch what sleep you can. The choice before us is victory or death.'

The last act of Raisa and Elena as political officers that evening was to hand out leaflets on which was printed Trotsky's final order:

I give warning that if any unit retreats without orders, the first to be shot down will be the commissary of the unit, and next the commander. Brave and gallant soldiers will be appointed in their places. Cowards, dastards and traitors will not escape the bullet. This I solemnly promise in the name of the entire Red Army.

As they made their way back through the military camp, Raisa tugged at Elena's sleeve.

'Should we ask somebody else to leaflet our own unit?'

'No, fuck the bastards. We're their political officers. Anishin as commissar won't look kindly on comrades who shirk their duties. Tomorrow, we storm Kazan. What's a few small-minded fools in comparison?'

So they handed out the rest of their leaflets. Raisa found herself standing before Konstantin as he lounged in his blanket.

'Well, are you going to take it?' she asked.

He laced his fingers behind his head and looked up at her.

'Shove it down the front of my trousers. I'll read it later.'

Raisa was stuck for words until Elena stepped forward.

'Maybe I'll shove it up your arse then you can keep it for use as toilet paper.'

They walked away to ribald laughter from the other men.

The assault began at three-thirty in the morning, with artillery fire blasting the walls of the city. Under Raskolnikov's command, a detachment of Kronstadt sailors joined the barrage from their flotilla on the river. Flashes filled the darkness and the roar of the guns shocked the hearts of the Red forces waiting to go into action.

'Are you scared?' Raisa whispered, as she crouched next to her lover, waiting for the order to advance.

'Fucking shitting myself,' Elena said. 'No matter what happens here, I love you for all time.'

Raisa glanced along the line. 'We can't kiss.'

Elena gave the men a scornful look and snorted.

'Can't we?'

She kissed Raisa passionately on the lips and glared at the watching faces.

'What's the matter with you fuckers then? Jealous?'

Konstantin spat. 'Dirty cunts.'

Elena tapped her forehead. 'And you've got a dirty mind and a foul mouth, *Comrade*.'

Finally, the barrage was at an end and they started to move, scrambling over rubble, stumbling through artillery smoke and the acrid stench of cordite. Defensive fire from the White emplacements was spitting, zinging, ricocheting around them, raising puffs of greyish-white masonry smoke. Elena flattened herself against a wall.

'Machine gun!'

The rattle and metallic snarl of the gun had the advancing Reds penned in. The defenders had a perfect vantage point, on slightly raised ground, looking down at the Reds' path. Anishin scrambled forward to see what was holding them up.

'We've got to take that nest,' he observed redundantly.

Elena caught Raisa's eye before weighing up the situation. She rested her foot against the door behind her then kicked it open.

'Raisa, take a couple of men and lay down fire from the upstairs windows.'

'What about you?'

Elena took a deep breath. 'We're going to storm that nest.'

Horror filled Raisa. This was a frontal assault up a hill. She almost said *be careful*, but there was no point. The Fates were already juggling the dice in their fists. She led the way up the stairs. Within seconds, she and two other soldiers were sniping down at the nest. The machine gun fire became wilder, the gunner forced to shelter from the hot lead raining in. Seizing on a lull in the firing, Elena sprinted towards the gun. Konstantin and three others followed in her wake. Elena was first into the machine gun post, pumping shots into the gunner and his feeder. Hearing the crunch of a boot, she spun round and killed a third defender as he rose from behind a hastily-erected barricade. Raisa was about to leave her vantage point when she spotted half a dozen Whites moving towards the machine gun emplacement from the right. She yelled a warning.

'Whites!'

Konstantin was the last to register the movement. A bullet thumped into his shoulder and he spun round, blood pumping out. Instantly, Raisa and her comrades set about pinning down the Whites, but Konstantin was in no man's land, trying to crawl towards cover. A second gunshot rang out and a puff of scarlet rose from his leg.

'Fuck!'

'Covering fire,' Elena shrieked, handing her rifle to a comrade.

Ducking low, she raced into the line of fire, seizing Konstantin's wrists.

'You're not dying on me, fucker,' she screamed. 'You're going to live long enough to apologise for what you called me.'

Then she was dragging him towards the row of houses, face contorted with the effort. Raisa thundered down the stairs, heart in mouth and ran into the street, pumping out shots to keep the Whites' heads low. She could hear Elena grunting, panting as she tried to get Konstantin inside. She was skidding on his blood trail.

'Well, somebody help her.'

Finally, they had Konstantin inside. After some shouted messages down the line, a medic ran up.

'How is he?' Elena demanded, taking Konstantin's rifle to replace her own. 'I hope the wound's painful, but not fatal.'

The medic looked up, startled.

'She's got a strange sense of humour,' Raisa said, heart still slamming after what she had seen. She turned to Elena. 'Do you have to take such risks?'

'What am I meant to do, leave the small-minded shit to die?'

Konstantin was blinking through the pain. 'You risked your life for me.'

Elena sat heavily next to him. 'Yes, I did, didn't I? Shows what a bloody idiot I am.'

Somebody was lighting Konstantin a cigarette.

'Looks like you're going to live,' Raisa told him. 'Not as if you deserve it, of course.'

He had tears in his eyes. 'I should never…'

Elena cut him off. 'There's no need for speeches. Just don't call me a cunt, not now, not ever, because if you do, I'll cut your fucking bollocks off. Got that?'

Konstantin nodded through the pain. Elena looked round the other men.

'That goes for the rest of you too. We are Communists. We are your comrades. Nothing else needs saying. Do you fucking understand me?'

Nobody was arguing. Anishin arrived with another man, lugging an ammunition box.

'What's this?' he asked. 'I thought you were going to take that machine gun post.'

He blinked with confusion at the laughter that followed.

Kolya

He was sitting on the bed, looking down at Svetlana.

'How can you feel more exhausted when you wake up than when you go to bed?'

Svetlana prodded his stomach with her fingers.

'That comes from rolling around with me for half an hour before you sleep. Besides, we're screwing in the middle of the day. There's no pattern to your life, my brave Chekist.'

Kolya gave a thin smile. 'We have to take our chances when we can. Klara is always asking where I'm going.' He squeezes his eyes. 'I'm serious though. Even on days when I manage six hours' sleep, I am still exhausted.'

Svetlana scrambled into a sitting position, pressing her chest against his back and wrapping her arms round him.

'We're all tired, lover. Did I show you the figures for the Petrograd party? Membership is down by half, just six thousand when we used to have thirteen thousand. Forty per cent of the members are October recruits. I find it hard to trust comrades who joined after the revolution. There are so many opportunists among them.'

She rested her chin on his shoulder.

'It seems like an age since we had tens of thousands of committed comrades in every factory and mill, men and women who had shared common hardship together. Where are they now?'

'Drawn into the apparatus of government like you and me or spread across the country same as your Volodya, fighting the Whites.'

'I wish I were there alongside him,' Svetlana said. 'I would rather have a rifle in my hand than waste my time trying to get the state bureaucracy to work. I hate all this crap.'

'You don't show it,' Kolya said.

'I feel it. I was proud to be a woman worker and a Bolshevik. Suddenly, old friends turn on me. Do you know how many women members we have now? Seven hundred in the whole city! Hardly any of them work in the factories any more. We've lost comrades like Albina, real revolutionaries with years of organising behind her. The last time I saw her, she walked right past me as if I wasn't there.'

Kolya turned to kiss her. 'I thought you were meant to be cheering me up.'

She tousled his hair.

'What's this about, my love? Is Klara still demanding to know why you never go home?'

Kolya shook his head.

'I don't know what I am becoming. Did you know they had to close down the Cheka Weekly?'

'I thought you'd be happy. Their hysterical shit is a betrayal of the revolution.'

Kolya answered with a sigh. 'It revels in killing. More blood. More blood. Lenin demands ruthlessness, but even he shrank back from the madness in its pages. Comrade Boky estimates that we have killed eight hundred prisoners in Peter alone. I've got blood on my hands, so much blood.'

'You had blood on your hands before you joined the Cheka, my love. We fought the counter-revolution at Pulkovo Heights. You helped suppress the cadet rising.'

He gazed at her with a bleak, broken look. 'I was fighting our enemies. I knew what I was doing was right. Svetlana, some of those I have seen go to the wall, I know they were innocent.'

'Then you must speak out.'

Kolya watched the changing expressions in her honest face and deep, brown eyes.

'I spoke to Comrade Boky about the situation. I spoke about Leonid in particular. He is without conscience, Svetlana.' Another sigh. 'But Boky is no longer head of the Commission and Zinoviev is demanding no slowing of the pace of repression.' The next words he said were full of foreboding. 'Svetlana, what if men like Leonid are the future?'

'We will not allow brutes like him to stain our reputation. This is a difficult moment in our revolution, but we will recover.'

Kolya sat hunched. 'I wish I had your conviction.'

'This is a turnaround,' Svetlana said. 'You were always so certain. You boasted your iron will. Everything you just said about Leonid, Pavel Sergeyevich says about you.'

Kolya stared at her. 'Maybe there's something in it. All this killing, Svetlana, it is making me a monster.'

'You're no monster, Kolya,' Svetlana said soothingly, 'not while you have a conscience.'

'I have to go,' he told her. 'We have to deal with the sailors.'

Svetlana's eyes widened. 'Don't tell me the discontent has reached Kronstadt!'

'Of course not. If we lost Kronstadt, we would lose our very souls. There are grumbles, but nothing that can't be handled. They are the glory of the revolution. No, the problem is with some of the sailors garrisoned here in Petrograd. The Second Baltic Fleet detachment is up in arms. The more the counter-revolution chokes us, the more we are reduced to turning on one another.'

He disentangled himself gently from her embrace. 'I think Klara knows about us.'

Svetlana lay on her back, displaying her nakedness to him.

'You're a wanton woman.'

'I am relaxed with you, Kolya.' She shoved at his chest with her foot. 'Do you think she will come after me and slap me, the way I did her?'

Kolya gave a hollow laugh. 'She wouldn't dare. You'd break her jaw.'

He leaned forward, hoisted a lazy thigh onto his shoulder and bent to kiss her goodbye.

Leonid was waiting for him at the Second Fleet barracks. The building was already surrounded by troops and a smattering of Chekists.

'You had better fill me in,' Kolya said wearily.

'The cheek of the bastards, parading down the Nevsky, making nuisances of themselves. They've been shouting anti-Bolshevik slogans. This time they went further, beating the shit out of Comrade Flerovsky.'

Kolya gave a nod of resignation. Smacking the commissar of the Baltic Fleet around was the act of a madman.

'Take the building,' Kolya instructed. 'Arrest the ringleaders.'

Leonid gave his humourless smile. He had an appetite for the rough stuff. There was little resistance and Kolya made his way through the barracks in the aftermath of the failed rebellion, leaving the mopping up to Leonid. The barracks came as something of a shock. They were filthy and dark. There was excrement in the corners. One of the sailors was still at liberty.

'How long since this place has been cleaned?' Kolya asked, his face a rictus of disgust.

'You tell me,' the sailor grunted, none too happy at being interrogated by one of the Chekists who had just seized his leaders.

Kolya continued to explore the pitiful conditions, bunks without mattresses, blankets, pillows, water oozing from cracked ceilings. He found no evidence of cups or plates, soap or towels.

'How do you live like this?' Kolya asked.

The sailor stared at him, as if he had just landed from Planet Wet-Behind-The-Ears. 'You *are* Cheka, aren't you?'

Kolya nodded. 'Why do you ask?'

A shrug. 'We don't usually get much sympathy from you bastards.'

'We're not all the same,' said Kolya. He paused at the door. 'Oh, one piece of advice, if you meet any other Chekists today, don't call them bastards. They're not all as patient as me.'

He found Leonid waiting for him and was handed a printed leaflet.

'I found another of these.'

Kolya read through the sailors' resolution.

'Shameful peace, suffering of toiling people, violence of hired bureaucrats.' He glanced at Leonid. 'I think it means us.'

He read through to the end;

We demand the reestablishment of genuine Soviet power!
Down with the Brest noose!
Long live the International Socialist Revolution!

Leonid took the leaflet back.

'Printed on a Left SR duplicator,' he said. 'Same fucking terrorists who shot Uritsky and Lenin.'

'They're getting a hearing because people are pissed off with war and hunger,' Kolya reminded him.

Leonid folded the leaflet and put it in his pocket. 'You're sounding a bit like an SR yourself, Comrade.'

Kolya ignored the jibe. 'Let's get the ringleaders back to Gorokhovaya. We'll interrogate them there.'

The first interrogation involved a former Black Fleet sailor, Yakov Shashkov.

'Name?' Kolya asked.

Shaskov glared. 'Don't play games. You know my name.'

Leonid was standing behind him. He administered a meaty slap to Shashkov's head.

'There's no need for that,' Kolya said.

'The cheeky fucker needs reminding who's in charge here,' Leonid protested.

Kolya rested his chin on steepled fingers. 'I'll do the reminding.' He turned his attention to Shashkov. 'You're not a serving sailor?'

'No.'

'So what were you doing, involving yourself in the demonstrations?'

'I was fighting for the socialist revolution,' Shashkov replied. 'Do you remember when that's what you believed in too?'

'It's what I still believe in,' Kolya told him. 'I have many friends fighting the White armies, risking their lives to protect the gains of the revolution.'

'And whose fault is that? We should have been fighting a revolutionary war against all the imperialists.'

'Instead, your party comrades carry out futile assassinations.' He pretended to be reading a list. 'Volodarsky, the diplomat Mirbach, Uritsky....' A Pause. 'Lenin.'

'Lenin's alive.'

Leonid took a step forward, making Shashkov flinch.

'No thanks to you, you counter-revolutionary twat.'

Kolya frowned his disapproval at Leonid and pretended to write a note. 'You take over a section of the Kremlin and attempt open rebellion. Is that your socialist revolution? I call it treason.'

'The traitors wear leather coats these days,' Shashkov retorted pointedly. 'You think a bit of fucking animal hide gives you the right to torture and kill.'

'Are you sure I can't hit him?' Leonid asked.

'Let him be,' Kolya said.

'You were arrested with a consignment of rifles,' Kolya said, scanning his notes. 'What were the rifles for?'

'What do you think?' came the defiant answer. 'Shooting.'

Kolya chose to overlook Shashkov's sarcasm.

'Shooting...*whom*?'

Shashkov was growing uneasy about Leonid who had taken up a position behind him.

'They were for self-defence,' he said.

'Self-defence against...*whom*?' Kolya waited a few seconds then made a note. 'The suspect refused to answer.' The only sound was the scrape of his pen. 'Tell me about what happened to Comrade Flerovsky.'

Shashkov looked uncomfortable. This was an attack on a senior official. 'He tried to run off. Some of the lads may have gone over the top.'

'So you admit that the anti-Soviet insurrection....'

'The what!' Shashkov's face drained of blood.

'You had a consignment of rifles. You beat the commissar of the Baltic Fleet. How would you describe it?'

'We were protesting against hunger. What fucking insurrection? It was about shit living conditions.'

Kolya met his gaze. 'Were they *your* shit living conditions?'

'No, but...'

Kolya made a note. 'No.' He pushed back his chair and rose to his feet. 'When you chose to interfere, you made yourself an outside agitator, an enemy of the people. Do you understand the seriousness of your actions, Citizen?'

Shashkov reacted to being addressed as citizen, rather than comrade. 'I know you shot our comrades in Moscow.'

'Fania Kaplan tried to assassinate Lenin,' Kolya reminded him. 'The SRs rose in open revolt and occupied the Kremlin. An SR assassinated Comrade Volodarsky. Is this the way a party in a coalition government behaves? Do you expect clemency, Comrade?'

Shashov swallowed. 'From a lousy, fucking Bolshevik? No.'

That produced a guttural laugh from Leonid. 'You got that right.'

'Do you have anything to say in your defence?' Kolya asked.

'Defence?' Shashkov replied. 'I didn't know this was a court.'

'This is the Cheka,' Kolya said. 'It is anything it wants to be.' He gestured to Leonid. 'Take him away.'

It wasn't long before there was a cry of pain from outside the room. The moment Leonid reappeared, Kolya demanded to know what had happened.

'The daft bugger fell. He's got a bit of a shiner.'

'How many times do I have to tell you, Comrade? You are not to take justice into your own hands.'

'He fell,' Leonid said provocatively.

He glanced at Kolya's report over his shoulder.

'Where's the recommendation?'

'There isn't one,' Kolya said.

'Why?'

'Is there much point?' Kolya asked. 'We both know what's in store for the leaders of the rebellion.'

'There should still be a recommendation,' Leonid insisted.

'To what purpose?'

Leonid glared as if Kolya was being wilfully obstructive. 'Because we are the Cheka. We take responsibility for our actions. Our job is to behead the counter-revolution. If I were in your place, I would be proud to sign off on the bastards' executions.'

'Then maybe it is a good job you are not in my place, Leonid.'

'What's that supposed to mean?'

The hostility between them was coming close to violence. Kolya took his time to answer, closing Shashkov's file. 'I think you like your job too much.'

'Maybe you don't take yours seriously enough, Nikolai Nikolayevich.'

Kolya made his way to the door.

'So which one are you seeing tonight?' Leonid asked. 'Svetlana or Klara?'

'Is that any of your business, Comrade?'

Leonid started to button his jacket, ready to step out into the autumn chill. 'None at all. I'm interested, that's all. Call it morbid curiosity.'

Kolya set off down the corridor, remembering the way Leonid had stared at Svetlana's body. 'Or jealousy.'

Kolya strode out to his car, passing some of the other prisoners. He picked up Klara from her building.

'I didn't expect you to come for me,' she said.

'Are you complaining?'

She smiled. 'Of course not. I'm just glad to see you once in a while.'

'Oh, for fuck's sake, Scorpion, don't start that again.'

Klara ignored the warning.

'I know you're seeing her again.'

Kolya shook his head in exasperation. 'And I saw you when I was with her. Why don't you kick me out if you're so bothered?'

Tears were welling up in Klara's eyes. 'I love you!'

He laughed. 'Isn't life a bitch?'

At that, she dissolved into tears. Kolya sighed and watched the city flashing by. They reached her flat twenty minutes later. As Kolya closed the door behind him, he slipped his arms around her waist.

'Are you angry with me, Scorpion?'

'Yes.'

'What if I were to give you some good news?'

She wriggled round to face him, face alight with expectation.

'What kind of good news?'

'I have been offered a room at the Astoria. There is a corridor for officials of the Cheka.'

Klara squealed with delight, all thoughts of Svetlana banished.

'Is it true the Party has special rations?'

'It isn't luxury living, but yes, I believe that there are certain minor advantages to living there.'

Klara hugged him, her tears forgotten. The feel of her inflamed him. After the moral filth of the interrogation room, he wanted to burn away the shame.

'I want you,' he said.

Klara squirmed. 'Not like this.'

'Why not?'

'I want to wash my face first.'

She struggled free and approached the washstand. She was soaking a flannel in the bowl when she felt Kolya behind her, lifting her skirts.

'Stop that!'

He didn't stop. She could feel him hard against her.

'Kolya...'

His hand was between her legs, insistent, demanding. Now he was gripping her hips, bending her forward. He took her like that, silently and without endearments. There was no sound except for a grunt of exertion. When he had finished, he stumbled away, buttoning his flies. Klara turned and stared at him.

'Why?' she demanded. 'What made you treat me like my punters used to, as if I was nothing?'

Kolya slumped into a chair and gazed across the room blankly.

Klara's cheeks were damp with tears.

'Tell me, what was that about?'

He made no attempt to reply. The answer was in an interrogation room at Gorokhovaya.

Raisa

The Whites were in full retreat, falling back across the bridge.

'Now we sweep them out of the city,' Elena said, eyes sparkling with the thrill of victory.

Enemy machine-gunners were hurriedly swinging their weapons onto their shoulders and running clumsily under their weight. They reminded Raisa of clowns, the way their trousers billowed as they ran.

'We will proceed with caution,' Anishin said, gesturing to some of the men to go forward and check for snipers hiding in the girders of the bridge's structure.

'Let Anishin take charge,' Raisa hissed, creeping forward to stand by Elena's side. 'He is the commissar. Let him make the decisions.'

The Elena before her was like a coiled spring, in no mood to let the counter-revolutionaries slip out of her hands.

'You don't win a war by letting the enemy retreat in good order,' she retorted. 'With an armoured car or some good, fast horsemen, we could cut them off and break their resistance here. Why let them escape so they can shoot our people down another day? Have you forgotten our misguided generosity so early, the way we let Krasnov go to raise counter-revolution?'

Raisa watched her lover almost trembling with eagerness for the fight. She feared for Elena, so brave yet so rash. The Whites were clearing out, some mounting their horses and galloping away, others scurrying after them in panic. Anishin had his arm in the air, signalling to the men to wait. when tyres screamed on the cobbles.

'Who is in command here?'

The accent was Latvian. The officer stared hard-eyed at the delay.

'I am Comrade Anishin, commissar of...'

'Commissar of standing here with his thumb up his arse,' the Latvian snapped. 'Get your men moving.' Seeing Elena and Raisa crouching against the railings, he gave a low whistle. 'I'll change that. Get your *comrades* moving. I wish we had soldiers like those two in the Rifle Division.'

'Well?' Elena asked, trying not to say 'I told you so,' 'now do we move?'

There was some sniggering at Anishin's obvious discomfort. The entire unit was moving forward across the bridge. There was no resistance. On the far bank of the river, there were piles of abandoned equipment. The Whites had fled, spooked by the Red torpedo boats skimming the waters of the Volga. None of them wanted to face Raskolnikov's sailors.

'It's their turn to run,' Elena said, eyes glittering.

Now, she was the very fire of revolution, her impatient gaze sweeping the street before her. Raisa was uneasy. It all seemed so quiet. The houses opposite would provide excellent cover for snipers. Anishin instructed two teams of fighters to rush the doors and kick their way inside.

'All clear,' the first team shouted after a few moments.

'Clear here too,' called the second.

Everywhere, the Red soldiers were straightening up, rubbing sweat from their faces, checking on reserves of ammunition, searching for a cigarette. Anishin walked through the calm.

'You've got five minutes to get your breath then we continue sweeping the streets.' He glanced at his political officers. 'What you did for Konstantin, Elena, it won you the respect of the men.'

Elena refused to be placated by a facile compliment.

'It's a battle I should not have had to win twice,' she said. 'If I had been a man, it wouldn't have been like this.'

Anishin tipped his head briefly. 'You may be right. Either way, it's done now.'

They progressed through empty streets. It reminded Raisa of the night at the Winter Palace. They had expected a firestorm and found themselves walking to victory. Was this going to be a repeat? Could they really bring this war to a speedy end?

'Keep your eyes peeled,' Anishin warned. 'I find it hard to believe the Whites have simply cleared out without a fight. Fierce fighting is reported in other parts of the city.'

The thunder of hooves alerted them to a counter-attack. Mounted Whites swept round a corner, sabres hissing from scabbards, roars climbing into the chill air.

'Rapid fire!' Anishin yelled.

The Reds' first volley tore through the approaching cavalry, the horses' pitiful screams mixing with the last cries of their riders. Dead and dying horses crashed to the ground, spilling men across the road. The second wave of mounted soldiers jumped the sudden obstacles and careered into the ranks of the riflemen. Sabres flailed, flashing in the light. Now Reds screamed. Brutal chaos filled the street. Mayhem replaced the clear divisions of a moment before. Anishin was at the heart of the fighting, picking off the wheeling riders with precise, unhurried shots. The charge was broken. As the Whites peeled away and retreated down the road, Elena rested a hand on his shoulder.

'If I ever doubted your leadership,' she said, 'I apologise.'

Anishin started to reload the pistol. 'Don't tell anyone, but I was shitting myself.'

Raisa listened as if in a dream, peering through a window at eerie spectres in a fantasy world.

'But I am part of it,' she murmured.

'What did you say?' Elena asked brightly.

Raisa permitted herself an embarrassed smile. 'Nothing. I was thinking out loud.'

Elena squeezed her arm and looked around. 'Half a dozen dead. Shit.'

'Fifteen of the enemy,' Anishin noted.

'Do you think I even care anymore?' Elena asked. 'After all the dead I've seen, I've only got tears for my own comrades.'

'They are all human,' Raisa said.

Elena tossed her head.

'You're too soft for war, my sister.'

Raisa frowned.

'We can't kill them all, Elena. One day we will have to make peace.'

Anishin's face was grim. 'The only way we will make peace is through the victory of the proletarian revolution. Move out.'

The flotilla manned by the Kronstadt sailors was maintaining withering fire from the river, silencing many of the pockets of White resistance. From time to time, a shell would punch into the surface of the river, throwing up fountains of foam, a reminder that the operation was far from over. Already, some of the bluejackets were scrambling up the bank on the city side to support the advance from Sviazshk.

'More women, eh?' one sailor said, winking at Raisa. 'We had Comrade Reissner on our vessel earlier. I'd keep her company any day.'

'Don't go giving Reissner the eye,' another warned him, only half-seriously. 'Raskolnikov would hang your nuts from the nearest tree.'

The advance was less tense now, almost relaxed. Armoured vehicles were rolling forward in the wake of the men on horseback. Raisa would like to have said cavalry, but these were no Cossacks. They plodded rather than charged through the detritus-littered streets. They encountered another officer from the Rifle Division, who was returning from a foray into the centre of the city.

'Keep a look-out for snipers. We've cleared most of them, but I don't have enough men to search all the buildings.'

They had reached an open square. There was a dead horse, spilled entrails still steaming, lying beside an overturned cart. The pitiful contents were strewn across the cobbles. There were some dead Whites. Children were stripping them of their boots. Raisa felt a tug of apprehension.

'Something's wrong,' she murmured.

'Get off the street,' Anishin was telling the children. 'Move, you little buggers.'

Holstering his pistol, he moved forward to clear them out of harm's way.

'You kids, it's dangerous. Clear off before you get yourselves shot.'

Still, they tugged at dead men's boots. Anishin looked back at his unit, waving them behind cover and inching into the square. There was exasperation in his body language.

'Will you get away from there? Kids....'

Before he could finish, a bullet thumped into his chest, spinning him round. He fell heavily, head cracking against the ground. His body was jerking, boots drumming on the paving stones. Without any hesitation, Elena started to run towards him.

'Cover me!'

A cry broke from Raisa's throat. 'Wait!'

'Cover me, for fuck's sake!'

Then Raisa was pumping shots at the unseen gunman, desperate rounds punching more holes into already pockmarked walls. Elena tried hoisting Anishin on her shoulders, but he was too heavy. She was reduced to tugging at his ankles. His body was limp, leaving a trail of blood as Elena dragged him out of the line of fire. Her breathing was tortured as she heaved at the dead weight. Two more shots from the upper floors overlooking the square thudded into the ground nearby.

'He's dead,' Raisa cried. 'Can't you see? Vassily's gone. Come back!.'

Elena shook her head stubbornly. 'He's breathing. He's...'

A third gunshot hit her in the back, throwing her to the ground as if she had been punched. A terrified scream tore Raisa's throat.

'No!'

Elena was flailing like a swimmer, all strength spent. Raisa dodged through the remorseless fire. There were two snipers at least. She had hold of Elena. Even now, her lover-comrade refused to give up on her commissar.

'What about Vassily? I won't leave him!'

'Look at him,' Raisa yelled. 'Face facts, my love. He's dead.'

She finally succeeded in dragging her wounded lover clear. 'Where are you hit?'

Elena sagged in her arms.

'My side. I think they broke a rib. It stings like a son of a bitch.'

Raisa sobbed with relief. 'You'll be OK. You'll live.' She turned. 'Medic! Somebody help me here.'

'Don't fuss,' Elena said, swatting Raisa away. 'I'm fine.'

But she didn't seem fine. Her words were beginning to slur. She was heavy against Raisa. That's when Raisa felt the wetness against her stomach. Blood was pumping out, coming in fast, ugly spurts. Elena's eyes were dimming.

'Help me!'

By now, they were both drenched in blood.

'No!'

Elena was inert, impossible to support. They slumped to their knees while the men crowded round. One started to tug at Elena's clothing to examine the wound.

'Fuck! There's a hole you could get two fingers in.'

The blood was unstoppable. Raisa continued to press down on her lover's body, desperate to staunch the outflow. She was slithering in the sticky puddle around Elena's now inert form. Tears were spilling down her cheeks because she knew, she *knew*. Finally, there was help.

'I am Zhukhov. I am a doctor here in Kazan.'

'You have to save her. I order you to save her.'

But there was no salvation coming from Zhukhov's hands. After a brief examination, he told Raisa what she already knew.

'I am so sorry,' he murmured. 'Your friend is dead.'

'No,' Raisa pleaded. 'She can't be. I didn't get to speak to her, to tell her I love her. Tell me it's not true.'

There were reassuring hands on her shoulders, but she didn't feel them.

She was numb.

There was a funeral. Scarlet banners snapped in the wind. Red commissars gave their orations, full of fire and confidence in the world revolution to come. Raisa didn't hear a word, just the dull boom of their voices. She would have to leave Elena there, alongside her fallen comrades in a common grave. When the official, military funeral started to break up, Anishin's command stayed. It was Konstantin who urged Raisa to speak.

'You are the political officer, Comrade Raisa. You have the words.'

Raisa moved like a sleepwalker, stumbling to the edge of the pit where the gravediggers waited to cover the fallen.

'Do I have words?' she asked. 'Words are easy enough. We use them all the time. We use them to stir ourselves to battle, to summon our strength to walk into Hell.'

She registered the bowed heads.

'That's what we do, Comrades, isn't it? To save our revolution, we walk into Hell. Can you imagine people who rush towards shards of red hot metal, machine gun fire that can tear them in half, the points of bayonets? It's crazy. Most of us are not even soldiers, we are trying to become soldiers. We do it, because we believe in the liberation of humanity, in the worldwide socialist revolution. We walk into Hell in the hope of a Heaven on Earth.'

Her voice broke and she threw back her head, loose hair whipping her face.

'We lost good comrades today, the best mankind could offer to the jackals of war. You will all have names you would want mentioned. I will talk of just two. Comrade Anishin was my friend. He was reliable, honest and true. He wasn't a soldier, either. He was a metalworker from the Vyborg. He died because he tried to guide some children to safety.'

Before she could finish, she broke down completely, throwing her arms up twice, three times as she tried to find her voice, but it kept drowning in uncontrollable sobs.

'But Elena, my Elena, she was life to me. I know there are those among you that don't understand our love, you fear it, but she was me and I was her. How many chances in one lifetime do you get to have a love like that? Sometimes, in these moments, orators try to find some speck of comfort. Comrades, there is none. There is no other place where we will meet again. There is no consolation. I must walk alone without her for the remainder of my days, somebody I thought would always be at my side.'

Again, she succumbed to loss and despair, her voice a shriek like the keening of a seagull on the wind.

'But we who live on, we will endure. We will be the memory of our comrades. We will make their spirits live through our example. They died so that a socialist world could rise from the flames and ashes of war.'

The soldiers mumbled their way through the Internationale and walked away. Some struggled to look Raisa in the eye. Konstantin, still bandaged from his wounds, took her hand for a moment and wept openly.

'Forgive me for the things I said about you, the things I said about Elena.'

Raisa squeezed his hand and nodded. He walked away into the mist, a grey figure slowly fading from view. She turned to watch the burial detachment tossing shovelfuls of earth onto the row of corpses.

'Words,' she murmured.

Did she even believe them herself?

Pavel

The repetitive clickety-clack of the train was making him drowsy. Moscow was already far behind. He was going back to red Petrograd, not as a victor, but as a survivor. Blood and fire had consumed the Don and the Kuban, devoured the lives of comrades, but he was on his way back, at least for a few days.

'Are you asleep?' Mikhail asked.

'No,' Pavel said. 'I'm not like you. I can't sleep on trains. How do you do it?'

'I just empty my mind.'

'Easier for you than me,' Pavel taunted, earning him a backhanded slap across the head.

'You should be happy,' Mikhail asked. 'You're going home to your wife and child. I'm a single man, nothing to go back to.'

Pavel's cheek was damp from the condensation on the window and he had a sour taste in his mouth.

'We've lost too many good men to be happy, Mikhail Vassilievich.'

Mikhail rubbed the back of his skull on the headrest to relieve an itch.

'I think about them too, you know.'

Pavel was still brooding over their weeks in the Don and the Kuban, the great victory at Ekaterinodar and the lives their generals had thrown away in the aftermath.

'I was their commanding officer. I bear responsibility for my unit.'

'You take it too much to heart,' Mikhail said. 'War's shit, whichever way you look at it.'

Pavel remembered the morning the Whites came. 'I had Nikita's blood all over me. We had to watch while they shot our men and left their bodies in a fucking ditch.'

That's when Abram returned from the toilet and dropped into the seat next to him. 'There's one death you don't have on your conscience, isn't there?'

Pavel summoned a half-smile. 'I still find it hard to believe you got out of there alive. It can't have been more than a matter of a split-second, an instant.'

Abram nodded. 'It was the strangest moment of my life. The sunlight flashed on the barrel of the gun the way I predicted. I squeezed my eyes shut and waited for the end. Then that shot rang out and I thought, what the fuck, is this the afterlife?'

Mikhail laughed heartily. 'Bollocks to the afterlife. It was a Red sharpshooter blowing the White officer's fucking head off.'

Pavel remembered the moment. He was already beginning to squeeze the trigger when the Red sniper saved Abram's life. In one easy movement, Pavel had shifted his target and shot a second White through the eye socket, sending terror crackling through the enemies' ranks.

'Our comrades came from nowhere,' Mikhail said.

'Not quite,' Pavel said, correcting him. 'The commanding officer told me they'd been moving forward through the grass for some time. It was the strangest game of cat and mouse I've ever seen. The Whites were creeping up on us and the Reds were following them. We must be the luckiest bastards alive.'

'Four of us left,' Abram said, holding up his fingers. 'Four out of our entire unit. That's more than lucky.'

Pavel nodded. 'All the rest are ghosts who are going to stand at the bottom of my bed every night for the rest of my life.' He turned Abram's way. 'Is it the same for you, Abram? Do you see their faces?' He turned to Mikhail. 'Do you?'

The answer lay in the ensuing silence, the bowed heads and thought-clouded eyes of the three men. Abram finally broke the silence.

'You must be looking forward to seeing Nina and your kid.'

He followed the brief exchange of glances between Pavel and Mikhail.

'Am I missing something?'

Mikhail nudged his friend. 'Pavel here wants to have his cake and eat it. He's got a wife who loves him, but his affections are elsewhere.'

Abram remembered strained conversations on nights before battle. This made sense.

'Raisa?'

'Yes, Raisa.'

'What's she like?'

Abram saw Pavel's hesitation. Soldiers usually like to talk about their women, to boast, to remember, to imagine intimacy denied. Pavel was strangely reticent about the women in his life.

'She's beautiful.'

'Any woman is beautiful to a man in love.'

'She loves another woman.' Pavel fumbled for a cigarette. 'Isn't that a bastard?' He was surprised at the lack of reaction from Abram. 'You don't seem surprised.'

'It's not that,' Abram answered. 'I have nothing to say.'

'Mikhail laughs at me,' Pavel said.

That brought a protest. 'No, I don't!'

'Enough of me,' Pavel said. 'What about you? Do you have a sweetheart?'

'I do,' Abram said. 'She is a long way away from here.'

'In England?'

Abram nodded. 'London. She lives in Bloomsbury.'

'Strange kind of name. What's it like?'

'It is a good place to live. It is very quiet and bourgeois in the English way.'

Mikhail was interested. 'What's her name? What does she do?'

'Her name is Rebecca. She wants to be a writer. Her father has a bookselling business so there is no great pressure on her to find employment.'

'Is she a Communist?'

'She is a member of the Labour Party.' He saw Mikhail's frown. 'You would call her a Menshevik.'

'And what do you call her?' Pavel asked.

Abram leaned forward. 'Anything she wants so long as she lets me kiss her.'

'A kiss? Is that all you get?'

Abram frowned. 'That's my business.'

'The way I feel,' Mikhail said, 'I want more than a kiss the first time I meet a woman.'

'What woman?'

Mikhail grinned. 'Any bloody woman who'll have me.'

Pavel closed his eyes and smiled. 'Ah, a desperate one.'

The three of them laughed.

'What's so funny?' Volodya asked, sliding in next to Pavel.

'Well, look who's just surfaced. How did you do chatting up that little nurse?'

Volodya shrugged. 'She's got a fiancé in Kiev. Faithful to him too. That was a waste of half an hour.'

Pavel shook his head and the train rumbled on towards Moscow and, beyond that, red Petrograd.

Pavel walked through the locomotive steam flanked by his comrades. To his surprise, Nina was waiting for him. In her arms was a healthy-looking baby boy, just a few months old. She rushed towards Pavel and embraced him with her free arm, planting a kiss on his lips.

'How did you know when I would arrive?' Pavel asked.

'After I got your letter, I came here each and every day to meet the troop trains.'

Mikhail cleared his throat. 'Hear that, Pavel Sergeyevich? I wish I had a woman here in Peter who loved me that much.'

Nina was suddenly self-conscious as she became aware of the other men accompanying her husband.

'You know Mikhail, of course,' Pavel said. 'And Volodya, Svetlana's boy. This is Abram.'

'And this,' Nina said, 'is your son, Roman.'

Pavel took the boy. To his surprise, despite his absence at the Front, there was no resistance and there were no tears.

'He seems to know his father,' Abram said.

Roman wrapped his hand round Pavel's finger.

'Will you look at that?' Pavel said, beaming. 'What a grip!' He turned his son this way and that. 'He's well fed.'

'That's Svetlana's doing,' Nina said. 'But for her help and Anna's, I don't know what we would have done. There are children dying of starvation across this city.'

'Watch you don't attract the attention of the Cheka,' Mikhail said. 'They put people up against the wall for getting more than their fair share of food. They've got men at roadblocks confiscating supplies.'

They walked past men hanging huge, red banners from the station walls. They proclaimed the first anniversary of the Great October Revolution.

'Of course,' Pavel said. 'It's a year already.'

'It seems like an age,' Mikhail said. 'There were times I didn't think I would make it back to Peter.'

'Was it terrible out there?' Nina asked.

Pavel nodded slowly. 'Let's talk about happier things. We are alive and the revolution is a year old. What's planned?'

'There are going to be processions to commemorate the fallen,' Nina told him. 'Then there will be a torchlight parade.' She hugged Roman. 'And fireworks. Our little boy is going to see his first firework display.'

'There were plenty of fireworks in Cossack country,' Mikhail said ruefully.

'They are going to rename the streets,' Nina said, as they walked towards the tram stop. 'The Nevsky Prospect is going to be called October 25th Prospekt. Liteiny will be Volodarsky Prospect to celebrate our fallen comrade's life. Palace Square will be Uritsky Square because that is where he died.' She winked at Pavel. 'You'll like this one, the Police Bridge is going to be the People's Bridge.'

'Police are people,' Pavel said, 'I suppose.'

'Not the Cheka,' Mikhail said.

'Knock it off,' Pavel said. 'They're on our side.'

'The Chekists have only got one side,' Mikhail retorted, 'and that's their own. I don't like the bastards.'

'So when do the celebrations begin?' Abram asked, keen to move the conversation away from the dangerous subject of the Extraordinary Commission.. 'I barely know what day it is any more.'

'It's tonight,' Nina said. 'You just got home in time.'

Pavel glanced at his comrades. 'Lucky us.'

At the tram stop, Mikhail embraced Pavel.

'I'll be on my way,' he said. 'You never know. I might just find myself a good woman.' He laughed. 'Or the temporary loan of some other man's good woman. Or a very bad one. It doesn't matter either way. Let's hope they give us a decent spell of leave before they ship us back out to some fly-blown hell-hole to get shot at again.'

Volodya was on his way a few moments later.

'How long can you stay?' Nina asked.

'A week,' Pavel told her. 'Two at most. The pressure on some Fronts is easing. The German and Hungarian revolutions have begun.'

'So why can't you stay?'

'The war isn't done with us yet.' Pavel glanced at Abram. 'What about you, my friend?'

'I will stay with my uncle. He lives on the Vyborg side.'

'Will you be looking for somebody to share your bed?'

'Comrade, I have a sweetheart,' Abram said. 'I will read and play the piano.'

'You play?'

'Yes, quite well actually. Maybe I will entertain the two of you sometime.'

There was another embrace then the three comrades parted, carrying with them the scars of war, the ones you could touch and the ones nobody could see. They passed women collecting for the soldiers at the Front.

'You don't need to donate,' the one nearest them told Pavel as he started to fumble for change. 'You are already making your contribution.'

'I'll still chip in,' Pavel told her. 'Every penny is needed.'

He knew what lay in store, of course. Nina put Roman to bed for a nap and they made love. Later, the three of them sat at the window, watching the fireworks exploding in the black emptiness of the northern sky. They could just make out the sound of an orchestra playing the Internationale.

'It is a shame it had to rain,' Nina said.

'It is Petrograd in autumn,' Pavel said. 'What do you expect?'

They returned Roman to bed, but his sleep was interrupted by the fireworks and he cried incessantly for a while.

'The only thing that settles him is to take him into my bed,' Nina said. 'Do you mind?'

'Of course not.' He gazed at the window. 'I think I'll go for a walk anyway. I would like to see the celebrations.'

Nina tensed, just for a moment. 'Of course. Don't be too long.'

Pavel wandered among the crowds on pavements still gleaming with the recent rains. There was a chill in the air, but he walked with his greatcoat open and flapping. It was good to be back in red Peter, the city that was, according to every fluttering scarlet banner, the cradle of the world socialist revolution. He stopped to hear Zinoviev speak.

'We will definitely live to see the moment when not only we but the French, English and the American have their own Smolny,' he declared.

Pavel had always thought Zinoviev something of a windbag and he found it hard to forgive him for initially opposing the revolution. There seemed to be something genuine about the hope in his voice, however. Maybe there would at last be some respite for beleaguered October.

'Long live the revolutions that are approaching and those that have already arrived!'

The orchestra struck up the Internationale once more and Pavel walked on. There were hydroplanes skipping over the black waters of the Neva and necklaces of lights strung across the decks of the ships. Faces lit and dimmed as searchlights slashed the darkness. Even after the privations and disillusion of war, Pavel felt his heart leap. October lived. Beyond the borders of Russia, the world working class was at last stirring. Petrograd, drab and hungry for so many months was gaudy with hope. He was passing the Palace of Labour when he heard a shout from across the road.

'Pavel Sergeyevich!'

He turned to see Svetlana and waved. Coincidences could be happy, after all. Imagine his joy when he saw who was with her.

'Raisa, you are returned.'

Yet her face did not light. Her eyes were dim. She was thinner, gaunt somehow, as if all vitality had been drained from her. Pavel searched for an explanation for this transformation. Svetlana drew him aside.

'It's Elena,' she explained. 'She died in the taking of Kazan.'

Pavel immediately seized Raisa's hands and kissed them.

'Forgive me,' he cried. 'I had no idea. Raisa. How did it happen?'

Svetlana put an arm round Raisa's shoulder.

'Talk to Pavel,' she said. 'I will wait over there.'

The beam of the searchlight caught Raisa's face and she spoke falteringly.

'I am lost,' she said, 'quite lost. She was my heart, my soul. I thought we would be together forever. Life is cruel, Pavel Sergeyevich. How could I have such happiness and have it torn away after so short a time?'

They found somewhere to sit amid the bustling crowds.

'Were you there?' Pavel asked. 'Did you see her fall?'

Raisa nodded, tears spilling down her cheeks.

'She tried to speak, but only blood came. It was her eyes. She knew she was dying, but she tried to pretend. For me.' She clawed at her hair. 'Anishin perished too, shot by the same sniper. It was all so futile.'

Pavel turned and looked at Svetlana. There was not the same pain in her eyes, just sadness and regret. She had been fond of poor Vassily, but she didn't love him. Raisa, on the other hand, was beside herself with grief.

'I can't accept it,' Raisa sobbed. 'She was there, Pavel. She was right there beside me, so alive, so full of hope for the future. How can that be?' She had her hands out in front of her. 'There is a human life. Then...then in a moment...it is gone.'

'How long have you been home?'

'Almost a month,' Raisa said. 'I work. I see to the needs of the children, but Pavel, I don't live. I don't know how any more. Elena was my whole life. I can't...'

He let her slump against him and ran his hands over her hair. So many times, he had dreamed of this moment, but it was reduced to ashes. He loved Raisa and she loved a ghost.

'I try to find her,' Raisa said. 'Is that not foolish, Comrade? I am a Marxist and a materialist, but I will her every moment to rise from her grave and haunt me. I imagine I can turn back the hands of time and hold her in my arms just once more, but that can never be, can it?'

'Raisa....'

Her words continued to gush out, desperate, anguished, a torrent of pain.

'I would give up everything I am and everything I have. I would create God himself, just to have her rise like Lazarus. Is that wrong of me, to wish for something that can never be?'

'No,' Pavel said. 'It is not wrong. Grief and loss are terrible things.'

'This pain,' Raisa said, 'it is unimaginable. Why must the world be so unforgiving? I was reduced to living on the street. Men used me as if I were their plaything. Should there not be some reward for that? It is as if I am lying in an open grave while shovel after shovel of dirt falls on me. Where is justice, Pavel? Where?'

She drew back from him.

'But for the children, I would have thrown myself into the Neva by now.' She shook her head. 'Do you see? I am not even allowed to end it. There are young lives that depend on me.'

Pavel stammered out a single platitude.

'Things will get better, Raisa.'

She stared at him as if he was mad.

'Will they?' she cried. 'How do you know? How can you? It is a month and time does not heal. It gets worse, not better. She was my friend, my comrade, my only true love and she is gone.'

The searchlight roamed once more along the riverside and caught her face. Pavel wanted to protect her, to discover some wise words that would reconcile her to her loss, but that was beyond his gifts. Finally, Svetlana made her way over.

'Are you done?'

Raisa nodded and got to her feet. Pavel noticed how Svetlana steadied her and linked her arm.

'I am sorry for your loss too, Svetlana,' he said. 'This war is consuming lives like a furnace swallowing fuel.' He squeezed Raisa's arm. 'Can I call on you while I am on leave?'

Raisa nodded absently then started walking. Svetlana whispered into Pavel's ear before hurrying to catch up.

'Please do. She needs a friend.' She shook her head. 'I have lost a beloved niece. She has lost everything.'

Pavel walked aimlessly after that, pausing in front of the Winter Palace where crowds had gathered.

'Hard to imagine, isn't it?' a soldier in uniform said.

'What's that?'

'A year. Look how much has changed,'

Pavel's mind was still full of Raisa's tearstained features.

'The autocracy gone. The provisional government gone. The Romanovs dead. Do you think we should have shot them, Comrade, I mean, kids and all?'

'Fuck knows,' Pavel answered. 'The Whites were advancing. Maybe they could have made Nicholas a figurehead for the counter-revolution.'

'Yes, but kids, for fuck's sake... Have you got kids?'

'A little boy.'

'I haven't. I don't want them either, not in a world that's gone to shit. These bastard imperialists are never going to accept our place in the world. Do you think we'll ever have peace?'

'Don't ask me, Comrade, I'm just a foot soldier like you.'

'Where did you serve?'

'Transcaucasus. You?'

'Nowhere yet. We're shipping out to Siberia soon. Lucky me, eh? Siberia in winter. I'll probably end up dead with my bollocks frozen to the ice on Lake Baikal.'

'Cheerful bastard, aren't you?' Pavel said.

The soldier clapped him on his shoulder.

'Happiest bugger in the whole of purgatory, that's me.'

He left without even saying his name. By the time Pavel got home, Nina was fast asleep, Roman curled up in the crook of her arm. Pavel found a blanket, wrapped himself in it and dozed fitfully in the chair opposite them.

Somewhere in the distance a cannon boomed.

Kolya

He opened the office door to see Leonid inside, back turned as he examined something on the desk. Kolya's hand lingered on the doorknob as his fellow Chekist went through his papers. For the last few weeks, they had barely talked. Leonid was an ugly feature of Kolya's life, like a cockroach in the larder. Deciding it was time to announce his presence, he slammed the door and walked to the middle of the room, head tilted to one side in a show of curiosity. If he had been expecting Leonid to jump, display one iota of embarrassment or try to cover up what he was up to, Kolya was in for disappointment. The intruder was untroubled at being discovered.

'So you're keeping cuttings, now, are you?' Leonid said, turning casually. 'Once a student, always a student. What's it for?' He grinned coldly as he flicked through the sheaf of newspaper articles. 'What is it? Academic research? Maybe you are planning to write a history of the commission.'

'I don't see that it is any of your business,' Kolya said. 'What do you think you're doing going through my desk drawers without permission?'

'I didn't have to open the drawers,' he sniffed, infuriatingly calm. 'You left it on top for all to see. If you want to hide your papers from prying eyes, you need to lock them away where nobody can see them. I was curious, that's all.'

Kolya could have called Leonid out as a liar, but what was the point? The man was a brutally effective operative, a rising star among killers.

'You marked this article in particular,' Leonid said. 'Why?'

Kolya took the cutting and ran his eyes over it. It was from *Krasnaya Gazeta*: 'The bourgeoisie has been taught a cruel lesson...Let our enemies leave us in peace to build a new life. If they do so, we shall ignore their simmering hatred and stop hunting them out. The Red Terror is over, at least until the White Terror begins again. The destiny of the bourgeoisie is in its own hands.'

'I don't see why you picked this one out from all the others,' Kolya said.

It wasn't true. He knew exactly why it was of interest.

'Why this one?' Leonid repeated. He took the folder back off Kolya. 'Why not a more representative article from some time earlier? 'Let there be floods of blood of the bourgeoisie –

more blood, as much as possible.' They are both from the same newspaper.'

Why did Kolya suddenly feel like a prisoner undergoing interrogation? He was Leonid's superior. Nevertheless, he found himself having to tread carefully.'And I am under no obligation to answer your questions,' Kolya answered acidly. 'It is because I agree with the *Gazeta*'s sentiments in the later article. Red terror is a response to the terror of our enemies, to English, American and Japanese boots on our soil, to the assassinations of our leaders...'

'There are enemy boots on our soil right now,' Leonid reminded him. 'The Whites are still butchering workers.'

'Our measures have stabilised the situation here in Peter,' Kolya said. 'What is the point of killing for killing's sake?'

'That's what Uritsky was saying just before a SR terrorist gunned him down in the street.' Leonid set the folder down on the desk. 'You're too soft-hearted to suppress counter-revolution, Kolya.'

'I am as determined as you, Comrade,' Kolya countered. 'The difference between us is that I see terror as a temporary weapon, a scalpel to cut out a cancerous growth. The moment my enemy blinks and accepts defeat, I will put it aside. What about you?'

Leonid chuckled. 'I'm a plain, blunt working man, Kolya, not an intellectual like you. I just take orders. I'm not interested in fancy words, only actions.' He inspected his fingernails. 'That reminds me. I've got something here for you.'

He reached into his breast pocket, drew out a sheet of paper folded into quarters, and offered it to Kolya. Was that a smirk playing on his lips? Kolya felt a worm of unease squirming inside him. The instant he unfolded the note, apprehension turned to horror.

'What is this?'

Leonid was enjoying Kolya's reaction.

'Surely it needs no explanation, Comrade. It is a delivery note, one of several in my possession.'

Kolya found himself blinking rapidly, trying to recover his composure.

'It is a little odd, don't you think? The rations for institutions such as children's homes are set out quite clearly. What I fail to understand is why rations for thirty individuals are being delivered to a home with – let me see – thirteen, fourteen, fifteen, yes, sixteen children. It is something of an anomaly, don't you think?'

'It is a supplement to the diet of hungry children. Would you begrudge them a little extra food?'

'It's not for me to make such decisions,' said Leonid. Then, pointedly, he added. 'Or you, Comrade. The rations are established by a higher authority. It's not for us to change the rules. Imagine how it looks though. Our remit includes the suppression of corruption, after all.'

'What do you want?' Kolya demanded, desperate to force the demons back into their box.

'Let's not jump the gun, Comrade,' Leonid said. 'Examine please the names on this note. You will see that the home's founder and current manager is one Raisa Alexeyevna Kulakova. I think you know her.'

Kolya wanted to tell him to cut the crap, but there was worse to come.

'It seems Comrade Kulakova was, until recently, acting as a political officer on the Volga Front. All this at the tender age of seventeen too. She must be quite a woman. We wouldn't want to see her get into trouble over something as trivial as a delivery note. I mean, a hero of the Red Army brought down by an irregularity.'

He waited a beat before continuing.

'Let's see. What else? Oh yes, while she was gone, the home's supervisor was Comrade Svet....'

'Enough!' Kolya snapped. 'You can stop playing your bloody games, Leonid. We both know who was good enough to put a roof over those kids' heads and food in their mouths. We....'

This time, it was Leonid's turn to interrupt. 'I am sure that the comrades had the best of intentions. I am not made of stone, Kolya, but you can see how it looks. As I just said to you, the Cheka has a responsibility to stamp out corruption with all the means at its disposal. You know as well as me that four members of this very commission were shot for corruption recently.'

That set Kolya's flesh crawling. Leonid cleared his throat and produced a second sheet of paper.

'We now come to an issue of some delicacy, Comrade. It seems that the deliveries have been signed off by an employee at the Commissariat of Food Supplies. You may recognise the name.' He pointed out a signature. 'It is here.'

'Cut to the chase, Leonid. We both know Klara took care of it as a favour to me. What do you want?'

Leonid put on a mask of affronted innocence.

'Comrade!' he said. 'Whatever do you mean? I did not approach you in pursuit of personal gain. I am simply a member of the Extraordinary Commission doing his duty. You can see how this looks. If I can prevent a colleague being subjected to embarrassment or worse, that is what I will do.'

'It is quite innocent, Leonid,' Kolya answered, 'as you very well know. Those kids were on the verge of starvation. Everybody does these things to survive. We both know Party members who purchase bread from the bagmen. Yes, there are even Chekists who use the black market. Svetlana begged me to intervene on the children's behalf...'

'And you did it out of the goodness of your heart. I do understand. After all, what possible services could you demand in return?'

Kolya braced as if hit. 'How dare you insinuate that I wanted anything in return!'

Unmoved, Leonid crossed his arms.

'Here's the thing, the Commissariat of Public Welfare is struggling to provide enough food for the children at a number of homes in the city, but nowhere do I see such generous rations. Maybe they could all do with the patronage of a member of the Cheka.' He took the sheets back and thrust them in his pocket. Then he hesitated, took one sheet out again and gave a theatrical frown.

'There is one invoice that is more problematic than the others, Kolya.'

Kolya's heart thudded. What did Leonid have on them?

'You see, Klara seems to have been struggling to get enough food for the home on one occasion and re-routed supplies from a Red Army consignment.'

Kolya could feel his neck burning. There had been quite a scandal in the Party press about the theft of foodstuffs urgently needed for the Front.

'Embezzlement of supplies, Kolya,' Leonid drawled. 'That incurs the death penalty, as I am sure you know. I thought it best to put this material before you now, Kolya, because we are friends. I simply want your advice. What should I do with it?'

Kolya's mind was racing as he tried to anticipate Leonid's next move. When it came, it took him by surprise.

'Let me leave it with you,' he said. 'Think it over. We will speak again quite soon.'

Kolya met Svetlana in his new room at the Astoria.

'What's this about?' she demanded. 'There was a message on my desk. If you think I am breaking off work to climb in the sack with you, think again.' She closed the door with her hip. 'And why the Astoria, of all places? Klara is bound to find out I have been here.'

Kolya was agitated. 'Svetlana, I need you to hear me out. This is serious. Forget Klara. She knows anyway. This is the only place I could think of. The flat at Mrs Turisheva's has been occupied by new tenants. My office is out of the question.'

'You've got five minutes,' Svetlana said. 'If this is just a trick to get me into bed, I'm out of here.'

'Svetlana, please sit down,' Kolya said. 'This affects both of us, Raisa too.'

At that, Svetlana frowned. 'Kolya, you've got me worried. What is this?'

'It's Leonid,' he explained. 'He's got something on us.'

At the mention of Leonid's name, Svetlana's face filled with dismay. This was the man that had stripped her naked with his eyes. She listened as Kolya explained the situation. Within moments, her eyes were wide with concern.

'Embezzlement of supplies,' she repeated.

'Exactly,' Kolya said, 'and didn't friend Leonid love reminding me it carries the death penalty.'

'Does he wield so much power?' she asked. 'I thought he was just a driver.'

'Was,' Kolya replied. 'He's working his way up. The man is a sadist and a bully. He is also as cunning as a fox. So long as Dzerzhinsky and Uritsky, even Boky, ran things at Gorokhovaya, there was some kind of control over the likes of Leonid. Things are changing. You know there is corruption, I suppose?'

'Of course, but how does that affect us?'

'He has a record of everything delivered to the home.'

'We were feeding hungry children!'

'Believe me, a man like Leonid can make even that seem sinister.'

Svetlana ran her hands through her hair, trying to think things through.

'So he is blackmailing us?'

'He's a clever bastard. He is manipulating us, pulling our strings as if we were dancing puppets.'

'To what purpose?'

Kolya was surprised that a woman who had been through so much could be so naïve.

'Do I need to spell it out to you? Leonid is a man on the make. He will let us dangle then he will set out his terms.'

'Let him do his worst,' Svetlana retorted. 'You have your position. I have been in the Party longer than either of you. Nobody would think me corrupt. Why should we worry about some petty functionary?'

Kolya took her hands, willing her to grasp the gravity of the situation. 'Hear me out, Svetlana.' After a moment's hesitation, he continued. 'In normal times, nobody would believe Leonid's accusations. In the atmosphere of hysteria created by the war, the Cheka has got free rein. There have been members of the Cheka itself arrested or even shot for less than this. Leonid has proof that we gave Raisa's kids preferential treatment. Peter is starving. Think how it looks.'

Svetlana cast a meaningful glance at Kolya's rooms. 'Preferential treatment, you say? What will you be eating tonight, *Comrade*?'

Kolya overlooked the jibe. 'If Leonid is half as clever as I think, he has other things he could use. I interceded on behalf of that corrupt factory manager, Nagorny and his storeman Ionov. This was in a factory given over to war production. Do you see how he could twist it to make us look like enemies of the revolution?'

'And I was at the factory that day,' Svetlana said, her eyes darkening.

'So was Raisa. Do you see what I mean?'

'Shit!'

Now he had her attention. 'There was a time Moisei Uritsky had my back. Even Peters had a soft spot for me. Those days are gone, Svetlana. Men like Leonid increasingly have the ear of the Presidium. You said it yourself, the culture of the Party is decaying. You and I are steeped in the ideals of October. The same can't be said of Leonid.'

'He is the one who is corrupt, not us!'

'He has evidence. We don't.'

'Then we will go over his head.'

'To whom, Svetlana? You don't have Vassily Anishin to protect you. What would Comrade Lunacharsky think if those notes were put before him? This looks like a conspiracy to steal food out of the mouths of our troops. Then there is Zinoviev. He loves men like Leonid who are willing to play the part of the revolution's attack dogs. We must come to an accommodation with Leonid. We have no choice.'

Svetlana had a hand over her mouth as she digested Kolya's words. 'How do I tell Raisa? She has lost Elena. Those kids are all she has left. If their rations are cut...'

She didn't need to spell it out.

'It won't come to that,' Kolya told her. 'Leonid wants me to turn a blind eye to his activities. That means he needs me.'

'But for how long? I know men like this. He will just keep demanding more and more until he has no more use for you. Then what?'

They sat for some time, side by side, gazing into a bleak future.

'The reason Leonid can wield so much power is because of the weakness of the revolution,' Kolya said. 'War and famine are bleeding it dry. The best comrades are at the Front or running the machinery of the state. The likes of Leonid thrive like bugs in a worn-out mattress. Once the Whites are crushed and the international revolution comes to our aid, these opportunist bureaucrats will be tossed aside.'

'So what do you propose?'

'Just this,' Kolya said, 'we make some temporary concession so that we can see out this difficulty. Look at the news from the West. The red flag flies in Kiel. The German workers will come to the aid of Soviet Russia. It's worth it, Svetlana. We must buy ourselves some time.'

'And if it doesn't work out?'

Kolya stared at the carpet, fingers interlaced on his knees.

'Kolya, what if red Russia is left to stand alone? What if nothing comes of the events in Berlin, Vienna, Budapest. What if this is the way things are going to be?'

'Put aside your doubts, Svetlana,' Kolya urged. 'The German workers will save us then men like Leonid will be blown away like chaff. We didn't make a revolution to line the pockets of scoundrels. The future is ours, my love.'

He took her face in his hands and pressed his lips to hers.

'I promise.'

That is how Klara found them on opening the door. Her face drained of blood at the sight of Kolya's hands on Svetlana's cheeks.

'Well, isn't this fucking cosy,' she snarled.

'Klara…'

'Don't say it isn't how it looks,' Klara snapped. 'I know you're screwing that bitch.' She turned on Svetlana. 'You can hit me all you like, you Red whore, but you won't silence me.'

'Klara, stop shouting. Please.'

Kolya rose to his feet and reached out to touch her. She pushed him away.

'Let go of me, you bastard.'

Then Kolya was pinning her arms to her side.

'Listen to me, will you? The reason Svetlana's here is because that lousy fucker Leonid has found out about the extra rations going to the children's home.'

A flash of fright blew Klara's anger away.

'That's right,' Kolya said. 'He has an invoice that proves you redirected Army supplies to the home. Why did you take such a risk, Klara? That's sabotaging the war effort.'

'You told me the children were starving!'

Kolya softened his tone. 'I know. I'm sorry. I didn't mean to yell. Look, we could be in mortal danger, every one of us. I've told you about Leonid. He's dangerous. So you need to calm the fuck down and listen to me.'

If there was one thing that motivated Klara more than jealousy, it was self-preservation.

'What does he want?' Klara asked, face taut with anxiety.

'We don't know yet,' Kolya said, 'but we soon will.'

Raisa

'What do you think?' Dina asked.

The children gathered around the banner, anxious to hear Raisa's opinion.

'Children of the revolution,' Raisa read. 'That's beautiful.'

The slogan was painted in bright scarlet on a golden background. Raisa touched Iskra's nose affectionately.

'That's you and Dina and me and….all of you. How wonderful? How did you manage to make it without me finding out?'

'We waited until you were busy,' Dina replied.

'And you are always busy,' Iskra said. 'So it was easy.'

Raisa inspected the two faces painted either side of the slogan. 'And who are these two, I wonder. They don't look like children.'

'They're not,' Dina said.

'Could this be Comrade Kollontai?' Raisa ask, 'And this one Krupskaya?'

'Neither,' Iskra said.

'Comrade Reissner? Comrade Stasova?'

'It's you!' Iskra cried, pointing to the woman with the blond hair. 'And this is Elena.'

The little girl's voice trailed off. 'Is that all right?'

Raisa ran her fingers over the crude portrait of Elena and she smiled.

'Oh children, it is wonderful. You wanted to keep her alive. I love you all so much.'

Tears spilled down her cheeks, for her wonderful, fallen Elena, for herself. It was as if her heart tore, but in the cleft of pain was Elena's breath, her voice, her touch. Anna appeared with Svetlana at her side.

'The truck is here. We have to go.'

The truck had been lavishly decorated, transforming it from a military vehicle into a float. The procession of the proletarian children was part of the celebrations of the first anniversary of the revolution. Raisa's flock scrambled aboard, the girls in their white dresses, the boys in black trousers and white shirts, all excited that they were getting a break from the privations and drudgery of starving Petrograd. They all wore red kerchiefs. Iskra had a posy of chrysanthemums. As the vehicle rolled slowly towards Uritsky Square, Dina instructed two of the children to raise their banner. It earned generous applause from the crowds lining the street. Raisa, Svetlana and Anna sat in the background as the float progressed through the city streets.

'They all wanted to celebrate Elena's life,' Svetlana said. 'Dina organised them.' She lowered her voice to a whisper. 'They weren't sure how you would react.'

Raisa managed a smile. 'I know you have all been tiptoeing around me. I won't break, you know. My Elena lived and died the way she wanted. The time I had with her was the most precious in my whole life.'

'My niece had more life than a dozen others,' Svetlana sighed. 'I can't believe I will never see her again.'

Raisa's chin crumpled, but she managed to prevent the tears coming.

'Have you told Iskra the news?' Svetlana asked.

Raisa shook her head. 'I thought it would be a lovely surprise.'

As they moved from Uritsky Square down 25 October Prospect, there was renewed applause from the huge crowd as the floats full of children appeared to the strains of the Internationale. Banners and flags rippled in the chill wind. Handheld placards announced the young state's successes in literacy.

'Every child in the home can read,' Anna said. 'That is a great achievement. And they are all well-fed.'

Raisa and Svetlana swapped glances, but Anna continued, oblivious to their reaction and unaware of the crisis that was haunting them.

'We are giving these little ones a future,' she said. 'We will win this war. We will prevail. I know it.'

The band in front of them struck up the Internationale again and the children joined in, waving to the crowd.

'Can it really be only a year?' Raisa said, wondering at the banners commemorating twelve months since the October revolution. 'It is as if I have experienced three lives.'

'We all feel the same,' Svetlana agreed. 'During the Paris Commune, the workers won a city. We have won a great nation of one hundred and thirty million souls. In our lifetime, who knows, we may win the whole world.'

Raisa leaned her head against Svetlana's shoulder. 'This talk seems so unreal. Sometimes, we can't even put bread on the table. The gap between our dreams and the day to day reality is....' She searched for the word. 'It is beyond imagining.'

211

'We must be victorious,' Svetlana answered. 'Either we succeed or the capitalist nations will crush us underfoot. There is no middle way.' She pointed. 'There's Pavel with his wife and child, such a bonny little boy.'

Raisa caught Pavel's eye and wondered what it was, this bond between them. Nina held Roman's hand and got him to give them a wave. At the end of the procession, there were speeches, songs and dramatic tableaux. Everyone there knew the celebration concealed desperate privation.

'Have you all had a good time?' Raisa asked.

There was a chorus of enthusiastic voices. As it subsided, she turned to Iskra.

'I have a surprise for you.'

She waved and a smiling woman in her fifties appeared.

'Babushka!'

Iskra ran into her grandmother's arms.

'Svetlana searched for her every day,' Raisa explained. 'She got in touch with every factory, but there was no sign of Mrs Osipova. Then somebody remembered her at the Staryi Lessner plant and Svetlana went through the records.'

'I had to return to my village,' Mrs Osipova said, hugging Iskra. 'Imagine my surprise when Svetlana arrived to tell me my granddaughter was alive and well. I am here to take you home.'

For a few moments, Iskra seemed torn.

'I love my *babushka*,' she said, 'but there is everyone at the home too.' Her eyes blurred with tears. 'Do I have to choose?'

Raisa embraced her. 'You can't live in two places, many miles apart, little one. Mrs Osipova is your family, Iskra. We all love you, but it is right that you go back with her.'

Iskra sobbed against Raisa's body for a few moments then she wiped away her tears.

'You be a brave girl,' Raisa said. 'Your *babushka* will bring you back to visit.'

Iskra glanced hopefully at Mrs Osipova, who nodded. Before long, it was time for them to go. Iskra waved until she was lost from sight.

'You did a beautiful thing, Svetlana,' Raisa said. 'With everything else you have to do, I don't know how you found her.'

'Kolya helped,' Svetlana answered.

Raisa gave her a sideways look. 'I don't know how you can have anything to do with that man. He betrayed you.'

'Kolya has his flaws,' Svetlana said, 'as do we all.'

'I could never forgive something like that,' Raisa insisted.

'You are young,' Svetlana said, stroking Raisa's cheek. 'Life rubs off our edges.'

They arrived back at the home, weary but happy. Raisa's happiness didn't last long, Once the children were in bed, Svetlana told Raisa about their problem with Comrade Ahmetov.

'Does Anna know?' she asked.

'No,' Svetlana said, 'and I'd like to keep it that way.'

Raisa sat at her desk. While she was away on the Volga Front, Svetlana had organised the renovation of the house and Raisa now had a small office. She worked for a while then she opened the drawer and took out the medal with its red and white ribbon. Comrade Trotsky had awarded the Order of the Red Banner posthumously to Elena for her valour in saving Konstantin and in giving her own life to try to carry Ashinin from danger. Raisa held it to her breast and the tears fell, tears she had hidden from the children, from Anna and Svetlana.

'Why did you have to be so brave?' she sobbed. 'Why did you have to race to the front ranks in every battle?' There wasn't just sadness in her voice, but rage too, the rage of someone who has been robbed of a great joy. 'We were meant to be forever. We were meant to grow old together. We were meant to see a new world take shape.'

She kept the medal pressed to her heart, willing Elena's face to appear before her.

'I can't see you,' she moaned. 'Oh, my love, why must I live when you are gone? If I struggle to imagine your face now, what will I have left a year from now, five years, ten?'

She rocked back and forth 'I am seventeen and a half. I have lost a mother, been enslaved, loved and lost my heart and soul. Now, this Leonid Ahmetov wants to destroy everything I have built. He wants to take the food out of the mouths of children. What more can I endure?'

Snowflakes were dancing outside. She went to the window and gazed across the rooftops. The city looked so innocent, cloaked in white. Raisa's hand was on the pane. Suddenly, with a cry, she sank to her knees, palm sliding down the wall.

'I don't know how to go on,' she said. 'I am meant to keep these children safe, to educate and protect them, but I am little more than a child myself. I am scared.'

At that moment, she felt a light touch on her shoulder and saw the pale fingers, like lines of frost on her dress.

'Dina. How much did you hear?'

'Everything,' Dina answered. 'I know your heart is breaking, Raisa, but you must live for us. We worship you.'

She knelt beside Raisa and they embraced. They stayed that way for some time, oblivious to the cold.

'Is this the medal they gave her?' Dina asked. 'May I see?'

Raisa opened her palm.

'It is such a little thing,' Dina said, 'for a life.' She searched Raisa. 'You won't leave us, will you? You wouldn't....'

'Hush,' Raisa said. 'I am not going to take my life. I told you a story once, before I went away to Kazan. I thought a story was the way to talk to children, but you deserve better, don't you Dina? Like me, you have lived more than one life. You have had to grow up far too quickly. My heart broke when Elena died. It is broken now. It will never mend, but I will live. I will go on. We fought together for a cause greater than two silly little people....'

'You're not silly!'

Elena laid her palm on Dina's cold, hollow cheek.

'All human beings are flawed and silly and sad, but there is such glory inside us, such wonder. Great things can happen. I want to see what flawed silly, sad humanity can do. I will not give up. I will do anything, anything, to protect you and fight for a socialist future. Do you understand what I am saying to you?'

Dina nodded. 'Of course I understand.' She glanced over her shoulder. 'I didn't come to spy on you. The other children say they can't sleep. They miss little Iskra. Anna is sharing one bed with Group One and some of Group Two. Will you get in with the rest of us?'

Raisa laughed. 'Of course. I think I need some company myself tonight.'

They climbed to their feet and Raisa put the medal away in the drawer. They squirmed their way into the overcrowded bed. Soon they were fast asleep.

All except Raisa.

Dina said she understood, but she didn't. Not really. She could not imagine what Raisa was prepared to do to keep her children safe. She lay awake for another hour, dwelling on the Comrade Ahmetov problem. Svetlana had even hinted he wanted to possess her as the price of keeping quiet about the extra food supplies. Raisa's insomnia went on and on, well into the dead, dark hours of the night.

Until she had made a decision. Nobody would be allowed to hurt the children in her care. Nobody had a right to starve them.

The next day, she had a job to do.

Leonid

He had a spring in his step as he walked down the corridor and into Comrade Markov's office. Kolya was working at his desk.

'How was Svetlana?' Leonid asked as he kicked the door shut behind him. 'I would love to have been a fly on the wall when little Klara walked in.'

There was something about Leonid's voice that made Kolya's flesh crawl at every word.

'You know about our meeting?' He met his tormentor's gaze with a frosty stare. 'Are you spying on me?'

'Not at all,' Leonid drawled. 'We've got plenty of Cheka comrades living at the Astoria now. You know how the rumour mill works. She's a beautiful woman, your Svetlana. Klara's quite a looker too. Some might say you've got a surfeit of riches there.' He smirked. 'You might want to throw one of them my way.'

Kolya reacted angrily. 'You're sick, you bastard!'

Leonid was enjoying Kolya's discomfort.

'I am a man in possession of certain documents. Did you read the recent circular, Kolya? And I quote: *'The embezzlement of Army supplies will be ruthlessly suppressed.'* Ruthlessly suppressed. I wonder what that looks like. We should negotiate, Comrade Kolya, not shout at one another. We both love women, Comrade, and we have similar tastes. I would happily take Svetlana off your hands.'

Kolya gripped the reins on his temper. Leonid watched with amusement as his face went taut with suppressed fury.

'My private life is none of your business,' Kolya snapped. 'I'm getting tired of your games. Just tell me your price and don't you dare mention either Svetlana or Klara again. You're not worth the dirt on their shoes. I don't trade in people's lives.'

Leonid inspected his fingernails.

'You are a member of the Cheka. That is precisely what you do. Look Kolya, we are Communists....'

'No,' Kolya said, interrupting. '*I* am a Communist. You are an opportunist. You joined after the revolution to further your own interests.'

'You should be careful what you're saying, Kolya,' Leonid said, his face suddenly like stone. 'I am the one with all the cards. Your tendency to show leniency has been noted by Comrade Zinoviev. There is also some concern about your, shall we say, *colourful* personal life.'

Kolya glared.

'Grigory Abramov – I seem to remember you know Comrade Grigory from your student days – he thinks you are responsible for a decline in Comrade Svetlana's work for the Party. You…distract her.'

'Get out!'

'Don't be silly, Kolya,' Leonid said. 'Do you really want me to go down the corridor and talk to a member of the Presidium about your arrangement with the children's home, the irregularities at the engineering plant? I can make you sound like a counter-revolutionary saboteur. All we are doing here is sorting out a little, local difficulty. Here is the way I see it. There are several elements to our discussion.'

He waited for an interruption, but there was none.

'I assume you want those kids to get their rations.'

Kolya gave a brief nod.'It would break Raisa's heart to see them starve.'

'Good,' Leonid said. 'That means there must be no more incriminating delivery notes.'

He plucked the documentation from his pocket. 'These, for example. We wouldn't want anyone getting the wrong idea about Klara, Svetlana or little Raisa now, would we?' He paused. 'There's a thought. If you want to keep Klara and Svetlana to yourself, maybe you could put in a word with Raisa for me.'

There was a second when Leonid thought he saw something in Kolya's expression, a little flame of knowledge, but he put it to the back of his mind. After all, he was the puppet master and he had these four inadequates dancing to his tune.

'Now,' Leonid said, 'on a completely unrelated matter, things are getting a bit strained with my wife at the moment. She doesn't appreciate the hours I keep, you see. I would like somewhere of my own to relax, away from the stresses of work and family, somewhere like a room at the Astoria perhaps. I am sure it is within your gift to recommend me for accommodation there.'

'You are not the only one who can enter another man's office,' Kolya said coldly. 'I saw the letter you were writing to request a room at the

Astoria.' He took a set of keys from his desk drawer and threw it Leonid's way. 'There.'

Leonid caught the keys, pocketed them and smiled.

'There is one more little thing,' he said.

He heard the sigh in Kolya's voice.

'Yes.'

'It is about scrutiny, you see.'

Leonid enjoyed the look of confusion.

'Yes,' he continued, 'I am a private kind of man. I like to get on with things on my own initiative. This isn't a criticism, you understand, but you seem to want to oversee everything I do. That's...restricting.'

'So you want me to cut you some slack?'

Leonid slapped his leg. 'There you go! I knew you would understand. Yes, I'd like more responsibility. It's these reports I have to write, detailing everything I do. Couldn't you accept summaries? Include the main points without cluttering the things with unnecessary detail?'

'Unnecessary detail...?' Kolya laid his hands palm down on his desk. 'Do you have anything in mind?'

'No,' purred Leonid, 'nothing in particular. It's a general thing. We can meet once a week, say, and go through what I've been doing. There's no need for all this burdensome red tape, is there?'

This was an easy promise for Kolya to fulfil. Leonid knew he kept the most rigorous records on the whole section.

'That is not a problem.'

Leonid beamed and thrust out a hand. Kolya flicked a glance at the huge palm and thick fingers, but he kept his hands to himself. Leonid simply laughed.

'I am so pleased that we could iron out this little problem. I think I'll get a bottle of Vodka to celebrate.'

Buttoning his coat, a satisfied Leonid crunched through the snow to the corner of Gorkhovaya and took a swig of Vodka from the bottle.

'I need to celebrate,' he announced to the darkness, flushed with his victory. 'Let's see. What shall I do?'

That's when he saw her.

'A celebration is it, Comrade?' Azure eyes flashed. 'Maybe I can help you with that.'

'Can you now?' Leonid said, looking the woman up and down.

She had the most entrancing eyes. She was wearing a rather fine coat, fur hat and a scarf wound round the lower part of her face. The effect was quite tantalising.

'You are obviously a man of some influence,' she said, 'coming out of the Cheka headquarters armed with a full bottle of Vodka.'

She ran her hands down her stomach and planted them on her hips. Even in her warm winter coat, Leonid could detect a fine figure beneath. He produced the keys to his Astoria room and jangled them in front of her.

'I can promise you a late-night snack,' he said, 'some Vodka and a very comfortable bed with crisp, white sheets. The Astoria is a good hotel. There aren't many young women who are lucky enough to access such comfort.'

His throat was dry. She really did have the most entrancing gaze. She reminded him of someone. He took a step forward and held out the Vodka, swinging the bottle to and fro.

'Would you like a sip?' he asked. 'There is nothing better for making us forget our troubles.'

'Later,' she said, her breath frosting as she spoke.

Leonid noticed that a lock of blond hair had escaped from her hat.

'I like blondes,' he said, indicating the wisp of hair.

'You're in luck then,' she said. 'I am a natural blonde…everywhere'

She was inflaming his senses. Why wouldn't she peel off that infuriating scarf?

'Show me your face, darling,' he said.

'Why are you in such a hurry?' she answered. 'Just be patient. You won't be disappointed.' She gave another coquettish smile. 'It's nice at the Astoria, you say?'

'Very nice,' Leonid said, his pulse quickening. He couldn't wait to run his hands through her hair. Fuck that, he couldn't wait to feel that trim, little body under him. He was already hard. 'There aren't many women in the whole of Peter who will find a place half as comfortable to lay their heads tonight. Did you know the hotel was built to accommodate tourists coming to Russia for the Romanov tercentenary?' He chuckled. 'I bet the owners didn't think the hotel would still be going long after the autocracy had fallen.'

She gave a cute, little sway of her hips. 'You've got me interested, Comrade.'

'Why don't you take off that scarf, my dear? If the rest of your face matches your eyes, you must be quite something.'

She turned and walked to the corner of an alley.

'I assume you would like to examine the goods before you purchase,' she said.

His throat went dry as she leaned against the wall, unbuttoning the top three buttons of her coat. She winked and turned the corner.

'Coming?' she called.

Leonid hurried through the snow, stumbling once and producing a delightful laugh from the object of his desire. He followed her into the alley. To his surprise, she was nowhere to be seen.

'Hello?' he said. 'Where are you hiding?'

He turned slowly.

'You like games, do you? Well, come along to the Astoria and we can play.' He was getting frustrated. 'Oh, come out, for fuck's sake. I'm freezing my bollocks off out here.'

That's when he became aware of movement behind him and turned, a broad grin on his face.

'There you are. A real little tease, aren't you?'

She was standing in a doorway, watching him.

'Well,' Leonid said, 'let's see what you've got.'

She held open her coat and he ran his eyes down her body, from her bare throat to the line of cleavage revealed by her dress.

'Beautiful,' he said. 'Now the face.'

He watched the way she peeled away her muffler, saw her full lips and frowned.

'You're...Raisa!'

'Well remembered,' she said, 'Kolya tells me you wanted me in exchange for your silence.'

'Well well, so you're happy with the transaction, are you? Let's have a kiss and a cuddle then, cutie, get you in the mood for a night of passion at the Astoria.'

'I am Raisa Alexeyevna Kulakova, Communist. I don't sell myself to any man, my friend, especially not a prize prick like you.'

Leonid scowled. 'What did you say?' He stepped forward, raising a meaty hand. 'Oh, I am going to teach you a lesson, you little bitch.'

At that moment, he saw the gun.

'What the fuck!'

Raisa squeezed the trigger and he felt a burning pain in his stomach. Looking down in horror, he saw the band of scarlet spreading. Then the gun roared again and his face hit the snow. The bullet had torn away his balls.

'No more games for you, Leonid.'

His senses were dimming.

'Why? Wh...'

Then she was kneeling beside him.

'Oh, come on, Leonid,' Raisa said. 'Kolya said you were intelligent, cunning even. You can work it out surely. I called on him yesterday. He explained how you wanted to take the food from my children's mouths and blackmail my friends. We formed our little plan then and there to solve a problem called Leonid Ahmetov. Didn't you think you got the keys to your Astoria room just a little too easily?'

'Help me,' Leonid croaked, as he lay in the pool of blood. 'Please.'

'Nobody can help you, Leonid. When you threatened my children's future, you signed your death warrant. Let me explain it to you. About now, Kolya is standing on the steps with his comrades from the Cheka. That's his alibi. Not that he needs one. The Cheka is beyond the law. The entire group will have heard gunshots. Another assassination! Counter-revolution! They will be on their way by now.'

By then, Leonid was barely conscious.

'In a moment, I will put a bullet in your head and tiptoe away along the far wall. Do you see how deep the drifts are on this side of the alley? Yet the wind has left the far side quite clear. I will make my way home and tuck up the children, safe in the knowledge that nobody will ever put them on the street or steal the food from their mouths.'

She stood. All Leonid could see now was her boots. His gaze was dimming.

'Kolya will arrive with the other Chekists. He will issue an instruction to round up the usual counter-revolutionary suspects. By then, of course, you will be quite dead, you piece of shit.'

'You can't do this. You're just a girl.'

'I am a woman and a revolutionary. You stain our cause, you and all your kind. I am going to finish you off because you put the children in my care in danger. When Kolya described your filthy lust for Svetlana, for Klara and for me, it only confirmed me in my decision. You had to die. I killed once before, you know, to earn the right to life. I will kill again to give my children their right to life.'

'You don't have children!'

Raise stared him down, eyes blazing with contempt.

'I didn't bear them,' she said, 'but they are mine.'

'You're crazy.'

'I assure you that I am quite sane,' Raisa said. 'I am going to finish you off because you threatened my friends and endangered my children. Oh, and I will finish you off because you are a disgrace to the name Communist.'

The last thing Leonid heard in this world was a roar like rolling thunder.